高一同學的

U0097629

> 1. 熟背「高中常用7000字」
>
> 2. 月期考得高分
>
> 3. 會說流利的英語

1.「用會話背7000字①」書+ CD 280元

以三個極短句為一組的方式，讓同學背了會話，同時快速增加單字。高一同學要從「國中常用2000字」挑戰「高中常用7000字」，加強單字是第一目標。

2.「一分鐘背9個單字」書+ CD 280元

利用字首、字尾的排列，讓你快速增加單字。一次背9個比背1個字簡單。

3. rival

> rival[5] (ˈraɪvḷ) n. 對手
> arrival[3] (əˈraɪvḷ) n. 到達 } 都有 rival
> festival[2] (ˈfɛstəvḷ) n. 節日；慶祝活動

> revival[6] (rɪˈvaɪvḷ) n. 復甦
> survival[3] (səˈvaɪvḷ) n. 生還 } 字尾是 vival
> carnival[6] (ˈkɑrnəvḷ) n. 嘉年華會

> carnation[5] (kɑrˈneʃən) n. 康乃馨
> donation[6] (doˈneʃən) n. 捐贈 } 字尾是 nation
> donate[6] (ˈdonet) v. 捐贈

3.「一口氣考試英語」書+ CD 280元

把大學入學考試題目編成會話，背了以後，會說英語，又會考試。

例如：

> What a nice surprise! (眞令人驚喜！)【常考】
> I can't believe my eyes.
> (我無法相信我的眼睛。)
> *Little did I dream of seeing you here.*
> (做夢也沒想到會在這裡看到你。)【駒澤大】

4. 「一口氣背文法」書+ CD 280元

英文文法範圍無限大，規則無限多，誰背得完？
劉毅老師把文法整體的概念，編成216句，背完
了會做文法題、會說英語，也會寫作文。既是一
本文法書，也是一本會話書。

1. 現在簡單式的用法

I *get up* early every day.	我每天早起。
I *understand* this rule now.	我現在了解這條規定了。
Actions *speak* louder than words.	行動勝於言辭。

【二、三句強調實踐早起】

5. 「高中英語聽力測驗①」書+ MP3 280元

6. 「高中英語聽力測驗進階」書+ MP3 280元

高一月期考聽力佔20%，我們根據大考中心公布的
聽力題型編輯而成。

7. 「高一月期考英文試題」書 280元

收集建中、北一女、師大附中、中山、成功、景
美女中等各校試題，並聘請各校名師編寫模擬試
題。

8. 「高一英文克漏字測驗」書 180元

9. 「高一英文閱讀測驗」書 180元

全部取材自高一月期考試題，英雄
所見略同，重複出現的機率很高。
附有翻譯及詳解，不必查字典，對
錯答案都有明確交待，做完題目，
一看就懂。

高二同學的目標——提早準備考大學

1. 「用會話背7000字①②」
   書+CD，每冊280元

「用會話背7000字」能夠解決
所有學英文的困難。高二同學
可先從第一冊開始背，第一冊
和第二冊沒有程度上的差異，
背得越多，單字量越多，在腦
海中的短句越多。每一個極短句大多不超過5個字，1個字或
2個字都可以成一個句子，如：「用會話背7000字①」p.184，
每一句都2個字，好背得不得了，而且與生活息息相關，是
每個人都必須知道的知識，例如：成功的祕訣是什麼？

11. What are the keys to success?

Be *ambitious*.	要有**雄心**。
Be *confident*.	要有**信心**。
Have *determination*.	要有**決心**。
Be *patient*.	要有**耐心**。
Be *persistent*.	要有**恆心**。
Show *sincerity*.	要有**誠心**。
Be *charitable*.	要有**愛心**。
Be *modest*.	要**虛心**。
Have *devotion*.	要**專心**。

當你背單字的時候，就要有「雄心」，要「決心」背好，對
自己要有「信心」，一定要有「耐心」和「恆心」，背書時
要「專心」。

背完後，腦中有2,160個句子，那不得了，無限多的排列組
合，可以寫作文。有了單字，翻譯、閱讀測驗、克漏字都難
不倒你了。高二的時候，要下定決心，把7000字背熟、背
爛。雖然高中課本以7000字為範圍，編書者為了便宜行事，
往往超出7000字，同學背了少用的單字，反倒忽略真正重要
的單字。千萬記住，背就要背「高中常用7000字」，背完之
後，天不怕、地不怕，任何考試都難不倒你。

2.「時速破百單字快速記憶」書 250元

字尾是 try，重音在倒數第三音節上

entry [3] ('ɛntrɪ) n. 進入【No entry. 禁止進入。】
country [1] ('kʌntrɪ) n. 國家；鄉下【ou 讀 /ʌ/，為例外字】
ministry [4] ('mɪnɪstrɪ) n. 部【mini = small】

chemistry [4] ('kɛmɪstrɪ) n. 化學
geometry [5] (dʒɪ'amətrɪ) n. 幾何學【geo 土地，metry 測量】
industry [2] ('ɪndəstrɪ) n. 工業；勤勉【這個字重音當唸錯】

poetry [1] ('po‧ɪtrɪ) n. 詩
poultry [4] ('poltrɪ) n. 家禽　}字尾 y 表「集合名詞」
pastry [5] ('pestrɪ) n. 糕餅

3.「高二英文克漏字測驗」書 180元

4.「高二英文閱讀測驗」書 180元
全部選自各校高二月期考試題精華，英雄所見略同，再出現的機率很高。

5.「7000字學測試題詳解」書 250元
一般模考題為了便宜行事，往往超出7000字範圍，無論做多少份試題，仍然有大量生字，無法進步。唯有鎖定7000字為範圍的試題，才會對準備考試有幫助。每份試題都經「劉毅英文」同學實際考過，效果奇佳。附有詳細解答，單字標明級數，對錯答案都有明確交待，不需要再查字典，做完題目，再看詳解，快樂無比。

6.「高中常用7000字解析【豪華版】」書 390元
按照「大考中心高中英文參考詞彙表」編輯而成。難背的單字有「記憶技巧」、「同義字」及「反義字」，關鍵的單字有「典型考題」。大學入學考試核心單字，以紅色標記。

7.「高中7000字測驗題庫」書 180元
取材自大規模考試，解答詳盡，節省查字典的時間。

TEST 1

說明： 第 1 至 5 題，每題一個空格。請依文意在文章後所提供的 (A) 到 (F) 選項中分別選出最適當者。

It was a beautiful day, so I decided to have a picnic at a small park near my office. I headed for a hot dog stand and ordered one for lunch. I watched the vendor put together the perfect hot dog, just the way I wanted it. ___1___ "It looks a little on the cool side," he said, "so never mind paying me." I said thanks and dug into my food. While I was eating, I was distracted by a man sitting alone nearby, looking at me. I could tell that he hadn't eaten for days. Another homeless person, I thought, like all the others you see in cities. ___2___ But when I went to the garbage can to throw away my lunch bag, I heard a voice ask, "There isn't any food in the bag, is there?" ___3___ I didn't know what to say. I guessed he couldn't bear to see anything thrown away. ___4___ I went across to the hot dog stand, bought a hot dog,

crossed back to the garbage can, and gave the hungry
man the food.   5   That day I learned how generosity
can go farther than the person you give to. By giving,
you teach others how to give as well.

    (A) I didn't pay much more attention than
        that.

    (B) It was the man who had been watching
        me.

    (C) I felt bad for the man, and suddenly
        I had an idea.

    (D) But when I took out money to pay him,
        the man surprised me.

    (E) The homeless person was ignorant of my
        irritation.

    (F) I thought I should pass on the kindness
        that someone had given to me.

TEST 1 詳解

It was a beautiful day, *so* I decided to have a picnic *at a small park near my office.* I headed *for a hot dog stand and* ordered one *for lunch.*

那天天氣很好，所以我決定在辦公室附近的一個小公園野餐。我走向一個熱狗攤，點了一份熱狗堡當午餐。

* picnic[2] 〔'pɪknɪk〕 n. 野餐　　*head for* 向…走去；前往
hot dog 熱狗　　stand[2] 〔stænd〕 n. 露天攤位
order[1] 〔'ɔrdə〕 v. 點 (餐)

I watched the vendor put *together* the perfect hot dog, *just the way I wanted it.* [1](D) *But when I took out money to pay him,* the man surprised me. "It looks *a little* on the cool side," he said, "*so never mind paying me.*"

我看著小販組合出正是我想要的完美熱狗。但是當我拿出錢要付給他時，小販讓我很驚訝。「它看起來有點冷了，」他說，「所以不用付錢給我。」

* vendor[6] 〔'vɛndə〕 n. 小販　　*put together* 組合；拼裝起來
perfect[2] 〔'pɝfɪkt〕 adj. 完美的　　surprise[1] 〔sə'praɪz〕 v. 使驚訝
a little on the cool side 【口語】有一點冷；有一點涼
never mind 不用啦

I said thanks *and* dug into my food. *While I was eating*, I was distracted *by a man sitting alone nearby*, *looking at me*. I could tell *that he hadn't eaten for days*. Another homeless person, I thought, *like all the others you see in cities*. [2](A) I didn't pay *much more* attention *than that.*

我說了謝謝，然後就大口吃我的食物。當我正在吃的時候，我因為一個獨自坐在附近，正看著我的男人而分心。我可以看得出來，他已經好幾天沒吃東西了。我心想，又是一個無家可歸的人，就像在城市裡看到的其他無家可歸的人一樣。我沒有在多加注意。

* *dig into* 開始大吃　　distract[6] 〔 dɪˈstrækt 〕 v. 使分心
　alone[1] 〔 əˈlon 〕 adv. 獨自地　　nearby[2] 〔ˈnɪrˈbaɪ 〕 adv. 在附近
　tell[1] 〔 tɛl 〕 v. 看出；知道
　homeless 〔ˈhomlɪs 〕 adj. 無家可歸的　　*pay attention* 注意

But when I went to the garbage can to throw away my lunch bag, I heard a voice ask, "There isn't any food *in the bag*, is there?" [3](B) It was the man *who had been watching me.*

但是當我去垃圾桶要扔掉我的午餐袋時，我聽到一個聲音在問：「袋子裡沒有任何食物了吧，有嗎？」就是那個一直在看我的人。

* *garbage can* 垃圾桶　　*throw away* 丟棄
　voice[1] 〔 vɔɪs 〕 n. 聲音

I didn't know **what** to say. I guessed *he couldn't bear to see*

anything thrown away. [4](C) I felt bad *for the man,* **and** *suddenly*

I had an idea.

我不知道該說什麼。我猜他無法忍受看到有東西被扔掉。我很同情那個
男人，然後突然間我有個想法。

* guess[1] 〔 gɛs 〕 v. 猜　　bear[2] 〔 bɛr 〕 v. 忍受
  feel bad for 同情　　suddenly[2] 〔'sʌdṇlɪ 〕 adv. 突然地

I went *across to the hot dog stand,* bought a hot dog, crossed *back to*

the garbage can, **and** gave the hungry man the food. [5](F) I thought *I*

should pass on the kindness **that** *someone had given to me.*

我去對面的那個熱狗攤，買了一份熱狗堡，又回到垃圾桶那裡，然後把
食物給那個飢餓的人。我覺得我應該把別人給我的善意傳遞下去。

* **go across** 橫越到對面　　**pass on** 傳遞
  kindness[2] 〔'kaɪndnɪs 〕 n. 善意；友好的行為

That day I learned **how** generosity can go *farther* **than** *the person you*

give to. By giving, you teach others **how** to give as well.

那天我了解到慷慨的影響力，可以遠超過你所給予的人。藉由給予，你
也教會別人如何給予。

* generosity[4] 〔,dʒɛnə'rasətɪ 〕 n. 慷慨
  farther[3] 〔'farðɚ 〕 adv. 更遠；在更大的程度上；在更大的範圍內
  as well 也 (= too[1])

TEST 2

說明： 第 1 至 5 題，每題一個空格。請依文意在文章後所提供的 (A) 到 (F) 選項中分別選出最適當者。

Electronic communication, because of its speed, is far more efficient than paper-based communication. ___1___ Questions can be answered quickly, and a rapid dialogue can take place.

However, one of the drawbacks of e-mail is that your correspondent won't be able to use normal status cues such as diction or dialect. Thus, he or she may make assumptions based on your name, address, and above all, facility with language. ___2___

___3___ It lacks vocal inflection and gestures. Your correspondent may have difficulty telling if you are serious or kidding, happy or sad. ___4___

Another difference between e-mail and older media is that what the sender sees when composing a message might not look like what the reader sees. With e-mail,

the software and hardware that you use for composing,

sending, storing, downloading, and reading may be

completely different from what your correspondent uses.

___5___

(A) Sarcasm is particularly dangerous to use
     in e-mail.

(B) Sloppiness with the language may result
     in a rather harsh judgment.

(C) E-mail also does not convey emotions
     nearly as well as face-to-face or even
     telephone conversations.

(D) Therefore, your message's visual qualities
     may be quite different by the time it gets
     to someone else's screen.

(E) Because the turnaround time can be so
     fast, e-mail is also more conversational
     than traditional paper-based media.

(F) Nowadays, text messaging is even more
     popular than e-mail.

TEST 2 詳解

Electronic communication, *because of its speed*, is *far more*

efficient *than paper-based communication*.

電子通信因為其速度，比紙本通信有效率得多。

* electronic³ (ɪ,lɛk'trɑnɪk) *adj.* 電子的
  communication⁴ (kə,mjunə'keʃən) *n.* 溝通；通信
  because of 因為　　speed² (spid) *n.* 速度
  efficient³ (ə'fɪʃənt) *adj.* 有效率的
  based¹ (best) *adj.* 以…為基礎的；以…為主要手段的
  paper-based *adj.* 紙本型態的

[1](E) ***Because** the turnaround time can be so fast*, e-mail is *also more*

conversational ***than** traditional paper-based media*.　Questions can

be answered *quickly*, *and* a rapid dialogue can take place.

由於往來的時間如此之快，電子郵件也比傳統的紙本媒體更像在交談。
問題可以被迅速回答，而且可以進行快速的對話。

* turnaround ('tɜnə,raʊnd) *n.* 往返
  e-mail⁴ ('i,mel) *n.* 電子郵件 (= *electronic mail*)
  conversational⁴ (,kɑnvə'seʃənḷ) *adj.* 會話的
  traditional² (trə'dɪʃənḷ) *adj.* 傳統的
  media³ ('midɪə) *n. pl.* 媒體　　rapid² ('ræpɪd) *adj.* 快的；迅速的
  dialogue³ ('daɪə,lɔg) *n.* 對話　　*take place* 發生；產生；進行

However, one *of the drawbacks of e-mail* is ***that*** *your*

correspondent won't be able to use normal status cues such as diction

or dialect.

然而，電子郵件的缺點之一，就是你的通信者將無法使用像是用字遣詞或方言之類的，一般狀態的線索。

* drawback[6] ('drɔ,bæk) *n.* 缺點
  correspondent[6] (,kɔrə'spandənt) *n.* 通信者
  be able to V. 能夠…　　normal[3] ('nɔrml) *adj.* 一般的；標準的
  status[3] ('stetəs) *n.* 狀況；狀態　　cue[4] (kju) *n.* 線索
  such as 像是　　diction ('dɪkʃən) *n.* 措辭；用語
  dialect[5] ('daɪə,lɛkt) *n.* 方言

Thus, he ***or*** she may make assumptions *based on your name, address,*

and *above all, facility with language.* [2](B) Sloppiness *with the*

language may result in a *rather* harsh judgment.

因此，他或她可能會根據你的名字、地址，以及最重要的語言能力，做出臆測。語言的隨便可能會導致相當嚴厲的批判。

* assumption[6] (ə'sʌmpʃən) *n.* 假想；臆測
  based on 根據　　address[1] (ə'drɛs) *n.* 地址
  above all 最重要的是　　facility[4] (fə'sɪlətɪ) *n.* 熟練；技巧
  sloppiness ('slapɪnɪs) *n.* 隨便【sloppy[5] *adj.* 邋遢的；隨便的】
  result in 導致；造成　　rather[2] ('ræðə) *adv.* 相當地
  harsh[4] (harʃ) *adj.* 嚴厲的；苛刻的
  judgement[2] ('dʒʌdʒmənt) *n.* 判斷；批判

[3](C) E-mail *also* does not convey emotions *nearly as well as*

face-to-face or even telephone conversations. It lacks vocal inflection

and gestures.

電子郵件也不能像面對面，或甚至是用電話交談，那樣表達情緒。
它缺乏聲音的抑揚頓挫和手勢。

* convey[4] 〔 kən've 〕 v. 傳達　　emotion[2] 〔 ɪ'moʃən 〕 n. 情緒
nearly[2] 〔'nɪrlɪ 〕 adv. 幾乎；差不多　　face-to-face adj. 面對面的
conversation[2] 〔ˌkɑnvɚ'seʃən 〕 n. 對話
lack[1] 〔 læk 〕 v. 缺乏
vocal[6] 〔'vokḷ 〕 adj. 聲音的
inflection 〔 ɪn'flɛkʃən 〕 n. 語調的抑揚變化
gesture[3] 〔'dʒɛstʃɚ 〕 n. 姿勢；手勢

| lack v. 缺乏 |
| = be lacking in |
| = be in lack of |

Your correspondent may have difficulty *telling if you are serious or*

kidding, happy or sad. [4](A) Sarcasm is *particularly* dangerous *to use*

in e-mail.

你的通信者可能很難分辨出，你是認真還是開玩笑，高興還是悲傷。在
電子郵件中使用諷刺，是特別危險的。

* *have difficulty (in) + V-ing* 很難～　　tell[1] 〔 tɛl 〕 v. 看出
serious[2] 〔'sɪrɪəs 〕 adj. 認真的　　kid[2] 〔 kɪd 〕 v. 開玩笑
sarcasm 〔'sɑrkæzəm 〕 n. 諷刺【sarcastic adj. 諷刺的】
particularly[2] 〔 pɚ'tɪkjələlɪ 〕 adv. 特別地

Another difference *between e-mail **and** older media* is ***that what***
*the sender sees **when** composing a message might not look like **what***
the reader sees.

電子郵件和較舊的通訊媒介另一個不同點是，寄件人在撰寫郵件
時，所看到的內容，可能看起來不像閱讀的人所看到的。

* sender〔'sɛndɚ〕*n.* 寄件人
compose[4]〔kəm'poz〕*v.* 組成；作（文）
message[2]〔'mɛsɪdʒ〕*n.* 訊息　　reader〔'ridɚ〕*n.* 閱讀的人

With e-mail, the software ***and*** hardware ***that** you use for composing,*
*sending, storing, downloading, **and** reading* may be *completely*
different *from **what** your correspondent uses.* [5]**(D)** *Therefore*, your
message's visual qualities may be *quite* different ***by the time** it gets*
to someone else's screen.

你用來撰寫、發送、儲存、下載，和閱讀電子郵件，所使用的軟體和硬
體，可能和與你通信的人所使用的完全不同。因此，你的訊息到達他人
的螢幕時，視覺品質可能會有很大的不同。

* software[4]〔'sɔft,wɛr〕*n.* 軟體　　hardware[4]〔'hɑrd,wɛr〕*n.* 硬體
store[1]〔stor〕*v.* 儲存　　download[4]〔'daʊn,lod〕*v.* 下載
completely[2]〔kəm'plitlɪ〕*adv.* 完全地
visual[4]〔'vɪʒʊəl〕*adj.* 視覺的　　quality[2]〔'kwɑlətɪ〕*n.* 品質；特質
quite[1]〔kwaɪt〕*adv.* 相當　　***by the time*** 到了⋯的時候
get to 到達　　screen[2]〔skrin〕*n.* 螢幕

TEST 3

說明： 第 1 至 5 題，每題一個空格。請依文意在文章後所提供的 (A) 到
(F) 選項中分別選出最適當者。

Hydropower is any energy created by moving water.
In Greek, "hydro" simply means water. The history of
hydropower dates back thousands of years. ___1___
Another common source of hydropower is water mills,
with which diverse activities such as grinding grain or
cutting lumber are made possible. To harness energy
from flowing water, however, the water must be
controlled. ___2___ The power of flowing water then
causes turbines to turn, making generators move. Usually
large and fast-flowing rivers produce the most power.

___3___ Similarly, hydroelectric power plants near
waterfalls can also create huge amounts of energy. A
famous example of this is the hydroelectric plant at
Niagara Falls. ___4___ Nowadays, hydroelectricity is
generally considered a clean and renewable energy source.

After the devastating earthquake in 2011 in Japan, people have had heated debates over whether or not nuclear power plants should be banned. ___5___

(A) First a large reservoir is created to make an artificial lake so that water can be channeled through tunnels in the dam.

(B) At this point, natural resources such as sunlight, wind or rain seem to provide better alternatives that are both environmentally safe and eco-friendly.

(C) Back in Roman times, people built water-driven turbines, not to generate electricity but to grind grains to make flour and breads.

(D) Another is the enormous Three Gorges Dam, the largest hydroelectric power plant in the world, which spans the Yangtze River in China.

(E) Water and its related imagery has long been a source of inspiration to Greek poets.

(F) The Columbia River, for instance, is a huge river that produces massive amounts of hydroelectric energy.

TEST 3　詳解

Hydropower is any energy *created by moving water*. *In Greek*,
"hydro" *simply* means water.

水力發的電是用流動的水創造的能源。在希臘語中，"hydro" 就是
指水。

* hydropower〔ˌhaɪdro'pauɚ〕*n.* 水力發的電
energy[2]〔'ɛnɚdʒɪ〕*n.* 能源　　create[2]〔krɪ'et〕*v.* 創造
moving[1]〔'muvɪŋ〕*adj.* 移動的　　Greek〔grik〕*n.* 希臘語
hydro〔'haɪdro〕*adj.* 水的；氫的
simply[1]〔'sɪmplɪ〕*adv.* 簡單地；只　　mean[1]〔min〕*v.* 意思是

The history *of hydropower* dates *back thousands of years.* [1]*(C) Back
in Roman times*, people built water-driven turbines, ***not** to generate
electricity **but** to grind grains to make flour **and** breads.*

水力發電的歷史可以追溯到幾千年前。過去在羅馬時代，人們建造水力
驅動的渦輪機，不是爲了發電，而是爲了研磨穀物，以製作麵粉和麵
包。

* history[1]〔'hɪstrɪ〕*n.* 歷史
date back 可追溯到　　back[1]〔bæk〕*adv.* 過去；以前
Roman〔'romən〕*adj.* 羅馬的　　times[1]〔taɪmz〕*n. pl.* 時代
drive[1]〔draɪv〕*v.* 驅動　　turbine〔'tɝbaɪn〕*n.* 渦輪機

not A but B 不是 A，而是 B　　generate[6]〔ˈdʒɛnəˌret〕v. 產生
electricity[3]〔ɪˌlɛkˈtrɪsətɪ〕n. 電　　grind[4]〔graɪnd〕v. 磨
grain[3]〔gren〕n. 穀物　　flour[2]〔flaʊr〕n. 麵粉

Another common source *of hydropower* is water mills, *with **which***

*diverse activities such as grinding grain **or** cutting lumber are made*

possible.
另一個常見的水力發電的來源，是水力磨粉機，有了這些水磨機，才可
以進行各種活動，像是使研磨穀物或切割木材。

　　* common[1]〔ˈkɑmən〕adj. 常見的　　source[2]〔sors〕n. 來源
　　water mill 水力磨粉機；水磨
　　diverse[6]〔dəˈvɜs〕adj. 各種的　　activity[3]〔ækˈtɪvətɪ〕n. 活動
　　such as 像是　　lumber[5]〔ˈlʌmbɚ〕n. 木材
　　make…possible 使…成為可能

To harness energy from flowing water, however, the water must be

controlled. [2](**A**) *First* a large reservoir is created *to make an artificial*

*lake **so that** water can be channeled through tunnels in the dam.*

然而，為了利用流水的能量，必須控制水。首先要創造一座大型的水
庫，做一個人造湖，以便水能經由通道進入水壩中。

　　* harness[5]〔ˈhɑrnɪs〕v. 利用　　flowing[2]〔ˈfloɪŋ〕adj. 流動的

reservoir⁶ 〔'rɛzə˞,vɔr , -,vwɑr 〕 *n.* 水庫
artificial⁴ 〔,ɑrtə'fɪʃəl 〕 *adj.* 人造的;人工的　　lake¹ 〔 lek 〕 *n.* 湖
so that 以便於　　channel³ 〔'tʃænl̩ 〕 *v.* 輸送;傳送
tunnel² 〔'tʌnl̩ 〕 *n.* 隧道;通道　　dam³ 〔 dæm 〕 *n.* 水壩

The power *of flowing water then* causes turbines *to turn, making*
generators move. *Usually* large ***and*** fast-flowing rivers produce the
most power. ³(F) The Columbia River, *for instance,* is a huge river
that *produces massive amounts of hydroelectric energy.*

接著流動的水的力量會使渦輪轉動,推動發電機。通常大型且快速流動
的河流,能產生最大的力量。例如,哥倫比亞河是一條巨大的河流,能
產生大量的水力發電。

* cause¹ 〔 kɔz 〕 *v.* 使　　generator⁶ 〔'dʒɛnə,retə˞ 〕 *n.* 發電機
move¹ 〔 muv 〕 *v.* 移動;運轉
produce² 〔 prə'djus 〕 *v.* 生產;製造
Columbia 〔 kə'lʌmbɪə 〕 *n.* 哥倫比亞
for instance 例如　　huge¹ 〔 hjudʒ 〕 *adj.* 巨大的
massive⁵ 〔'mæsɪv 〕 *adj.* 巨大的　　amount² 〔 ə'maʊnt 〕 *n.* 數量
hydroelectric 〔,haɪdroɪ'lɛktrɪk 〕 *adj.* 水力發電的

Similarly, hydroelectric power plants *near waterfalls* can *also* create
huge amounts *of energy.* A famous example *of this* is the hydroelectric
plant *at Niagara Falls.*

同樣地,瀑布附近的水力發電廠也可以創造大量的能源。在尼加拉大瀑
布的水力發電廠,就是一個有名的例子。

* similarly[2] (ˈsɪmələˌlɪ) *adv.* 同樣地
plant[2] (plænt) *n.* 工廠　　***power plant*** 發電廠
waterfall[2] (ˈwɔtəˌfɔl) *n.* 瀑布　　famous[1] (ˈfeməs) *adj.* 有名的
example[1] (ɪgˈzæmpḷ) *n.* 例子
Niagara Falls (naɪˈægrə ˈfɔlz) *n.* 尼加拉大瀑布

[4](**D**) Another is the enormous Three Gorges Dam, *the largest*

hydroelectric power plant in the world, ***which*** *spans the Yangtze*

River in China.

另一個是三峽大壩，這座橫跨中國長江，世界上最大的水力發電廠。

* enormous[4] (ɪˈnɔrməs) *adj.* 巨大的
gorge[5] (gɔrdʒ) *n.* 峽谷　　***Three Gorges Dam*** 三峽大壩
span[6] (spæn) *v.* (橋、拱等) 橫跨；跨越
the Yangtze River 長江；揚子江

Nowadays, hydroelectricity is *generally* considered a clean ***and***

renewable energy source. *After the devastating earthquake in 2011*

in Japan, people have had heated debates *over* ***whether or not***

nuclear power plants should be banned.

現在水力發電一般被認為是乾淨且可再生的能源。在 2011 年日本發生
破壞性極大的地震後，人們對於是否應該禁止核能電廠，已有激烈的爭
論。

* nowadays[4] ('nauə,dez) adv. 現今
hydroelectricity (,haɪdroɪ,lɛk'trɪsətɪ) n. 水力發電
generally[2] ('dʒɛnərəlɪ) adv. 一般地；普遍地
consider[2] (kən'sɪdə) v. 認爲
renewable[3] (rɪ'nuəbḷ) adj. 可更新的
devastating ('dɛvəs,tetɪŋ) adj. 破壞性極大的；毀滅性的
　　(= destructive[5])　　earthquake[2] ('ɝθ,kwek) n. 地震
heated[1] ('hitɪd) adj. 激烈的　　debate[2] (dɪ'bet) n. 辯論
whether or not 是否　　nuclear[4] ('njuklɪə) adj. 核子的
nuclear power plant 核電廠　　ban[5] (bæn) v. 禁止

---

[5]**(B)** *At this point*, natural resources *such as sunlight, wind **or** rain*

seem to provide better alternatives ***that** are both environmentally safe*

and eco-friendly.

此時此刻，天然資源，像是陽光、風或雨，似乎提供了更好的選擇，旣
環保又不損壞生態環境。

* point[1] (pɔɪnt) n. 時刻　　natural[2] ('nætʃərəl) adj. 天然的
resource[3] (rɪ'sors) n. 資源　　sunlight[1] ('sʌn,laɪt) n. 陽光
provide[2] (prə'vaɪd) v. 提供
alternative[6] (ɔl'tɝnətɪv) n. 可選擇的事物；替代物
environmentally[3] (ɪn,vaɪrən'mɛntḷɪ) adv. 環境上
safe[1] (sef) adj. 安全的
environmentally safe 對環境安全的；環保的
　　(= environmentally friendly)
eco-friendly ('iko,frɛndlɪ) adj. 不損壞生態環境的；環保的

TEST 4

說明： 第 1 至 5 題，每題一個空格。請依文意在文章後所提供的 (A) 到
(F) 選項中分別選出最適當者。

____1____ In the back of the property, the CEO has the
largest swimming pool any of them has ever seen. The
huge pool, however, is filled with hungry alligators.

The CEO says to his executives, "____2____ Courage is
what made me CEO. So this is my challenge to each of
you: if anyone has enough courage to dive into the pool,
swim through those alligators, and make it to the other
side, I will give that person anything he or she desires.
My job, my money, my house, anything!"

Everyone laughs at the outrageous offer and proceeds
to follow the CEO on the tour of the estate. ____3____
Everyone turns around and sees the CFO (Chief Financial
Officer) in the pool, swimming for his life. He dodges
the alligators left and right and makes it to the edge of
the pool with seconds to spare. ____4____

The CEO approaches the CFO and says, "You are amazing. I've never seen anything like it in my life. You are brave beyond measure and anything I own is yours. Tell me what I can do for you."

The CFO, panting for breath, looks up and says, "＿＿5＿＿"

(A) The CEO's check bounces and he is on the verge of bankruptcy.

(B) You can tell me who pushed me in the pool!

(C) Suddenly, they hear a loud splash.

(D) He pulls himself out just as a huge alligator almost bites his leg.

(E) A CEO throwing a party takes his executives on a tour of his mansion.

(F) I think an executive should be measured by courage.

TEST 4 詳解

[1](E) A CEO *throwing a party* takes his executives *on a tour of*

his mansion.

有位執行長舉行派對，帶著他的主管們參觀他的豪宅。

* **CEO** 執行長；總裁 (= *Chief Executive Officer*)
chief[1] 〔tʃif〕 *adj.* 主要的
executive[5] 〔ɪg'zɛkjutɪv〕 *adj.* 執行的；經營管理的 *n.* 主管
officer[1] 〔'ɔfəsə〕 *n.* 官員；高級職員
throw a party 舉辦派對 (= *hold a party*)
tour[2] 〔tur〕 *n.* 旅行；參觀　　mansion[5] 〔'mænʃən〕 *n.* 豪宅

In the back of the property, the CEO has the largest swimming pool

any of them has ever seen. The huge pool, *however*, is filled *with*

hungry alligators.

在花園住宅的後面，執行長擁有一座他們所見過最大的游泳池。然而，
巨大的游泳池中，卻充滿了飢餓的短吻鱷。

* property[3] 〔'prɑpətɪ〕 *n.* 財產；花園住宅
huge[1] 〔hjudʒ〕 *adj.* 巨大的
be filled with 充滿了
alligator 〔'ælə,getə〕 *n.* 短吻鱷

alligator 〔'ælə,getə〕 *n.* （美洲）短吻鱷
crocodile 〔'krɑkə,daɪl〕 *n.* （亞洲或非洲）鱷魚

The CEO says *to his executives*, "[2](F) I think an executive should be measured *by courage*. Courage is *what* made me CEO.

執行長對他的主管們說：「我認爲應該以勇氣來衡量一個主管。勇氣是使我成爲執行長的原因。

* measure[2,4] 〔'mɛʒɚ〕 v. 測量；衡量　　courage[2] 〔'kɝɪdʒ〕 n. 勇氣
make[1] 〔mek〕 v. 使成爲

So this is my challenge *to each of you*: *if anyone has enough courage to dive into the pool, swim through those alligators*, *and make it to the other side*, I will give that person anything *he or she desires*. My job, my money, my house, anything!"

所以這是我對你們每個人的挑戰：如果有人有足夠的勇氣跳入游泳池中，游過那些鱷魚，到達泳池的另一邊，我將會給那個人任何他/她想要的。我的職位、我的錢、我的房子，任何東西！」

* challenge[3] 〔'tʃælɪndʒ〕 n. 挑戰　　dive[3] 〔daɪv〕 v. 跳水；潛水
make it to 到達　　desire[2] 〔dɪ'zaɪr〕 v. 渴望；想要

Everyone laughs at the outrageous offer *and* proceeds to follow the CEO *on the tour of the estate*.

每個人都對這個駭人聽聞的提議一笑置之，然後繼續跟著執行長走訪豪宅。

　* laugh[1] 〔 læf 〕 v. 笑 < *at* >
　outrageous[6] 〔 aʊtˈredʒəs 〕 adj. 駭人聽聞的
　offer[2] 〔 ˈɔfɚ 〕 n. 提議　　proceed[4] 〔 prəˈsid 〕 v. 繼續
　follow[1] 〔 ˈfɑlo 〕 v. 跟隨　　estate[5] 〔 əˈstet 〕 n. 地產；財產

[3](C) *Suddenly, they hear a loud splash.* Everyone turns *around and*

sees the CFO (*Chief Financial Officer*) *in the pool, swimming for his*

life.

　　突然間，他們聽到一聲巨大的撲通聲。每個人都轉身，看到在泳池
裡，財務長（CFO）正在拼命游泳。

　* suddenly[2] 〔 ˈsʌdn̩lɪ 〕 adv. 突然地
　loud[1] 〔 laʊd 〕 adj. 大聲的　　splash[3] 〔 splæʃ 〕 n. 落水的撲通聲
　turn around 轉身　　*CFO* 財務長（= *Chief Financial Officer* ）
　financial[4] 〔 faɪˈnænʃəl 〕 adj. 財務的
　for one's *life* 拼命地

He dodges the alligators *left and right and* makes it to the edge *of the*

pool with seconds to spare. [4](D) He pulls himself *out just as a huge*

alligator almost bites his leg.

　　他左閃右避短吻鱷，剩不到幾秒鐘的時間，就到達了泳池邊。正當有隻
巨大的短吻鱷幾乎要咬到他的腿時，他從泳池裡爬了出來。

　* dodge[3] 〔 dɑdʒ 〕 v. 躲避　　edge[1] 〔 ɛdʒ 〕 n. 邊緣

second[1] 〔'sɛkənd〕 n. 秒　　spare[4] 〔spɛr〕 v. 剩下
pull out 使撤退；使退出　　bite[1] 〔baɪt〕 v. 咬

The CEO approaches the CFO *and* says, "You are amazing.

I've *never* seen anything *like it in my life.* You are brave *beyond*

measure *and* anything *I own* is yours. Tell me *what I can do for you.*"

執行長接近財務長，然後說：「你真棒。我生平從未見過這樣的
事。你非常勇敢，我的就是你的。告訴我，我能為你做什麼。」

* approach[3] 〔ə'protʃ〕 v. 接近
amazing[3] 〔ə'mezɪŋ〕 adj. 驚人的；令人吃驚的
brave[1] 〔brev〕 adj. 勇敢的
beyond[2] 〔bɪ'jɑnd〕 prep. 超過…的範圍；出乎…之外
measure[2] 〔'mɛʒɚ〕 n. 測量
beyond measure 非常地；無法衡量的

The CFO, *panting for breath,* looks up *and* says, "[5]**(B) You can tell**

me *who pushed me in the pool*!"

上氣不接下氣的財務長抬起頭說：「你可以告訴我，是誰把我推到泳池
裡！」

* pant 〔pænt〕 v. 大口喘氣　　breath[3] 〔brɛθ〕 n. 呼吸
pant for breath 上氣不接下氣
look up 抬頭看　　push[1] 〔puʃ〕 v. 推

TEST 5

說明 : 第 1 至 5 題，每題一個空格。請依文意在文章後所提供的 (A) 到
(F) 選項中分別選出最適當者。

Eating bugs is a common practice in many places.
Gross as it may sound, insects like wax moths,
grasshoppers, and even dragonflies are considered
delicacies by many people. Most Americans and
Europeans regard crustaceans such as lobster or crab as
fine food, yet supporters of insects argue that bugs are
much better food. ___1___ Ecologically speaking,
insects are better choices of food as well because it takes
plenty of resources, like food, water or energy to create
a pound of beef or chicken. ___2___ Conventional
livestock such as cattle or chicken are usually believed
to be primary sources of protein. ___3___ The truth is
that insects are probably much healthier than people
expect. They have been eaten in many countries
throughout India, much of Asia and Africa, and in South

America's rural populations. ____4____ If you are still not convinced that insects can be desirable food, scientists are working on growing clean insects in the laboratory to be added to other foods like bread. ____5____

(A) However, studies have shown that insects contain higher quantities of minerals and vitamins than many conventional meats that people eat.

(B) In Mexico, for instance, insects are so popular that they can be bought from street vendors and eaten in five-star restaurants.

(C) The reason is that lobsters tend to eat trash and dead things while insects feed on nature's salad bars.

(D) Maybe if people don't look the bugs in the eye while eating them, bugs can taste as good as French fries.

(E) By contrast, bugs rely mostly on nature, which in turn, reduces pollution.

(F) The fishing industry creates more jobs in warmer climates.

TEST 5 詳解

Eating bugs is a common practice *in many places.* *Gross as it*

may sound, insects *like wax moths, grasshoppers,* **and** *even dragonflies*

are considered delicacies *by many people.*

在許多地方，吃蟲子是常見的習俗。雖然吃蟲可能聽起來很噁心，但像大蠟螟、炸蜢，甚至蜻蜓等昆蟲，卻被許多人視爲美食。

* bug[1] 〔bʌg〕 n. 小蟲 　　common[1] 〔'kɑmən〕 adj. 常見的
　practice[1] 〔'præktɪs〕 n. 慣例；習俗；做法
　Gross *as* it may sound, ... 【as 作「雖然」解】
　= *Though* it may sound gross, ...
　gross[5] 〔gros〕 adj. 噁心的 　　insect[2] 〔'ɪnsɛkt〕 n. 昆蟲
　wax[3] 〔wæks〕 n. 蠟 　　moth[2] 〔mɔθ〕 n. 蛾
　wax moth 大蠟螟 　　grasshopper[3] 〔'græs,hɑpɚ〕 n. 炸蜢
　dragonfly[2] 〔'drægən,flaɪ〕 n. 蜻蜓
　consider[2] 〔kən'sɪdɚ〕 v. 認爲 　　delicacy 〔'dɛləkəsɪ〕 n. 佳餚

Most Americans **and** Europeans regard crustaceans *such as lobster*

or crab as fine food, *yet* supporters *of insects* argue **that** *bugs are*

much better food. [1](C) The reason is **that** *lobsters tend to eat trash*

and *dead things* **while** *insects feed on nature's salad bars.*

大部份的美國人和歐洲人，都把甲殼類動物，像是龍蝦或螃蟹，視爲美食，但昆蟲的支持者則認爲，蟲子是更好的食物。理由是龍蝦往往會吃垃圾和死掉的生物，而昆蟲則是以大自然的沙拉吧爲食。

* American〔ə'mɛrɪkən〕*n.* 美國人
European〔ˌjʊrə'piən〕*n.* 歐洲人
regard[2]〔rɪ'gɑrd〕*v.* 認為　　***regard A as B*** 認為 A 是 B
crustacean〔krʌs'teʃən〕*n.* 甲殼動物【crust[6] *n.* 甲殼】
such as 像是　　lobster[3]〔'lɑbstɚ〕*n.* 龍蝦
crab[2]〔kræb〕*n.* 螃蟹　　yet[1]〔jɛt〕*conj.* 但是
supporter[2]〔sə'portɚ〕*n.* 支持者；擁護者
argue[2]〔'ɑrgju〕*v.* 主張；認為　　reason[1]〔'rizn̩〕*n.* 理由
tend to V. 易於…；傾向於…　　trash[3]〔træʃ〕*n.* 垃圾
while[1]〔hwaɪl〕*conj.* 然而　　***feed on*** 以…為食
nature[1]〔'netʃɚ〕*n.* 大自然　　***salad bar*** 沙拉自助吧

Ecologically speaking, insects are better choices *of food as well*

because it takes plenty of resources, *like food, water **or** energy to*

*create a pound of beef **or** chicken.*

就生態方面而言，昆蟲也是更好的食物選擇，因為要製造一磅的牛肉或
雞肉，需要許多的資源，像是食物、水，或能量。

* ecologically〔ˌikə'lɑdʒɪkl̩ɪ〕*adv.* 在生態方面
【ecology[6]〔ɪ'kɑlədʒɪ〕*n.* 生態（學）】
ecologically speaking 就生態方面而言
choice[2]〔tʃɔɪs〕*n.* 選擇　　***as well*** 也（= too[1]）
take[1]〔tek〕*v.* 需要　　***plenty of*** 許多的
resource[3]〔rɪ'sors〕*n.* 資源
energy[2]〔'ɛnɚdʒɪ〕*n.* 能量　　create[2]〔krɪ'et〕*v.* 創造
pound[2]〔paʊnd〕*n.* 磅【重量單位，1磅等於0.454公斤】
beef[2]〔bif〕*n.* 牛肉　　chicken[1]〔'tʃɪkən〕*n.* 雞；雞肉

2(E) *By contrast*, bugs rely *mostly* on nature, *which in turn, reduces pollution.*

對比之下，蟲子大多依賴大自然，因而減少了污染。

> * *by contrast* 對比之下　　　*rely on* 依賴
> mostly[4] (ˈmostlɪ) *adv.* 大多　　*in turn* 因此；因而
> reduce[3] (rɪˈdjus) *v.* 減少；降低
> pollution[4] (pəˈluʃən) *n.* 污染

Conventional livestock *such as cattle or chicken* are *usually* believed to be primary sources *of protein.*

傳統的家畜，像是牛或雞，通常被認為是蛋白質的主要來源。

> * conventional[4] (kənˈvɛnʃənḷ) *adj.* 傳統的 (= *traditional*[2])
> livestock[5] (ˈlaɪvˌstɑk) *n.* 家畜【集合名詞】
> cattle[3] (ˈkætḷ) *n.* 牛【集合名詞】
> primary[3] (ˈpraɪˌmɛrɪ) *adj.* 主要的 (= *main*[2])
> source[2] (sors) *n.* 來源　　protein[4] (ˈprotiɪn) *n.* 蛋白質

3(A) *However*, studies have shown *that insects contain higher quantities of minerals and vitamins than many conventional meats that people eat.* The truth is *that insects are probably much healthier than people expect.*

然而，研究已經顯示，昆蟲含有礦物質和維生素的量，比人們吃的許多傳統肉類還要多。事實上，昆蟲可能比人們預期的更有益健康。

* study[1]〔'stʌdɪ〕 *n.* 研究　　show[1]〔ʃo〕 *v.* 顯示
contain[2]〔kən'ten〕 *v.* 包含　　quantity[2]〔'kwɑntətɪ〕 *n.* 量
mineral[5]〔'mɪnərəl〕 *n.* 礦物質　　vitamin[3]〔'vaɪtəmɪn〕 *n.* 維生素
truth[2]〔truθ〕 *n.* 事實　　probably[3]〔'prɑbəblɪ〕 *adv.* 可能
healthy[2]〔'hɛlθɪ〕 *adj.* 健康的；有益健康的
expect[2]〔ɪk'spɛkt〕 *v.* 期待；預期

They have been eaten *in many countries throughout India, much of*

*Asia **and** Africa, **and** in South America's rural populations.*

許多的國家都吃昆蟲，遍及印度、亞洲和非洲的大部分地區，以及南美洲農村地區的人。

* throughout[2]〔θru'aʊt〕 *prep.* 遍及　　India〔'ɪndɪə〕 *n.* 印度
Asia〔'eʃə〕 *n.* 亞洲　　Africa〔'æfrɪkə〕 *n.* 非洲
South America〔saʊθ ə'mɛrɪkə〕 *n.* 南美洲
rural[4]〔'rʊrəl〕 *adj.* 鄉村的【urban[4]〔'ɝbən〕 *adj.* 都市的】
population[2]〔ˌpɑpjə'leʃən〕 *n.* 人口

[4]**(B)** *In Mexico, for instance,* insects are *so* popular ***that** they can be*

*bought from street vendors **and** eaten in five-star restaurants.*

例如，在墨西哥，昆蟲非常受歡迎，所以可以在路邊攤買到，在五星級餐廳吃到。

* Mexico〔'mɛksɪˌko〕 *n.* 墨西哥【中美洲國家】
for instance 例如　　*so…that* 如此…以致於

popular[2,3] (ˈpɑpjələ) *adj.* 受歡迎的

vendor[6] (ˈvɛndə) *n.* 小販　　five-star *adj.* 五星級的

*If you are still not convinced **that** insects can be desirable food,*

scientists are working on growing clean insects in the laboratory to

be added to other foods like bread.

如果你還不相信昆蟲是理想的食物，科學家們正在實驗室裡，設法飼養乾淨的昆蟲，要把它們添加到像是麵包等的其他食物中。

* convinced[4] (kənˈvɪnst) *adj.* 相信的

desirable[3] (dɪˈzaɪrəbl̩) *adj.* 合意的；令人滿意的

work on 致力於　　grow[1] (gro) *v.* 栽培；飼養

laboratory[4] (ˈlæbrəˌtorɪ) *n.* 實驗室　　add[1] (æd) *v.* 加 < *to* >

[5](D) *Maybe **if** people don't look the bugs in the eye **while** eating them,*

bugs can taste as good as French fries.

也許如果當人們在吃蟲子時，沒有直視它們，那麼蟲子嚐起來的味道，可能會像薯條一樣好。

* ***look*** *sb.* ***in the eye*** 直視某人的臉

taste[2] (test) *v.* 嚐起來

French fries 薯條

常見的食用蟲
beetle *n.* 甲蟲
caterpillar *n.* 毛毛蟲
cicada *n.* 蟬
cricket *n.* 蟋蟀
tarantula *n.* 狼蛛
termite *n.* 白蟻

TEST 6

說明： 第 1 至 5 題，每題一個空格。請依文意在文章後所提供的 (A) 到 (F) 選項中分別選出最適當者。

Modern people are not the only victims of noise. People who lived in Rome two thousand years ago were already complaining about the noise in their city. They had a difficult time sleeping with all that traffic in the streets. ___1___ It is known that the sounds of an average city are loud enough to cause serious damage to the inhabitants' hearing. The situation is getting worse all the time since noise increases with the population.

___2___ We live surrounded by loud planes, trucks, motorcycles, buses, electric tools, radios, and pneumatic drills that roar day and night up to 90 or 100 decibels. The decibel is the unit used to measure the loudness of sound. A normal conversation reaches 55 decibels; a jet plane goes to 100 decibels and more, and an ordinary subway train approaching the station can be twice as loud as the loudest jet. At 120 decibels the ear stops hearing sound, and pain starts.

What's worse, it is not only hearing that is threatened. ___3___ Such problems have been observed among factory workers, prisoners in large prisons, and people who drive heavy trucks, operate pneumatic drills, or go to rock-and-roll concerts frequently.

To deal with the problem, quieter machines have been developed. __4__ Merchants point out that people who buy motorcycles, for instance, prefer the loudest ones because they sound powerful. Indeed, it takes everybody's efforts to keep city noise from increasing. __5__ The inhabitants may then have to shout to be heard at the dinner table.

(A) Yet the right to decide, most of the time, is in the hands of customers.

(B) Noise has also increased enormously in the 20th century with the development of machines.

(C) Some cities are trying to enforce their anti-noise laws more strictly.

(D) Even so, experts say, in twenty years the cities will be twice as loud as they are today because of the growth of the population.

(E) For them, noise was merely a disturbance; yet for modern people, it has become a real danger.

(F) According to research, loud noises, over a period of time, cause loss of sleep, anger, and many mental and physical problems.

TEST 6 詳解

Modern people are not the only victims *of noise*. People *who*
lived in Rome two thousand years ago were *already* complaining
about the noise *in their city*.

現代人不是噪音唯一的受害者。兩千年前,住在羅馬的人就已經在
抱怨城市裡的噪音了。

* modern[2] 〔'mɑdən 〕 *adj.* 現代的　　victim[3] 〔'vɪktɪm 〕 *n.* 受害者
noise[1] 〔 nɔɪz 〕 *n.* 噪音　　Rome 〔 rom 〕 *n.* 羅馬【義大利首都】
complain[2] 〔 kəm'plen 〕 *v.* 抱怨 < *about* >

They had a difficult time *sleeping with all that traffic in the streets*.

[1](E) *For them*, noise was *merely* a disturbance; *yet for modern people*,
it has become a real danger.

街道上往來的車輛,使他們難以入睡。對他們來說,噪音僅僅只是一種
干擾;然而對現代人來說,它已經變成真正的危險。

* *have a difficult time* (*in*) *+ V-ing* 做…有困難
traffic[2] 〔'træfɪk 〕 *n.* 交通;(往來的) 車輛
merely[4] 〔'mɪrlɪ 〕 *adv.* 僅僅　　disturbance[6] 〔 dɪ'stɜbəns 〕 *n.* 擾亂
yet[1] 〔 jɛt 〕 *adv.* 然而;但是　　real[1] 〔'riəl 〕 *adj.* 真的
danger[1] 〔'dendʒɚ 〕 *n.* 危險

It is known *that the sounds of an average city are loud enough to cause serious damage to the inhabitants' hearing.* The situation is

getting worse *all the time **since** noise increases with the population.*

大家都知道，一般城市的聲音，大到足以對居民的聽力造成嚴重損害。
因爲噪音會隨著人口的增加而增加，所以這情況一直在惡化中。

* average³ 〔'ævərɪdʒ 〕*adj.* 一般的　　loud¹ 〔 laʊd 〕*adj.* 大聲的
  cause¹ 〔 kɔz 〕*v.* 造成　　serious² 〔'sɪrɪəs 〕*adj.* 嚴重的
  damage² 〔'dæmɪdʒ 〕*n.* 損害　　inhabitant⁶ 〔 ɪn'hæbətənt 〕*n.* 居民
  hearing¹ 〔'hɪrɪŋ 〕*n.* 聽力　　situation³ 〔,sɪtʃʊ'eʃən 〕*n.* 情況
  worse¹ 〔 wɝs 〕*adj.* 更糟的　　***all the time*** 一直
  increase² 〔 ɪn'kris 〕*v.* 增加　　population² 〔,pɑpjə'leʃən 〕*n.* 人口

²**(B)** Noise has *also* increased *enormously in the 20th century with*

the development of machines. We live *surrounded by loud planes,*

*trucks, motorcycles, buses, electric tools, radios, **and** pneumatic drills*

***that** roar day **and** night up to 90 **or** 100 decibels.*

　　隨著機器的發展，在二十世紀噪音也大幅增加。我們生活在吵雜的
飛機、卡車、摩托車、公車、電子工具、收音機，和氣壓式電鑽的周
遭，它們日夜持續發出的轟鳴聲，高達 90 或 100 分貝。

* enormously⁴ 〔 ɪ'nɔrməslɪ 〕*adv.* 巨大地
  century² 〔'sɛntʃərɪ 〕*n.* 世紀
  development² 〔 dɪ'vɛləpmənt 〕*n.* 發展
  machine¹ 〔 mə'ʃin 〕*n.* 機器　　surround³ 〔 sə'raʊnd 〕*v.* 圍繞

plane[1] 〔 plen 〕 n. 飛機　　truck[2] 〔 trʌk 〕 n. 卡車
motorcycle 〔'motɚ,saɪkḷ〕 n. 摩拖車
electric[3] 〔 ɪ'lɛktrɪk 〕 adj. 電動的　　tool[1] 〔 tul 〕 n. 工具
pneumatic 〔 nju'mætɪk 〕 adj. 氣壓式的　　drill[4] 〔 drɪl 〕 n. 電鑽
roar[3] 〔 ror 〕 v. 發出持續的轟鳴聲；吼叫
day and night 日夜；不停地　　**up to** 高達
decibel 〔'dɛsə,bɛl 〕 n. 分貝

The decibel is the unit *used to measure the loudness of sound.* A

normal conversation reaches 55 decibels; a jet plane goes to 100

decibels **and** more, **and** an ordinary subway train *approaching the*

station can be *twice as* loud *as the loudest jet.* *At 120 decibels* the

ear stops hearing sound, **and** pain starts.

分貝是用來衡量音量大小的單位。正常對話達到55分貝；一架噴射機
會到100分貝以上，一般的地鐵列車進站時，聲量可能是最吵的噴射機
的兩倍大。在120分貝時，耳朵會停止聽到聲音，然後開始疼痛。

* unit[1] 〔'junɪt 〕 n. 單位　　measure[2,4] 〔'mɛʒɚ 〕 v. 測量
　loudness 〔'laʊdnɪs 〕 n. 響度；音量
　normal[3] 〔'nɔrmḷ 〕 adj. 正常的
　conversation[2] 〔,kɑnvɚ'seʃən 〕 n. 對話　　reach[1] 〔 ritʃ 〕 v. 達到
　jet plane 噴射機（ = jet[3] 〔 dʒɛt 〕）
　ordinary[2] 〔'ɔrdn,ɛrɪ 〕 adj. 普通的　　subway[2] 〔'sʌb,we 〕 n. 地下鐵
　train[1] 〔 tren 〕 n. 火車；列車　　approach[3] 〔 ə'protʃ 〕 v. 接近
　twice as…as～ 是～的兩倍　　pain[2] 〔 pen 〕 n. 疼痛

What's worse, it is not only hearing **that** *is threatened.*

[3](F) *According to research*, loud noises, *over a period of time*, cause

loss *of sleep*, anger, *and* many mental *and* physical problems.

　　更糟的是，不僅是聽力受到威脅。根據研究，經過一段時間，大聲的噪音會造成睡眠喪失、憤怒，和許多心理和身體的問題。

> * *what's worse* 更糟的是　　threaten[3] 〔'θrɛtn̩〕 v. 威脅
> *according to* 根據　　research[4] 〔rɪ's3tʃ,'ris3tʃ〕 v. n. 研究
> period[2] 〔'pɪrɪəd〕 n. 期間　　loss[2] 〔lɔs〕 n. 喪失
> mental[3] 〔'mɛntl̩〕 adj. 心理的　　physical[4] 〔'fɪzɪkl̩〕 adj. 身體的

Such problems have been observed *among factory workers, prisoners*

in large prisons, and people who drive heavy trucks, operate pneumatic

drills, or go to rock-and-roll concerts frequently.

工廠工人、大型監獄囚犯、重型卡車的駕駛、操作氣壓電鑽機的人，或經常參加搖滾演唱會的人，都被觀察到有這種問題。

> * observe[3] 〔əb'z3v〕 v. 觀察　　factory[1] 〔'fæktrɪ〕 n. 工廠
> prisoner[2] 〔'prɪznə〕 n. 囚犯　　prison[2] 〔'prɪzn̩〕 n. 監獄
> *heavy truck* 重型卡車　　operate[2] 〔'ɑpə,ret〕 v. 操作
> rock-and-roll 〔'rɑkən'rol〕 adj. 搖滾樂的
> concert[3] 〔'kɑns3t〕 n. 音樂會；演唱會
> frequently[3] 〔'frikwəntlɪ〕 adv. 經常

To deal with the problem, quieter machines have been developed.

[4](A) *Yet* the right *to decide*, *most of the time*, is in the hands *of*

customers. Merchants point out *that* people *who* buy motorcycles, *for instance, prefer the loudest ones **because** they sound powerful.*

為了處理這個問題，已經研發了更安靜的機器。然而，大多數的時間，決定權還是在顧客的手中。例如，商人指出，購買摩托車的人比較喜歡聲音最大聲的，因為它們聽起來強而有力。

* ***deal with*** 應付；處理   quiet[1] 〔`kwaɪət`〕 *adj.* 安靜的
develop[2] 〔dɪ`vɛləp`〕 *v.* 研發   right[1] 〔raɪt〕 *n.* 權利
customer[2] 〔`kʌstəmə`〕 *n.* 顧客   merchant[3] 〔`mɜtʃənt`〕 *n.* 商人
point out 指出   ***for instance*** 例如 (= *for example*)
prefer[2] 〔prɪ`fɝ`〕 *v.* 比較喜歡
powerful[2] 〔`pauəfəl`〕 *adj.* 強有力的

Indeed, it takes everybody's efforts *to keep city noise from increasing.*

[5]**(D)** *Even so*, experts say, *in twenty years the cities will be twice as loud **as** they are today **because** of the growth of the population.* The

inhabitants may *then* have to shout *to be heard at the dinner table.*

的確，防止城市噪音增加，需要每個人的努力。即便如此，專家說由於人口的增長，再過二十年，城市噪音會是現在的兩倍。居民那時可能必須在餐桌上大吼，對方才聽得見。

* indeed[2] 〔ɪn`did`〕 *adv.* 的確   take[2] 〔tek〕 *v.* 需要
effort[2] 〔`ɛfət`〕 *n.* 努力   ***keep~from*** … 使~不要…
even so 儘管如此   expert[2] 〔`ɛkspɝt`〕 *n.* 專家
growth[2] 〔groθ〕 *n.* 成長

TEST 7

說明： 第1至5題，每題一個空格。請依文意在文章後所提供的(A)到
(F) 選項中分別選出最適當者。

Coral reefs are not just splendid rocks. They are
actually similar to skeletons and are composed of small
living organisms called polyps. ___1___

Unfortunately, the coral environments are in grave
danger from human activities. Overfishing damages them
as it removes certain species of fish, thus disturbing the
food chain. ___2___ Of course, these explosions also
destroy many other sea creatures as well as the coral reefs
themselves.

___3___ Fertilizers used in farming cause increased
nutrient flow into reef water, which harms the reefs'
chemical balance. Human waste leads to the growth of
algae, which takes light and oxygen away from coral reefs.

Finally, the biggest problem is increasing carbon
dioxide emissions. ___4___ It is impossible for organisms
to adapt rapidly to such fundamental chemical changes in
their environment.

So is there hope for the future of coral reefs? Some areas such as Ahus Island, Papua New Guinea, have restricted fishing for years in key reef areas. ___5___ But the threat of global warming and increasing carbon dioxide emissions may be too big a problem for government to solve.

(A) Coral reefs are also under threat of water pollution.

(B) Other governments have started reef restoration projects to enhance the growth rate of coral reefs.

(C) Some fishermen even use dynamite fishing, in which explosives are thrown in the water to kill fish.

(D) These result in irreversible change in the chemical composition of the reef water.

(E) Accordingly, coral reefs flourish even though they are surrounded by ocean waters that provide few nutrients.

(F) Coral reefs are important to the ocean ecology because they support rich undersea biodiversity, from plants to vast numbers of fishes.

TEST 7 詳解

Coral reefs are not *just* splendid rocks. They are *actually*

similar to skeletons *and* are composed of small living organisms

called polyps.

珊瑚礁不只是非常漂亮的岩石。它們實際上與骨骼相似，是由一種
叫作珊瑚蟲的微生物所構成。

* coral[5] (ˈkɔrəl) *n.* 珊瑚   reef[5] (rif) *n.* 礁
  splendid[4] (ˈsplɛndɪd) *adj.* 壯麗的；極美的
  actually[3] (ˈæktʃuəlɪ) *adv.* 實際上
  similar[2] (ˈsɪmələ) *adj.* 相似的 < to >
  skeleton[5] (ˈskɛlətn̩) *n.* 骨骸；骸骨
  compose[4] (kəmˈpoz) *v.* 組成
  be composed of 由…組成；由…構成
  organism[6] (ˈɔrgənˌɪzəm) *n.* 有機體；生物
  living organism 生物   *called~* 叫作~
  polyp (ˈpɑlɪp) *n.* 珊瑚蟲；水螅蟲

> be composed of
>   由…組成
> = be made up of
> = consist of

[1](F) Coral reefs are important *to the ocean ecology because they*

support rich undersea biodiversity, from plants to vast numbers of

fishes.

珊瑚礁對海洋生態很重要，因為它們維持了豐富的海底生物多樣性，從
植物到大量的魚類。

* ocean[1] (ˈoʃən) *n.* 海洋

ecology[6]〔 ɪˈkɑlədʒɪ 〕 *n.* 生態（學）；生態環境

spport[2]〔 səˈport 〕 *v.* 支撐；維持

rich[1]〔 rɪtʃ 〕 *adj.* 豐富的

undersea〔ˈʌndəˈsi〕 *adj.* 海裡的

biodiversity〔 baɪoˌdaɪˈvɜsətɪ 〕 *n.* 生物多樣性

vast[4]〔 væst 〕 *adj.* 巨大的　　***vast numbers of*** 大量的

Unfortunately, the coral environments are in grave danger *from human activities*. Overfishing damages them *as it removes certain species of fish, thus disturbing the food chain.*

　　遺憾的是，人類的活動使珊瑚的環境面臨重大危險。過度捕撈會傷害它們，因為這樣會消除某些魚類，因而干擾食物鏈。

* unfortunately[4]〔 ʌnˈfɔrtʃənɪtlɪ 〕 *adv.* 不幸地；遺憾地

environment[2]〔 ɪnˈvaɪrənmənt 〕 *n.* 環境

grave[4]〔 grev 〕 *adj.* 重大的　　***in danger*** 有危險

activity[3]〔 ækˈtɪvətɪ 〕 *n.* 活動

overfishing〔ˌovəˈfɪʃɪŋ〕 *n.* （魚的）過度捕撈

damage[2]〔ˈdæmɪdʒ〕 *v.* 損害　　remove[3]〔 rɪˈmuv 〕 *v.* 除去

certain[1]〔ˈsɜtn̩〕 *adj.* 某些　　species[4]〔ˈspiʃɪz〕 *n. pl.* 品種

thus[1]〔 ðʌs 〕 *adv.* 因此　　disturb[4]〔 dɪˈstɜb 〕 *v.* 打擾

chain[3]〔 tʃen 〕 *n.* 鏈子　　***food chain*** 食物鏈

[2](C) Some fishermen *even* use dynamite fishing, *in which explosives are thrown in the water to kill fish.* *Of course*, these explosions *also* destroy many other sea creatures *as well as* the coral reefs themselves.

有些漁夫甚至使用炸藥捕魚，就是丟炸藥到水裡殺死魚。當然，這些爆炸也摧毀了許多其他的海洋生物，以及珊瑚礁本身。

* fisherman[2] (ˈfɪʃəmən) *n.* 漁夫　　dynamite[6] (ˈdaɪnəˌmaɪt) *n.* 炸藥
explosive[4] (ɪkˈsplosɪv) *n.* 炸藥　　*of course* 當然
explosion[4] (ɪkˈsploʒən) *n.* 爆炸　　destroy[3] (dɪˈstrɔɪ) *v.* 摧毀
creature[2] (ˈkritʃə) *n.* 生物　　*as well as* 以及

[3](A) Coral reefs are *also* under threat *of water pollution.*

Fertilizers *used in farming* cause increased nutrient flow *into reef*

water, **which harms the reefs' chemical balance.**　Human waste leads

to the growth *of algae,* **which takes light and oxygen away from coral**

reefs.

　　珊瑚礁也受到水污染的威脅。農業使用的肥料會增加流入珊瑚礁水域中的養分，這會危害珊瑚礁的化學平衡。人類的廢棄物導致藻類的增加，這會奪走珊瑚礁的光和氧。

* threat[2] (θrɛt) *n.* 威脅　　　**be under threat** 受到威脅
pollution[4] (pəˈluʃən) *n.* 污染　　fertilizer[5] (ˈfɝtḷˌaɪzə) *n.* 肥料
farming (ˈfɑrmɪŋ) *n.* 農業　　increased[2] (ɪnˈkrist) *adj.* 增加的
nutrient[6] (ˈnjutrɪənt) *n.* 營養素　　flow[2] (flo) *n.* 流
harm[3] (hɑrm) *v.* 傷害　　chemical[2] (ˈkɛmɪkḷ) *adj.* 化學的
balance[3] (ˈbæləns) *n.* 平衡　　waste[1] (west) *n.* 廢棄物
lead to 導致　　growth[2] (groθ) *n.* 生長；增加
algae (ˈældʒi) *n. pl.* 海藻　　light[2] (laɪt) *n.* 光；光線
oxygen[4] (ˈɑksədʒən) *n.* 氧

Finally, the biggest problem is increasing carbon dioxide emissions. <u>[4](D) These result in irreversible change *in the chemical composition of the reef water.*</u> It is impossible for organisms *to adapt rapidly to such fundamental chemical changes in their environment.*

最後，最大的問題是日益增加的二氧化碳排放量。這會導致珊瑚礁水域的化學組成發生不可逆轉的變化。生物不可能迅速適應他們的環境中，這種重大的化學變化。

* increasing[2] (ɪnˋkrisɪŋ) *adj.* 漸增的；越來越多的
  carbon dioxide (ˋkɑrbən daɪˋɑksaɪd) *n.* 二氧化碳
  emission (ɪˋmɪʃən) *n.* 排放　　***result in*** 導致；造成
  irreversible (ˏɪrɪˋvɝsəbḷ) *adj.* 不可逆的
  change[2] (tʃendʒ) *n.* 改變
  composition[4] (ˏkɑmpəˋzɪʃən) *n.* 組成
  organism[6] (ˋɔrgənˏɪzəm) *n.* 生物
  adapt[4] (əˋdæpt) *v.* 適應 < to >
  rapidly[2] (ˋræpɪdlɪ) *adv.* 快速地
  fundamental[2] (ˏfʌndəˋmɛntḷ) *adj.* 基本的；重大的

adapt *v.* 使適應
adopt *v.* 採用；領養
adept *adj.* 精通的

So is there hope *for the future of coral reefs*? Some areas *such as Ahus Island, Papua New Guinea,* have restricted fishing *for years in key reef areas.* <u>[5](B) Other governments have started reef restoration projects *to enhance the growth rate of coral reefs.*</u>

　　所以珊瑚礁的未來有希望嗎？有些地區，像是巴布亞新幾內亞的奧胡斯島，多年來已經在重要的珊瑚礁地區限制捕撈。其他的政府已經開始進行珊瑚礁恢復計劃，以提高珊瑚礁的生長率。

* area[1] (ˋɛrɪə, ˋerɪə) *n.* 地區
  Ahus Island (əˋhus ˋaɪlənd) *n.* 奧胡斯島
  Papua New Guinea (ˌpæpjʊə ˌnju ˋgɪnɪ) *n.* 巴布亞紐幾內亞
  restrict[3] (rɪˋstrɪkt) *v.* 限制　　key[1] (ki) *adj.* 非常重要的
  government[2] (ˋgʌvənmənt) *n.* 政府
  restoration[6] (ˌrɛstəˋreʃən) *n.* 恢復
  project[2] (ˋprɑdʒɛkt) *n.* 計劃
  enhance[6] (ɪnˋhæns) *v.* 提高；增加　　rate[3] (ret) *n.* 比率

But the threat *of global warming **and** increasing carbon dioxide*

emissions may be *too* big a problem *for government to solve.*

　　但是全球暖化和日益增加的二氧化碳排放量的威脅，對政府來說，可能是一個太大，而無法解決的問題。

* global[3] (ˋglobl̩) *adj.* 全球的　　warm[1] (wɔrm) *v.* 變溫暖
  global warming 全球暖化　　carbon[5] (ˋkɑrbən) *n.* 碳
  dioxide (daɪˋɑksaɪd) *n.* 二氧化物
  carbon dioxide 二氧化碳
  too…to V. 太…以致於不~　　solve[2] (sɑlv) *v.* 解決

TEST 8

說明： 第1至5題，每題一個空格。請依文意在文章後所提供的(A)到
(F) 選項中分別選出最適當者。

There is a true story about a remarkable dog named
Bobby in Scotland that actually had a statue erected in
his honor. ___1___ He was nothing more than a street
dog without a master, who had to struggle to stay alive.

___2___ Somehow Bobby understood and appreciated
this single act of compassion in a world of cruelty. So
when Jock passed away, Bobby began to stand guard by
his grave. Day in and day out, in any kind of weather,
Bobby would hold to his lonely and brave post. ___3___
The townspeople were deeply moved by Bobby's
incredible devotion, so they buried him next to Jock and
built a statue in his memory.

___4___ When we receive help and kindness from
others—parents, friends, or perhaps strangers—do we
remain forever grateful and seek to return the favor in

any way possible? Or is it more likely that we forget
about the event after a few days?

    __5__   It is the basis for filial piety, and the reason
why we pay homage to our ancestors. If we forget this,
how can we compare to Bobby? Can we still claim to
have more of a soul than a street dog?

(A) This continued on until the day he died, fourteen
years later.

(B) What did Bobby do to deserve this recognition?

(C) For the Chinese, one of the most important virtues
is the ability to feel true gratitude.

(D) One day an old man named Jock noticed his plight
and bought him something to eat.

(E) This sniffer dog was selected from the litter at eight
weeks old and was trained in basic obedience.

(F) Are there many humans who can match Bobby's
dedication?

TEST 8 詳解

There is a true story *about a remarkable dog named Bobby in*

*Scotland **that** actually had a statue erected in his honor.*

有一則眞實故事，是關於在蘇格蘭一隻非常出色，名叫巴比的狗，
爲了紀念牠，還眞的立了一座雕像。

* remarkable[4] ﹝ rɪˋmɑrkəbḷ ﹞ *adj.* 出色的；卓越的
  named ~ 名叫~   Scotland ﹝ˋskɑtlənd ﹞ *n.* 蘇格蘭
  actually[3] ﹝ˋæktʃʊəlɪ ﹞ *adv.* 實際上；眞地
  statue[3] ﹝ˋstætʃʊ ﹞ *n.* 雕像
  erect[5] ﹝ ɪˋrɛkt ﹞ *v.* 豎立
  honor[3] ﹝ˋɑnɚ ﹞ *n.* 榮譽；敬意
  *in one's **honor*** 紀念~

> status ﹝ˋstetəs ﹞ *n.* 地位
> statue ﹝ˋstætʃʊ ﹞ *n.* 雕像
> stature ﹝ˋstætʃɚ ﹞ *n.* 身材

[1]**(B)** What did Bobby do *to deserve this recognition*? He was *nothing*

more than a street dog *without a master*, **who** *had to struggle to stay*

alive.

巴比做了什麼，值得這種認可？牠只不過是一隻沒有主人，必須爲了生
存而奮鬥的流浪狗。

* deserve[4] ﹝ dɪˋzɝv ﹞ *v.* 應得
  recognition[4] ﹝ˌrɛkəgˋnɪʃən ﹞ *n.* 承認；認可
  nothing more than 僅僅；只不過
  street dog 流浪狗 (= *stray dog*)   master[1] ﹝ˋmæstɚ ﹞ *n.* 主人
  struggle[2] ﹝ˋstrʌgḷ ﹞ *v.* 奮鬥；努力   ***stay alive*** 活著

²**(D)** *One day* an old man *named Jock* noticed his plight **and** bought him something *to eat.* *Somehow* Bobby understood **and** appreciated this single act *of compassion in a world of cruelty.* **So when** *Jock passed away*, Bobby began to stand guard *by his grave.*

有一天，一個名叫喬克的老人注意到巴比的困境，買東西給牠吃。不知道為什麼，巴比竟然能了解和感激，在這殘酷的世界中，這個很有同情心的行為。所以當喬克過世時，巴比開始在他的墳墓旁守衛。

* notice[1] 〔'notɪs〕 v. 注意到　　plight[6] 〔plaɪt〕 n. 困境；苦境
  somehow[3] 〔'sʌm,haʊ〕 adv. 不知道為什麼
  appreciate[3] 〔ə'priʃɪ,et〕 v. 感激　　single[2] 〔'sɪŋɡl〕 adj. 單一的
  act[1] 〔ækt〕 n. 行為　　compassion[5] 〔kəm'pæʃən〕 n. 同情
  cruelty[4] 〔'kruəltɪ〕 n. 殘酷　　**pass away** 去世
  guard[2] 〔ɡɑrd〕 n. 守衛；看守　　**stand guard** 站崗；守衛
  by[1] 〔baɪ〕 prep. 在⋯旁邊　　grave[4] 〔ɡrev〕 n. 墳墓

Day in **and** *day out*, *in any kind of weather*, Bobby would hold to his lonely **and** brave post. ³**(A)** This continued on *until the day he died, fourteen years later.*

日復一日，在任何一種天氣下，巴比都孤單又勇敢地堅守自己的崗位。這一直持續到十四年後，牠去世的那一天。

* **day in and day out** 日復一日　　weather[1] 〔'wɛðɚ〕 n. 天氣
  hold to 堅持　　lonely[2] 〔'lonlɪ〕 adj. 孤單的
  brave[1] 〔brev〕 adj. 勇敢的　　post[1] 〔post〕 n. 崗位
  on[1] 〔ɑn〕 adv.（繼續）下去　　later[1] 〔'letɚ〕 adv. ⋯之後

The townspeople were *deeply* moved *by Bobby's incredible devotion*, *so* they buried him *next to Jock and* built a statue *in his memory*.

巴比不可思議的奉獻深深地打動了鎮民，所以他們把牠埋葬在喬克旁邊，為紀念牠而建了一座雕像。

　　* townspeople〔'taʊnz͵pipḷ〕*n. pl.* 鎮民　　move[1]〔muv〕*v.* 使感動
　　incredible〔ɪn'krɛdəbḷ〕*adj.* 令人難以置信的
　　devotion[5]〔dɪ'voʃən〕*n.* 忠誠；奉獻（= *dedication*[6]）
　　bury[3]〔'bɛrɪ〕*v.* 埋葬　　***next to*** 在⋯旁邊
　　in** one's **memory 紀念～

[4](F) Are there many humans ***who can match Bobby's dedication***? ***When*** we receive help ***and*** kindness *from others—parents, friends, **or** perhaps strangers*—do we remain *forever* grateful ***and*** seek to return the favor *in any way possible*? ***Or*** is it *more* likely ***that*** we *forget about the event after a few days*?

　　有許多人能比得上巴比的奉獻精神嗎？當我們得到他人——父母、朋友，或許還有陌生人——的幫助和善意時，我們是不是會永遠感激，並找尋任何可能的方式來回報恩惠？或者我們更可能會在幾天之後，就忘記這件事？

　　* match[2]〔mætʃ〕*v.* 比得上
　　kindness[2]〔'kaɪndnɪs〕*n.* 善意；友好的行為
　　perhaps[1]〔pɚ'hæps〕*adv.* 也許　　stranger[2]〔'strendʒɚ〕*n.* 陌生人
　　remain[3]〔rɪ'men〕*v.* 保持　　forever[3]〔fɚ'ɛvɚ〕*adv.* 永遠

grateful[4] 〔'gretfəl 〕 *adj.* 感激的　　seek[3] 〔 sik 〕 *v.* 尋求
return[1] 〔 rɪ'tɜn 〕 *v.* 回報　　favor[2] 〔'fevə 〕 *n.* 恩惠
likely[1] 〔'laɪklɪ 〕 *adj.* 可能的　　event[2] 〔 ɪ'vɛnt 〕 *n.* 事件

[5](C) *For the Chinese*, one *of the most important virtues* is the

ability *to feel true gratitude.* It is the basis *for filial piety,* ***and*** the

reason ***why*** *we pay homage to our ancestors.*

　　對中國人來說，最重要的美德之一，就是能夠感受到真正的感激。
這是孝順的基礎，也是我們向祖先表示敬意的原因。

* virtue[4] 〔'vɜtʃu 〕 *n.* 美德　　ability[2] 〔 ə'bɪlətɪ 〕 *n.* 能力
gratitude[4] 〔'grætə,tjud 〕 *n.* 感激　　basis[2] 〔'besɪs 〕 *n.* 基礎
filial 〔'fɪljəl 〕 *adj.* 孝順的
piety[6] 〔'paɪətɪ 〕 *n.* 虔誠；孝順

pay homage to *sb.*
向某人表示敬意
= show/have respect for *sb.*
= respect *sb.*
= look up to *sb.*
= hold *sb.* in respect

filial piety 孝順
homage 〔'hɑmɪdʒ 〕 *n.* 尊敬
pay homage to 向⋯表示敬意
ancestor[4] 〔'ænsɛstə 〕 *n.* 祖先

If we forget this, how can we compare to Bobby? Can we *still* claim

to have more of a soul ***than*** *a street dog*?
如果我們忘記這一點，我們如何能與巴比相提並論呢？我們還可以聲稱
比流浪狗擁有更高尚的情操嗎？

* *compare to* 與⋯相比　　claim[2] 〔 klem 〕 *v.* 宣稱
soul[1] 〔 sol 〕 *n.* 靈魂；心靈；道義；高尚情操

TEST 9

說明： 第1至5題，每題一個空格。請依文意在文章後所提供的(A)到
(F) 選項中分別選出最適當者。

Flushing the toilet with the lid up can spray diarrhea-causing bacteria into the air! Researchers from Leeds Teaching Hospitals detected C. difficile—a germ that can cause diarrhea and even life-threatening inflammation of the colon—nearly 10 inches above the toilet seat after flushing lidless hospital toilets. ___1___

"The highest numbers of C. difficile were recovered from air sampled immediately following flushing," the researchers reported in the Journal of Hospital Infection. " ___2___ "

C. difficile was spotted on surrounding surfaces 90 minutes after flushing, with an average of 15 to 47 contaminated toilet water droplets landing in the nearby environment, according to the study.

"Lidless conventional toilets increase the risk of C. difficile environmental contamination, and we suggest that their use be discouraged, particularly in settings where C. difficile infection is common," the authors wrote.

___3___ Almost everywhere we go, except in some public spaces, we have lids on our toilets. But not everyone puts them down when they flush. ___4___

Lidless toilets do spray water onto surrounding surfaces, including toothbrushes, but the health risk was found to be negligible. ___5___ However, C. difficile infections might reduce if more people opt to drop the lid.

(A) Although the study focused on hospital toilets, experts say the findings extend to public restrooms and households.

(B) Brushing your teeth is not effective against C. difficile.

(C) "Control" toothbrushes removed from the restroom before the flush were also speckled with fecal bacteria.

(D) They declined 8-fold after 60 minutes and a further 3-fold after 90 minutes.

(E) Doing so will reduce this type of environmental contamination very substantially.

(F) C. difficile is frequently found in hospitals and long-term care facilities where antibiotics are common.

TEST 9 詳解

Flushing the toilet *with the lid up* can spray diarrhea-causing

bacteria *into the air*!

沖馬桶時馬桶蓋是掀開的，可能會將引起腹瀉的細菌噴灑到空中！

* flush[4] 〔 flʌʃ 〕 *v. n.* 沖水；沖洗（廁所）　　toilet[2] 〔ˈtɔɪlɪt 〕 *n.* 馬桶
　lid[2] 〔 lɪd 〕 *n.* 蓋子　　up[1] 〔 ʌp 〕 *adj.* 豎直的；直立的
　spray[2] 〔 spre 〕 *v.* 噴灑　　diarrhea 〔ˌdaɪəˈriə 〕 *n.* 腹瀉
　cause[1] 〔 kɔz 〕 *v.* 造成　　bacteria[3] 〔 bækˈtɪrɪə 〕 *n. pl.* 細菌
　air[1] 〔 ɛr 〕 *n.* 空氣　　*the air* 空中

Researchers *from Leeds Teaching Hospitals* detected C. difficile—a

germ ***that*** can cause diarrhea ***and*** even life-threatening inflammation

of the colon —*nearly 10 inches above the toilet seat after flushing*

lidless hospital toilets.

里茲教學醫院的研究人員發現困難梭狀芽孢杆菌——一種可能導致腹
瀉，甚至危及生命的結腸炎症的病菌——它們是在醫院廁所中，沖無蓋
的馬桶之後，在馬桶座上方約 10 吋的地方偵測到的。

* researcher[4] 〔 rɪˈsɜtʃɚ 〕 *n.* 研究人員
　Leeds Teaching Hospitals 里茲教學醫院
　detect[2] 〔 dɪˈtɛkt 〕 *v.* 偵測；發現
　difficile 〔ˌdɪfɪˈsɪl 〕 *adj.* 【法文】難弄的；難以相處的（ = *difficult* ）
　C. difficile 困難梭狀芽孢杆菌　　germ[4] 〔 dʒɝm 〕 *n.* 病菌
　life-threatening *adj.* 威脅生命的

inflammation〔͵ɪnfləˈmeʃən〕*n.* 發炎　　colon〔ˈkolən〕*n.* 結腸
nearly[2]〔ˈnɪrlɪ〕*adv.* 將近；差不多　　lidless〔ˈlɪdlɪs〕*adj.* 無蓋的

[1]**(F)** C. difficile is *frequently* found *in hospitals **and** long-term care*

*facilities **where** antibiotics are common.*

在抗生素常見的醫院和長期護理機構，經常會發現困難梭狀芽孢杆菌。

* frequently[3]〔ˈfrikwəntlɪ〕*adv.* 經常地
long-term〔͵lɔŋˈtɝm〕*adj.* 長期的　　care[1]〔kɛr〕*n.* 照顧
facilities[4]〔fəˈsɪlətɪz〕*n. pl.* 設備；設施
antibiotic〔͵æntɪbaɪˈatɪk〕*n.* 抗生素
common[1]〔ˈkamən〕*adj.* 常見的

"The highest numbers *of C. difficile* were recovered *from air*

sampled immediately following flushing," the researchers reported

in the Journal of Hospital Infection. "[2]**(D)** They declined 8-fold

*after 60 minutes **and** a further 3-fold after 90 minutes.*"

「沖馬桶之後，立即從空氣中，重新採樣到的困難梭狀芽孢杆菌數
量最高，」，研究人員在《醫院感染期刊》上報導說。「它們在 60 分鐘
後，下降了八倍，90 分鐘後，又再下降了三倍。」

* number[1]〔ˈnʌmbɚ〕*n.* 數量；數目
recover[3]〔rɪˈkʌvɚ〕*v.* 找回；重新獲得
sample[2]〔ˈsæmpl̩〕*v.* 採樣　　immediately[3]〔ɪˈmidɪɪtlɪ〕*adv.* 立刻
following[1]〔ˈfaloɪŋ〕*prep.* 在…之後
report[1]〔rɪˈport〕*v.* 報導；報告　　journal[3]〔ˈdʒɝnl̩〕*n.* 期刊

infection[4] 〔 ɪn'fɛkʃən 〕 *n.* 感染　　decline[6] 〔 dɪ'klaɪn 〕 *v.* 減少
-fold ⋯倍（的）　　further[2] 〔 'fɝðɚ 〕 *adj.* 更進一步的

C. difficile was spotted on surrounding surfaces 90 minutes
after flushing, with an average of 15 to 47 contaminated toilet water
droplets landing in the nearby environment, according to the study.

根據這項研究，沖完馬桶後 90 分鐘，發現困難梭狀芽孢杆菌在馬
桶周圍的表面，平均有 15 到 47 個受污染的水滴，落在附近的環境中。

* spot[2] 〔 spɑt 〕 *v.* 發現　　surrounding[4] 〔 sə'raʊndɪŋ 〕 *adj.* 周圍的
surface[2] 〔 'sɝfɪs 〕 *n.* 表面　　average[3] 〔 'ævərɪdʒ 〕 *n.* 平均（數）
contaminate[5] 〔 kən'tæmə͵net 〕 *v.* 污染
droplet 〔 'drɑplɪt 〕 *n.* 小水滴　　land[1] 〔 lænd 〕 *v.* 降落
nearby[2] 〔 'nɪr͵baɪ 〕 *adj.* 附近的
environment[2] 〔 ɪn'vaɪrənmənt 〕 *n.* 環境
according to 根據　　study[1] 〔 'stʌdɪ 〕 *n.* 研究

"Lidless conventional toilets increase the risk *of C. difficile*
environmental contamination, ***and*** we suggest ***that*** *their use be*
discouraged, particularly in settings ***where*** C. difficile infection is
common," the authors wrote.

「傳統無蓋式的馬桶，會增加困難梭狀芽孢杆菌污染環境的風險，
所以我們建議不要使用它們，尤其是在困難梭狀芽孢杆菌感染很常見的
環境中，」作者寫道。

* conventional[2]〔kən'vɛnʃənḷ〕*adj.* 傳統的
increase[2]〔ɪn'kris〕*v.* 增加　　risk[3]〔rɪsk〕*n.* 風險
environmental[3]〔ɪn,vaɪrən'mɛntḷ〕*adj.* 環境的
contamination[5]〔kən,tæmə'neʃən〕*n.* 污染
suggest[3]〔səg'dʒɛst〕*v.* 建議
discourage[4]〔dɪs'kɝɪdʒ〕*v.* 勸阻；使打消念頭
particularly[2]〔pə'tɪkjələlɪ〕*adv.* 尤其；特別是
setting[5]〔'sɛtɪŋ〕*n.* 環境　　author[3]〔'ɔθɚ〕*n.* 作者

[3]**(A)** ***Although*** *the study focused on hospital toilets*, experts say the findings extend *to public restrooms **and** households.*

雖然這項研究聚焦在醫院的廁所，但專家說，這些研究結果可延伸至公共廁所和家庭中。

* ***focus on*** 聚焦；集中　　expert[2]〔'ɛkspɝt〕*n.* 專家
findings〔'faɪndɪŋz〕*n. pl.* 研究結果
extend[4]〔ɪk'stɛnd〕*v.* 延伸；延長　　public[1]〔'pʌblɪk〕*adj.* 公共的
restroom[2]〔'rɛst,rum〕*n.* 廁所　　household[4]〔'haʊs,hold〕*n.* 家庭

Almost everywhere we go, except in some public spaces, we have lids *on our toilets.* ***But*** not everyone puts them *down **when** they flush.*

[4]**(E)** Doing so will reduce this type *of environmental contamination very substantially.*

幾乎無論走到哪，除了在一些公共場所以外，我們的馬桶都有馬桶蓋。但是並不是每個人在沖馬桶時，都會把蓋子放下。放下馬桶蓋會大幅減少這類的環境污染。

* space[1] 〔 spes 〕 *n.* 場所　　reduce[3] 〔 rɪ'djus 〕 *v.* 減少
substantially[5] 〔 səb'stænʃəlɪ 〕 *adv.* 大大地

Lidless toilets do spray water *onto surrounding surfaces*,

including toothbrushes, ***but*** the health risk was found to be

negligible.

　　無蓋的馬桶的確會噴水在周圍的表面上，包括牙刷，但已經發現，
這種危害健康的風險是可以被忽略的。

* toothbrush 〔'tuθ,brʌʃ 〕 *n.* 牙刷
negligible 〔'nɛglədʒəbl̩ 〕 *adj.* 可以忽略的【neglect[4] *v.* 忽略】

,

[5](C) "Control" toothbrushes *removed from the restroom before the*

flush were *also* speckled *with fecal bacteria.* *However*, C. difficile

infections might reduce ***if*** *more people opt to drop the lid.*

在沖馬桶之前，從廁所拿走的「受管制的」牙刷，也可能會被糞便細菌
污染。然而，如果有更多人選擇放下馬桶蓋，那麼困難梭狀芽孢杆菌的
感染情況可能就會減少。

* control[3] 〔 kən'trol 〕 *n.* 控制；管制
remove[3] 〔 rɪ'muv 〕 *v.* 移動；搬動；除去
speckle 〔'spɛkl̩ 〕 *v.* 使弄上斑點；玷污 *< with >*
fecal 〔'fikl̩ 〕 *adj.* 糞便的
opt 〔 ɑpt 〕 *v.* 選擇【option[6] *n.* 選擇】
drop[2] 〔 drɑp 〕 *v.* 使落下；放下

TEST 10

說明： 第 1 至 5 題，每題一個空格。請依文意在文章後所提供的 (A) 到
(F) 選項中分別選出最適當者。

For many years, McDonald's has attracted millions
of kids to eat there by giving them free toys. Knowing
they can get something to play with, kids have been
conditioned into associating McDonald's with fun.
____1____ In kids' heads, McDonald's is paradise, when
in fact it is obesity land in disguise. In the year 2011,
concerned consumer groups harshly attacked the practice
of giving free toys as a marketing strategy. ____2____ In
response to such criticism, the fast-food giant was quick
to come up with a solution. ____3____ This is quite a
tactful counterattack that has turned the tide around.
It has successfully reshaped the burger titan into
everybody's best friend again. ____4____ Now McDonald's
is planning a campaign to present its food as nutritious.
Exactly how they are going to hypnotize consumers into

buying this idea is unknown, but we can be sure that we will be bombarded with a series of ads, slogans, star endorsements, and sales. ___5___ With the right kind of gifts, who is to say that sober-minded grown-ups won't be tricked?

(A) Rumors have it that pretty soon there will be Happy Meals for adults.

(B) Not surprisingly, they try every means to drag their parents into one of the chain restaurants on a regular basis.

(C) It can only be imagined how reluctant the parents must have been.

(D) Only this time, they are friends to not only kids, but also the poor and the needy.

(E) They claimed that it was unjust for the restaurant to lure kids into eating unhealthy food through any means.

(F) Instead of giving toys for free, they charged parents 10 dimes for each toy and then donated the money to charity.

TEST 10 詳解

For many years, McDonald's has attracted millions of kids *to eat there by giving them free toys*. *Knowing they can get something to play with*, kids have been conditioned *into associating McDonald's with fun*.

多年來，麥當勞藉由給免費玩具，已經吸引了數百萬的孩子去那裡吃東西。孩子們知道，他們能得到一些可以玩的東西，所以已經習慣於把麥當勞和樂趣聯想在一起。

* McDonald's〔mək'dɑnḷdz〕*n.* 麥當勞
  attract³〔ə'trækt〕*v.* 吸引　　million²〔'mɪljən〕*n.* 百萬
  millions of 數百萬的　　free¹〔fri〕*adj.* 免費的
  toy¹〔tɔɪ〕*n.* 玩具　　***play with*** 玩
  condition²〔kən'dɪʃən〕*v.* 使習慣於；控制；制約
  associate⁴〔ə'soʃɪˌet〕*v.* 聯想＜*with*＞　　fun¹〔fʌn〕*n.* 樂趣

¹**(B)** *Not surprisingly*, they try every means *to drag their parents into one of the chain restaurants on a regular basis*. *In kids' heads*, McDonald's is paradise, ***when*** *in fact it is obesity land in disguise*.

不令人意外的是，孩子們會嘗試各種方法，定期把父母拖進麥當勞的其中一家連鎖餐廳。在小孩的腦海裡，麥當勞是樂園，實際上它是經過偽裝的，會讓人肥胖的地方。

* means[2] 〔 minz 〕 *n.* 方法；手段【單複數同形】
drag[2] 〔 dræg 〕 *v.* 拖；拉　　chain[2] 〔 tʃen 〕 *n.* 連鎖店
on a regular basis 定期地 (= *reqularly*[2])
paradise[3] 〔 'pærə,daɪs 〕 *n.* 天堂；樂園
obesity 〔 o'bisətɪ 〕 *n.* 肥胖
land[1] 〔 lænd 〕 *n.* 想像（或虛構）的地方
disguise[4] 〔 dɪs'gaɪz 〕 *n.* 偽裝　　**in disguise** 偽裝的

In the year 2011, concerned consumer groups *harshly* attacked the

practice *of giving free toys as a marketing strategy.* [2](E) They

claimed ***that*** *it was unjust for the restaurant to lure kids into eating*

unhealthy food through any means.

在 2011 年，擔心的消費者團體嚴厲攻擊，以贈送免費玩具作為行銷策略的做法。他們宣稱，餐廳以任何方式，引誘孩子吃不健康的食物，是不合理的。

* concerned[3] 〔 kən's͡ɜnd 〕 *adj.* 擔心的
consumer[4] 〔 kən'sumɚ,-'sjumɚ 〕 *n.* 消費者
harshly[4] 〔 'harʃlɪ 〕 *adv.* 嚴厲地　　attack[2] 〔 ə'tæk 〕 *v.* 攻擊
practice[1] 〔 'præktɪs 〕 *n.* 做法；慣例
marketing 〔 'markɪtɪŋ 〕 *n.* 行銷
strategy[3] 〔 'strætədʒɪ 〕 *n.* 策略　　claim[2] 〔 klem 〕 *v.* 宣稱
unjust 〔 ʌn'dʒʌst 〕 *adj.* 不公平的；不合理的

lure[6] 〔 lʊr 〕 *v.* 誘惑　　unhealthy[2] 〔 ʌn'hɛlθɪ 〕 *adj.* 不健康的
through[2] 〔 θru 〕 *prep.* 透過；藉由

In response to such criticism, the fast-food giant was quick to come
up with a solution.　[3](F) *Instead of giving toys for free*, they charged
parents 10 dimes *for each toy **and** then* donated the money *to charity*.
針對這種批評，這家速食界龍頭很快就想出解決辦法。他們不免費贈送
玩具，而是每個玩具向父母收取一美元，然後把錢捐給慈善機構。

　　* response[3] 〔 rɪ'spɑns 〕 *n.* 回答；回應
　　in response to 作為對⋯的回覆；作為對⋯的反應
　　criticism[4] 〔 'krɪtə,sɪzəm 〕 *n.* 批評
　　fast-food 〔 'fæst,fud 〕 *adj.* 速食的
　　giant[2] 〔 'dʒaɪənt 〕 *n.* 大公司　　*come up with* 提出；想出
　　solution[2] 〔 sə'luʃən 〕 *n.* 解決之道
　　instead of 不⋯而~　　*for free* 免費
　　charge[2] 〔 tʃɑrdʒ 〕 *v.* 收費；向⋯索取（費用）
　　dime 〔 daɪm 〕 *n.* 一角　　donate[6] 〔 'donet 〕 *v.* 捐贈
　　charity[4] 〔 'tʃærətɪ 〕 *n.* 慈善機構

This is *quite* a tactful counterattack *that* has turned the tide around.

It has *successfully* reshaped the burger titan *into everybody's best*
friend again. [4](D) *Only this time*, they are friends *to **not only** kids*,
***but also** the poor **and** the needy*.

這是一個相當機智的反擊，已經扭轉了形勢。這項策略已經成功把漢堡巨人，又重新塑造成大家最好的朋友。只有這一次，他們不僅是孩子們的朋友，也是窮困的人的朋友。

* tactful[6] ('tæktfəl) adj. 機智的
  counterattack ('kauntərə,tæk) n. 反擊
  【counter- = contra- (= against)】
  turn around 使好轉　　tide[3] (taɪd) n. 形勢
  successfully[2] (sək'sɛsfəlɪ) adj. 成功地
  reshape (ri'ʃep) v. 重新塑造　　burger[2] ('bɝgɚ) n. 漢堡
  titan ('taɪtn̩) n. 巨人；要人；重要組織
  not only…but also 不僅…而且
  the poor 窮人 (= poor people)
  needy[4] ('nidɪ) adj. 貧困的　　***the needy*** 貧困的人

Now McDonald's is planning a campaign *to present its food as*

nutritious.

現在，麥當勞正在策劃一項宣傳活動，以說明他們的食品是有營養的。

* plan[1] (plæn) v. 計劃
  campaign[4] (kæm'pen) n. 活動
  present[2] (prɪ'zɛnt) v. 呈現；顯示
  nutritious[6] (nju'trɪʃəs) adj. 有營養的

*Exactly **how** they are going to hypnotize consumers into buying this*

*idea is unknown, **but** we can be sure **that** we will be bombarded with*

*a series of ads, slogans, star endorsements, **and** sales.*

他們究竟要如何催眠消費者相信這個想法是未知的，但我們可以肯定，
我們將被一連串的廣告、標語、明星代言，和特價活動疲勞轟炸。

* exactly[2] 〔 ɪgˋzæktlɪ 〕 *adv.* 確切地　　hypnotize 〔ˋhɪpnəˏtaɪz 〕 *v.* 催眠
  buy[1] 〔 baɪ 〕 *v.* 相信 (= believe[1])
  unknown[1] 〔 ʌnˋnon 〕 *adj.* 未知的　　bombard[6] 〔 bamˋbard 〕 *v.* 轟炸
  be bombarded with 被…疲勞轟炸
  a series of 一連串的；一系列的
  ad[3] 〔 æd 〕 *n.* 廣告 (= advertisement[3])
  slogan[4] 〔ˋslogən 〕 *n.* (簡短而有吸引力的) 廣告標語
  star[4] 〔 star 〕 *n.* 明星
  endorsement 〔 ɪnˋdɔrsmənt 〕 *n.* 背書；保證；(對商品等的) 推薦
  sale[1] 〔 sel 〕 *n.* 降價出售；特價活動

[5]**(A)** Rumors have it *that pretty soon there will be Happy Meals for*

adults. With the right kind of gifts, **who** *is to say* **that** *sober-minded*

grown-ups won't be tricked?

有傳言指出，很快就會有快樂成人餐。有了正確的禮物，誰能說冷靜的
大人不會被騙？

* rumor[3] 〔ˋrumɚ 〕 *n.* 謠言　　　*rumor has it that* 謠言指出；謠傳說
  meal[2] 〔 mil 〕 *n.* 一餐　　adult[1] 〔 əˋdʌlt 〕 *n.* 成人
  sober-minded 〔ˋsobɚˋmaɪndɪd 〕 *adj.* 冷靜的
  grown-up 〔ˋgronˏʌp 〕 *n.* 成年人　　trick[2] 〔 trɪk 〕 *v.* 欺騙

TEST 11

One of the biggest challenges I face as a teacher is developing a sense of community among students in the classroom. Students today have the wonders of interactive information technology at their fingertips. ___1___ With the magic of the Internet, students can connect to others who may live on the other side of the world. ___2___ But does it? I have found that even in small classes, students seldom speak to each other.

___3___ Most students have spent hours and hours connecting to others via the Internet, yet they have become isolated from the physical presence of their classmates.

___4___ This can be done in several ways. Of course there are always the basic introductions. But one strategy that students find beneficial is working on a task in small groups. Students say that this not only helps them to get to know each other, but also teaches them to cooperate with others. In addition, each group must share their finished work with the rest of the class. Shy students say that speaking in front of the class in a group is better than standing alone. ___5___ Outgoing students praise groups as a place they can communicate more fluently and freely. But to many students, the best thing about group work is making new friends in the real world!

(A) They say group work helps them to develop confidence.

(B) They can google almost any subject they are interested in.

(C) Often they don't know the name of the person sitting next to them.

(D) Developing a sense of community in the classroom improves learning.

(E) Experts say that the world is shrinking and technology brings people closer together.

(F) The unique matchmaking platform combines modern social networking trends with ancient matchmaking traditions.

TEST 11 詳解

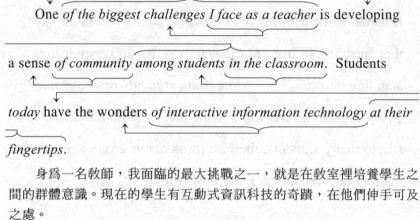

One *of the biggest challenges I face as a teacher* is developing a sense *of community among students in the classroom.* Students *today* have the wonders *of interactive information technology at their* fingertips.

身為一名教師，我面臨的最大挑戰之一，就是在教室裡培養學生之間的群體意識。現在的學生有互動式資訊科技的奇蹟，在他們伸手可及之處。

＊challenge³〔ˈtʃælɪndʒ〕*n.* 挑戰　face¹〔fes〕*v.* 面對
develop²〔dɪˈvɛləp〕*v.* 培養　sense¹〔sɛns〕*n.* 感覺
community⁴〔kəˈmjunətɪ〕*n.* 社區
a sense of community 社群意識
among¹〔əˈmʌŋ〕*prep.* 在…之間　wonder²〔ˈwʌndɚ〕*n.* 奇蹟
interactive〔ˌɪntɚˈæktɪv〕*adj.* 相互作用的；互動的
information⁴〔ˌɪnfɚˈmeʃən〕*n.* 資訊
technology³〔tɛkˈnɑlədʒɪ〕*n.* 科技　fingertip〔ˈfɪŋgɚˌtɪp〕*n.* 指尖
at *one's **fingertips*** 近在手邊；隨時可供使用

¹**(B)** They can google *almost* any subject *they are interested in.* With *the magic of the Internet*, students can connect to others ***who may live*** *on the other side of the world.*

他們幾乎可以用網路，搜尋到任何自己感興趣的主題。有了網路的魔法，學生可以連結到居住在世界另一邊的其他人。

* google〔'gugl〕v.（用網路搜尋引擎）搜尋
subject[2]〔'sʌbdʒɪkt〕n. 主題　　**be interested in** 對…有興趣
magic[2]〔'mædʒɪk〕n. 魔法　　Internet[4]〔'ɪntɚ,nɛt〕n. 網際網路
connect[3]〔kə'nɛkt〕v. 連結 < to >

[2](E) Experts say *that the world is shrinking and technology brings people closer together.* **But** does it? I have found *that even in small classes*, students *seldom* speak to each other.

專家說，世界正在縮小，而且科技使得人們更靠近。但真的是如此嗎？我發現，甚至在小班課堂上，學生也很少互相說話。

* expert[2]〔'ɛkspɚt〕n. 專家　　shrink[3]〔ʃrɪŋk〕v. 縮水；縮小
bring[1]〔brɪŋ〕v. 使　　even[1]〔'ivən〕adv. 甚至；即使

[3](C) *Often* they don't know the name *of the person sitting next to them.* Most students have spent hours **and** hours | *connecting to others via the Internet* |, **yet** they have become isolated *from the physical presence of their classmates.*

他們常常不知道坐在旁邊的人的名字。大多數學生已經花了數小時的時間，經由網路和其他人連結，然而他們卻和實際存在的同學隔離。

* via[5] (ˋvaɪə) *prep.* 經由 (= *by way of*)
isolated[4] (ˋaɪsḷ͵etɪd) *adj.* 隔離的；孤立的
physical[4] (ˋfɪzɪkḷ) *adj.* 身體的；有形的
presence[2] (ˋprɛzns̩) *n.* 存在

[4](**D**) Developing a sense *of community in the classroom* improves

learning. This can be done *in several ways.* *Of course* there are *always*

the basic introductions.

　　在課堂上培養群體意識，可以改善學習效果。這可以用幾種方式來完成。當然，總是會有基本的介紹。

* improve[2] (ɪmˋpruv) *v.* 改善　　basic[1] (ˋbesɪk) *adj.* 基本的
introduction[3] (͵ɪntrəˋdʌkʃən) *n.* 介紹

But one strategy *that students find beneficial* is working on a task

in small groups. Students say *that this not only* helps them to get to

know each other, *but also* teaches them to cooperate with others.

但是，有個學生覺得有益的策略，就是以小組的方式進行任務。學生指出，這不僅能幫助他們彼此認識，也教導他們要和別人合作。

* strategy[3] (ˋstrætədʒɪ) *n.* 策略　　find[1] (faɪnd) *v.* 覺得
beneficial[5] (͵bɛnəˋfɪʃəl) *adj.* 有益的　　***work on*** 致力於
task[2] (tæsk) *n.* 任務；工作　　***get to V.*** 得以～
cooperate[4] (koˋɑpə͵ret) *v.* 合作

In addition, each group must share their finished work *with the rest of the class*. Shy students say *that speaking in front of the class in a group* is better *than standing alone*. [5](A) They say *group work helps them to develop confidence.*

此外，每個小組都必須與班上其他的同學，分享他們完成的作業。害羞的學生說，一組人在全班面前講話，比自己單獨站在那裡要好。他們說，小組作業能幫助他們培養自信。

* ***in addition*** 此外　　share[2] 〔ʃɛr〕*v.* 分享
  finished[1] 〔'fɪnɪʃt〕*adj.* 完成的　　rest[1] 〔rɛst〕*n.* 其餘的人或物
  in front of 在…前面　　***the class*** 全班同學
  in a group 成群地　　alone[1] 〔ə'lon〕*adv.* 單獨地；獨自
  confidence[4] 〔'kɑnfədəns〕*n.* 自信；信心

Outgoing students praise groups as a place *they can communicate more fluently **and** freely*. ***But** to many students*, the best thing *about group work* is making new friends *in the real world*!

外向的學生稱讚小組作業，認為它是一個他們可以更流利、更自由溝通的地方。但對許多學生來說，關於小組作業最好的事情就是，能在現實世界中結交新朋友！

* outgoing[5] 〔'aʊt,goɪŋ〕*adj.* 外向的　　praise[2] 〔prez〕*v.* 稱讚
  communicate[3] 〔kə'mjunə,ket〕*v.* 溝通
  fluently[4] 〔'fluəntlɪ〕*adv.* 流利地　　***make friends*** 交朋友

TEST 12

說明： 第1至5題，每題一個空格。請依文意在文章後所提供的(A)到
(F) 選項中分別選出最適當者。

Farmers in India perform a complex routine practice
when there isn't enough rainfall for their crops. ___1___
However, the discharge of water from the pump is always
weak, so they can irrigate only a small part of their fields.

India has the most agricultural water pumps in the
world. ___2___ They not only suck ground water dry, but
also drain the farmers' pockets and endanger the country's
economy.

Watering crops has placed a heavy burden on the
Indian economy because the pumps take electricity from
the country's power grid yet function inefficiently.
Approximately 18 million of the 25 million pumpsets are
connected to the national electricity grid. Indian
government authorities calculate that farming constitutes
about 15 percent of gross domestic product, but it consumes
more than a quarter of the nation's electricity, mostly by
powering irrigation pumps. ___3___

On top of the economic problem, the country is also facing an infrastructure problem. ___4___ The system is likely to shut down at any time. In July 2012, more than half of India suffered the world's largest blackout ever. Smaller-scale blackouts are common and frequent, even in some of India's largest cities, arising from an outdated and overloaded power grid. ___5___

(A) The pumps cause a large number of problems.

(B) The nation's power system is unable to meet the demand for electricity from both agriculture and the ever-expanding manufacturing industry.

(C) There is not enough transportation available to the farmers.

(D) They rent a water pump from town, shoulder it laboriously, carry it to a corner of their land, and begin drawing out ground water.

(E) Easing energy demand from agriculture is indeed a top priority.

(F) In addition, electricity for farmers is usually free, but utilities providing power and the state electricity commissions are running at a huge loss.

TEST 12 詳解

Farmers *in India* perform a complex routine practice ***when** there isn't enough rainfall for their crops.* **[1](D) They rent a water pump from town**, shoulder it *laboriously*, carry it *to a corner of their land,* **and** begin drawing out ground water.

當降雨量不足以灌溉農作物時，印度的農民會進行複雜的例行工作。他們會從城裡租抽水機，費力地把它扛在肩上，帶到他們土地的一角，然後開始抽地下水。

* India〔ˈɪndɪə〕*n.* 印度　　perform[3]〔pəˈfɔrm〕*v.* 執行
complex[3]〔kəmˈplɛks, ˈkɑmplɛks〕*adj.* 複雜的
routine[3]〔ruˈtin〕*adj.* 例行的　*n.* 例行公事
practice[1]〔ˈpræktɪs〕*n.* 業務；工作
rainfall[4]〔ˈrenˌfɔl〕*n.* 降雨量　　crop[2]〔krɑp〕*n.* 農作物
rent[3]〔rɛnt〕*v.* 租　　pump[2]〔pʌmp〕*n.* 抽水機；幫浦
shoulder[1]〔ˈʃoldə〕*v.* 把…扛在肩上；挑起
laboriously〔ləˈbɔrɪəslɪ〕*adv.* 費力地
carry[1]〔ˈkærɪ〕*v.*（用手、肩等）挑；背；提
corner[2]〔ˈkɔrnə〕*n.* 角落　　draw[1]〔drɔ〕*v.* 汲取；引出 < *out* >
ground water 地下水

However, the discharge *of water from the pump* is *always* weak, ***so*** they can irrigate *only* a small part *of their fields*.

然而，抽水機抽出的水總是很小，所以他們只能灌溉一小部分的田地。

* discharge[6] (dɪs'tʃɑrdʒ) *n.* 流出
weak[1] (wik) *adj.* 虛弱的;微弱的
irrigate ('ɪrə,get) *v.* 灌溉　　field[2] (fild) *n.* 田地;田野

India has the most agricultural water pumps *in the world.*

[2](A) The pumps cause a large number of problems. They *not only*
suck ground water dry, *but also* drain the farmers' pockets *and*
endanger the country's economy.

印度是世界上農用抽水機最多的國家。這些抽水機造成許多的問
題。它們不僅吸乾地下水,還榨乾農民的錢,而且危害國家經濟。

* agricultural[5] (,ægrɪ'kʌltʃərəl) *adj.* 農業的
cause[1] (kɔz) *v.* 造成　　*a large number of* 許多的
suck[3] (sʌk) *v.* 吸　　drain[3] (dren) *v.* 使耗盡;使枯竭
pocket[1] ('pɑkɪt) *n.* 口袋;(可用於開銷的)錢
endanger[4] (ɪn'dendʒɚ) *v.* 危害　　economy[4] (ɪ'kɑnəmɪ) *n.* 經濟

Watering crops has placed a heavy burden *on the Indian economy*
because the pumps take electricity from the country's power grid *yet*
function inefficiently. Approximately 18 million *of the 25 million*
pumpsets are connected *to the national electricity grid.*

灌溉農作物已經給印度經濟帶來沉重的負擔,因為這些抽水機從國
家的輸電網路獲取電力,但運作的效率很低。在 2,500 萬台的抽水機組
中,大約有 1,800 萬台連接到國家的輸電網路。

* water[1] 〔ˈwɔtɚ〕 v. 給…澆水   place[1] 〔ples〕 v. 放置

burden[3] 〔ˈbɝdn̩〕 n. 負擔   ***place a burden on*** 增加…的負擔

electricity[3] 〔ɪˌlɛkˈtrɪsətɪ〕 n. 電

grid 〔grɪd〕 n. 輸電網   ***power grid*** 輸電網路

yet[1] 〔jɛt〕 adv. 但是   function[2] 〔ˈfʌŋkʃən〕 v. 運作；起作用

inefficiently[3] 〔ˌɪnəˈfɪʃəntlɪ〕 adv. 無效率地

approximately[6] 〔əˈprɑksəmɪtlɪ〕 adv. 大約

pumpset 〔ˈpʌmpˌsɛt〕 n. 抽水機組

connect[3] 〔kəˈnɛkt〕 v. 連接 < *to* >

national[2] 〔ˈnæʃənl̩〕 adj. 全國的

Indian government authorities calculate ***that*** *farming constitutes about*

15 percent of gross domestic product, ***but*** it consumes more than a

quarter of the nation's electricity, *mostly by powering irrigation pumps.*

印度政府當局統計，農業約佔國內生產毛額的15%，但其消耗的電力，

卻佔全國電力的四分之一以上，大多是提供動力給灌溉用的抽水機。

* government[2] 〔ˈgʌvɚnmənt〕 n. 政府

authorities[4] 〔əˈθɔrətɪz〕 n. pl. 當局

calculate[4] 〔ˈkælkjəˌlet〕 v. 計算   farming[1] 〔ˈfɑrmɪŋ〕 n. 農業

constitute[4] 〔ˈkɑnstəˌtjut〕 v. 構成   gross[5] 〔gros〕 adj. 全部的

domestic[3] 〔dəˈmɛstɪk〕 adj. 國內的

product[3] 〔ˈprɑdəkt〕 n. 產品

gross domestic product 國內生產毛額（= GDP）

consume[4] 〔kənˈsum, -ˈsjum〕 v. 消耗

quarter[2] 〔ˈkwɔrtɚ〕 n. 四分之一   mostly[4] 〔ˈmostlɪ〕 adv. 大多

power[1] 〔ˈpaʊɚ〕 v. 給…提供動力

irrigation 〔ˌɪrəˈgeʃən〕 n. 灌溉

[3](F) *In addition*, electricity *for farmers* is *usually* free, *but* utilities *providing power and* the state electricity commissions are running *at a huge loss.*

此外，給農民的電力通常是免費的，但是提供電力的公用事業公司和國家電力委員會，卻有龐大的虧損。

* *in addition* 此外（＝*moreover*[4]）　　free[1]〔fri〕*adj.* 免費的
　utility[6]〔ju'tɪlətɪ〕*n.* 公用事業；公用事業公司【鐵路、公車、
　　瓦斯、電力、自來水事業等】　　state[1]〔stet〕*adj.* 國家的
　commission[5]〔kə'mɪʃən〕*n.* 委員會
　run[1]〔rʌn〕*v.* 運作　　huge[1]〔hjudʒ〕*adj.* 巨大的
　loss[2]〔lɔs〕*n.* 損失；虧損　　*at a loss* 虧損

On top of the economic problem, the country is *also* facing an infrastructure problem. [4](B) The nation's power system is unable to meet the demand *for electricity from both agriculture and the ever-expanding manufacturing industry.* The system is likely to shut down *at any time*.

　　除了這個經濟問題之外，印度也面臨基礎建設的問題。國家的電力系統無法滿足農業和不斷擴大的製造工業的電力需求。電力系統可能會隨時關閉。

* *on top of* 除了…之外　　economic[4]〔ˌikə'nɑmɪk〕*adj.* 經濟的
　face[1]〔fes〕*v.* 面臨
　infrastructure〔'ɪnfrəˌstrʌktʃɚ〕*n.* 基礎建設（如鐵路、下水道等）
　system[3]〔'sɪstəm〕*n.* 系統　　*be unable to V.* 無法～

meet[1] ﹝ mit ﹞ v. 滿足　　demand[4] ﹝ dɪ'mænd ﹞ n. 需求
agriculture[3] ﹝ 'ægrɪ͵kʌltʃɚ ﹞ n. 農業
ever-expanding ﹝ 'ɛvɚɪk'spændɪŋ ﹞ adj. 不斷擴充的
manufacturing[4] ﹝ ͵mænjə'fæktʃərɪŋ ﹞ adj. 製造業的
industry[2] ﹝ 'ɪndəstrɪ ﹞ n. 產業；工業　　*be likely to V.* 可能…
shut down 關閉　　*at anytime* 隨時

In July 2012, more than half *of India* suffered the world's largest

blackout *ever*. Smaller-scale blackouts are common *and* frequent,

even in some of India's largest cities, arising from an outdated *and*

overloaded power grid. [5](E) Easing energy demand *from agriculture*

is *indeed* a top priority.

在 2012 年 7 月，印度有一半以上的地區，遭受全世界有史以來最大規模的停電。由於老舊和超載的輸電網路，甚至在一些印度最大的城市，小規模的停電也是常見而且頻繁的。緩解來自農業的能源需求，確實是要最優先處理的事。

　　* suffer[3] ﹝ 'sʌfɚ ﹞ v. 遭受　　blackout ﹝ 'blæk͵aʊt ﹞ n. 停電
ever[1] ﹝ 'ɛvɚ ﹞ adv. 迄今；有史以來　　scale[3] ﹝ skel ﹞ n. 規模
common[1] ﹝ 'kɑmən ﹞ adj. 常見的
frequent[3] ﹝ 'frikwənt ﹞ adj. 經常的　　*arise from* 起因於；由於
outdated ﹝ 'aʊt'detɪd ﹞ adj. 過時的
overloaded ﹝ 'ovɚ'lodɪd ﹞ adj. 負荷過重的
ease[1] ﹝ iz ﹞ v. 減輕；緩和　　energy[2] ﹝ 'ɛnɚdʒɪ ﹞ n. 能源
undeed[3] ﹝ ɪn'did ﹞ adv. 的確　　priority[5] ﹝ praɪ'ɔrətɪ ﹞ n. 優先事項
top priority 最優先事項

TEST 13

說明： 第 1 至 5 題，每題一個空格。請依文意在文章後所提供的 (A) 到
(F) 選項中分別選出最適當者。

Sir Richard Branson (born on July 18, 1950), a famed
British entrepreneur, is best known for his widely successful
Virgin brand, a banner that includes a variety of business
organizations.   1

He formed Virgin Atlantic Airways in 1984, launched
Virgin Mobile in 1999, and later failed in a 2000 bid to
handle the National Lottery. He has also started a European
short-haul airline, Virgin Express. Branson first got notoriety
with Virgin Records.   2   Known for his wacky exploits
used to promote his businesses, Branson is keen on playful
slogans, exemplified by his "Mine is bigger than yours" on
the new Airbus A340-600 jets used by his airline.   3
The hot air balloon, called the "Virgin Atlantic Flyer," was
the first hot air balloon ever to cross the Atlantic Ocean, and
was the largest ever flown at 60.513 m³ volume, reaching
speeds in excess of 209 km/h.

On September 25, 2004, he announced the signing of a
deal.   4

He has guest starred, playing himself, on several television shows, including *Friends*, *Baywatch* and *Only Fools and Horses*. ___5___

(A) Under it a new space tourism company, Virgin Galactic, will license the technology behind SpaceShipOne to take paying passengers into suborbital space.

(B) He has also made several unsuccessful attempts to fly in a hot air balloon around the world.

(C) He became Sir Richard Branson when he was knighted by the Queen in 1999 for his great business skill and passion of the spirit of the United Kingdom.

(D) He is also the star of a new reality television show on Fox called *The Rebel Billionaire* where sixteen contestants will be tested for their sense of adventure.

(E) It started out with multi-instrumentalist Mike Oldfield and introduced bands like the Sex Pistols and Culture Club to the world music scene.

(F) He temporarily retired in 2000 after his failure with the lottery.

TEST 13 詳解

Sir Richard Branson (*born on July 18, 1950*), *a famed British entrepreneur*, is best known *for his widely successful Virgin brand, a banner **that** includes a variety of business organizations.*

理察・布蘭森爵士（出生於 1950 年 7 月 18 日）是一位著名的英國企業家，以其非常成功的維珍品牌而聞名，維珍這個旗幟包括了各式各樣的商業組織。

* Sir[1] 〔 sæ, sɜ 〕 *n.* 爵士【貴族頭銜，用於姓名前】
  Sir Richard Branson *n.* 理察・布蘭森爵士【英國維珍集團的董事長，旗下企業包括維珍航空、維珍鐵路、維珍可樂、維珍唱片等】
  famed[4] 〔 fem 〕 *adj.* 著名的（ = *famous*[2] ）
  entrepreneur 〔 ˌɑntrəprə'nɜ 〕 *n.* 企業家
  British 〔 'brɪtɪʃ 〕 *adj.* 英國的　　***be well known for*** 以…而聞名
  widely[1] 〔 'waɪdlɪ 〕 *adv.* 廣泛地；非常地
  Virgin 〔 'vɜdʒɪn 〕 *n.* 維珍集團【英國財團】　　brand[2] 〔 brænd 〕 *n.* 品牌
  banner[5] 〔 'bænə 〕 *n.* 旗幟；橫幅　　include[2] 〔 ɪn'klud 〕 *v.* 包括
  variety[3] 〔 və'raɪətɪ 〕 *n.* 種類；多樣性　　***a variety of*** 各式各樣的
  organization[2] 〔 ˌɔrgənə'zeʃən 〕 *n.* 組織；機構

[1] **(C)** He became Sir Richard Branson *when he was knighted by the Queen in 1999 for his great business skill **and** passion of the spirit of the United Kingdom.*

因為在商業上的非凡能力，和代表著英國精神的熱情，所以他於 1999 年，被英女王授予爵位，成為理察・布蘭森爵士。

* knight³〔naɪt〕 *v.* 授予爵位　　skill¹〔skɪl〕 *n.* 技巧；技能
passion³〔'pæʃən〕 *n.* 熱情　　spirit²〔'spɪrɪt〕 *n.* 精神
the United Kingdom 英國

He formed Virgin Atlantic Airways *in 1984*, launched Virgin

Mobile *in 1999*, ***and*** *later* failed *in a 2000 bid to handle the National*

Lottery.

他於 1984 年成立維珍航空，1999 年開辦維珍電信，但後來在 2000
年，投標經營國家彩券時失敗了。

* form²〔fɔrm〕 *v.* 組織；成立　　Atlantic〔æt'læntɪk〕 *adj.* 大西洋的
airways⁵〔'ɛr,wez〕 *n.* 航空公司
Virgin Atlantic Airways 維珍航空　　launch⁴〔lɔntʃ〕 *v.* 開辦
mobile³〔'mobḷ〕 *adj.* 可移動的　 *n.* 行動電話
Virgin Mobile 維珍電信　　bid⁵〔bɪd〕 *n.* 競標
handle²〔'hændḷ〕 *v.* 應付；處理；經營
national²〔'næʃənḷ〕 *adj.* 國家的；全國性的
lottery⁵〔'lɑtərɪ〕 *n.* 彩券　　***National Lottery*** 國家彩券

He has *also* started a European short-haul airline, *Virgin Express*.
他還創辦了一家歐洲短程航空公司——維珍快捷。

* start¹〔stɑrt〕 *v.* 開始；創辦　　haul⁵〔hɔl〕 *n.* (拖運) 距離
short-haul〔'ʃɔrt'hɔl〕 *adj.* 短程的　　airline²〔'ɛr,laɪn〕 *n.* 航空公司
express²〔ɪk'sprɛs〕 *n.* 快遞；快運　　***Virgin Express*** 維珍快捷

Branson *first* got notoriety *with Virgin Records*. ²**(E)** It started out *with multi-instrumentalist Mike Oldfield **and** introduced bands like*

*the Sex Pistols **and** Culture Club to the world music scene.*

布蘭森第一次得到壞名聲，是因爲維珍唱片。它以多樂器演奏家麥克・
奧德菲爾德起步，並將像是性手槍和文化俱樂部等樂團，帶入世界音樂
的場景中。

* notoriety〔ˌnotəˈraɪətɪ〕*n.* 壞名聲【notorious[6] *adj.* 惡名昭彰的】
  Virgin Records 維珍唱片　　***start out*** 出發；開始
  multi- 多…的　　instrumentalist[2]〔ˌɪnstrəˈmɛntl̩ɪst〕*n.* 樂器演奏家
  introduce[2]〔ˌɪntrəˈdjus〕*v.* 引進；介紹　　band[1]〔bænd〕*n.* 樂團
  Mike Oldfield〔ˈmaɪkˈoldˌfild〕*n.* 麥克・奧德菲爾德【英國作曲
  　家、新世紀音樂家、電子音樂大師】　　pistol[5]〔ˈpɪstl̩〕*n.* 手槍
  Sex Pistols 性手槍【英國龐克搖滾樂團，被視爲流行樂史上最有影響
  　力的樂團之一，引發了英國的龐克運動】
  Culture Club 文化俱樂部【80年代英國 New Wave 樂團，因爲主唱
  　Boy George 的男扮女裝造型很引人側目】　　scene[1]〔sin〕*n.* 場景

Known for his wacky exploits used to promote his businesses, Branson

is keen *on playful slogans,* *exemplified by his "Mine is bigger **than***

yours" on the new Airbus A340-600 jets used by his airline.

布蘭森以古怪事績宣傳他的事業而聞名，他熱中於滑稽的標語，例如，
維珍航空的新型空中巴士 A340-600 噴射機上的「我的噴射機比你的
大」。

* wacky〔ˈwækɪ〕*adj.* 古怪的；滑稽可笑的；荒謬的
  exploit[6]〔ɪkˈsplɔɪt〕*n.* 功績；功勞

promote³〔prə'mot〕v. 促銷；推銷
keen⁴〔kin〕adj. 熱中的；沉迷的 < on / about >
playful²〔'plefəl〕adj. (言詞、行為) 滑稽的
slogan⁴〔'slogən〕n. 口號；標語
exemplify〔ɪg'zɛmplə,faɪ〕v. 以…為例
airbus〔'ɛr,bʌs〕n. 空中巴士　　jet³〔dʒɛt〕n. 噴射機

³(B) He has *also* made several unsuccessful attempts *to fly in a hot air balloon around the world.* The hot air balloon, *called the "Virgin Atlantic Flyer,"* was the first hot air balloon *ever to cross the Atlantic Ocean*, **and** was the largest *ever flown at 60.513 m³ volume, reaching speeds in excess of 209 km/h.*

他還在世界各地嘗試飛行熱氣球，但失敗了好幾次。這個熱氣球被稱為「維珍大西洋飛行物」，是有史以來第一個飛越大西洋的熱氣球，也是有史以來最大的，體積為 60.513 立方公尺，飛行時速超過 209 公里。

　　* attempt³〔ə'tɛmpt〕n. 企圖；嘗試
　　make an atttempt 企圖；嘗試　　balloon¹〔bə'lun〕n. 氣球
　　hot air balloon 熱氣球　　　***around the world*** 在世界各地
　　flyer〔'flaɪɚ〕n. 空中飛行物　　***the Atlantic Ocean*** 大西洋
　　ever¹〔'ɛvɚ〕adv. 迄今；有史以來
　　fly¹〔flaɪ〕v. 飛；駕駛（飛機等）【fly-flew-flown】
　　volume³〔'vɑljəm〕n. 體積　　speed²〔spid〕n. 速度
　　excess⁵〔ɪk'sɛs〕n. 過度；超過　　***in excess of*** 超過

On September 25, 2004, he announced the signing *of a deal.*

[4](A) *Under it* a new space tourism company, *Virgin Galactic*, will

license the technology *behind SpaceShipOne to take paying*

passengers into suborbital space.

　　在 2004 年 9 月 25 日，他宣布簽署一項協議。根據這項協議，一家新的太空旅遊公司「維珍銀河」，將授權太空船一號的技術，帶付費的乘客進入未在地球軌道的太空。

* announce[3] 〔əˋnaʊns〕 *v.* 宣布　　sign[2] 〔saɪn〕 *v.* 簽署
　 deal[1] 〔dil〕 *n.* 協議；交易　　under[1] 〔ˋʌndɚ〕 *prep.* 按照；依據
　 space[1] 〔spes〕 *n.* 太空　　tourism[3] 〔ˋtʊrɪzm〕 *n.* 觀光
　 galactic 〔gəˋlæktɪk〕 *adj.* 銀河的【galaxy[6] 〔ˋgæləksɪ〕 *n.* 銀河系】
　 license[4] 〔ˋlaɪsṇs〕 *v.* 批准；給…發許可證
　 suborbital 〔sʌbˋɔrbɪtl̩〕 *adj.* 未進入地球軌道的【orbit[4] *n.* 軌道】
　 suborbital space 次軌道太空；亞軌道太空

He has guest starred, *playing himself, on several television*

*shows, including Friends, Baywatch **and Only Fools and Horses.***

　　他曾經在幾個電視節目中客串演出過自己，包括《六人行》、《海灘遊俠》，和《只有傻瓜和馬》。

* guest[1] 〔gɛst〕 *adv.* 客串地　　star[1] 〔stɑr〕 *v.* 主演　*n.* 明星
　 play[1] 〔ple〕 *v.* 扮演…角色；飾演　　show[1] 〔ʃo〕 *n.* 電視（節目）
　 Friends 六人行【美國影集】　　***Baywatch*** 海灘遊俠【英國影集】
　 Only Fools and Horses 只有傻瓜和馬【英國情境喜劇】

[5](D) He is *also* the star *of a new reality television show on Fox called*

*The Rebel Billionaire **where** sixteen contestants will be tested for their*

sense of adventure.

他也是福斯電視台，新的眞人實境電視節目的明星，節目名叫《叛逆的
億萬富翁》，將會有十六名參賽者接受冒險感的測試。

　　* reality[2] 〔 rɪˈælətɪ 〕 *n.* 眞實　　　rebel[4] 〔 rɪˈbɛl 〕 *adj.* 反叛的
　　billionaire 〔ˌbɪljəˈnɛr 〕 *n.* 億萬富翁
　　contestant[6] 〔 kənˈtɛstənt 〕 *n.* 參賽者　　sense[1] 〔 sɛns 〕 *n.* 感覺
　　adventure[3] 〔 ədˈvɛntʃɚ 〕 *n.* 冒險

【補充資料】

理查・布蘭森，玩出維珍集團

　　他，在英國媒體的民調中被評選爲「英國最聰明的人」；他，曾經
裸奔宣傳公司產品；他，曾經駕駛熱氣球駛入紐約時代廣場；他，首次
環球航行，因爲熱氣球被電線纏住，落在阿爾及利亞沙漠成爲民兵俘
虜；他，1986 年駕著「維珍挑戰 2 號」，經過地獄般的 3 天 8 小時 31 分，
打破藍帶獎紀錄，拿到快艇賽冠軍；他，曾經在波灣戰爭時駕駛飛機進
入巴格達解救人質……布蘭森的傳奇色彩，是全球企業界的異數。

天生的商業頭腦

　　布蘭森掌管旗下 350 家以上的公司，營業項目涵蓋航空、鐵路、通
訊、金融服務及民生消費等。他從小就有商業頭腦，在一個復活節假
期，和朋友用賣報紙的錢買了樹苗，種了 400 棵耶誕樹，可是大部分樹
苗都被野兔吃掉，於是他們氣急敗壞地獵殺野兔，以一先令一隻賣出。
17 歲時，布蘭森離開學校，拿著媽媽給的 4 英鎊，在一個狹窄的地下室
創辦《學生雜誌》，因爲採訪與廣告策略的成功，讓《學生雜誌》的發
行量一度劇增到 20 萬份。一個偶然的機會，布蘭森發現當時唱片的零售
價過高，可以打折的郵購唱片業務比《學生雜誌》有賺頭，於是全力投
入。不久後，英國郵局罷工，讓他們的郵購業務被迫轉到唱片實體店。

唱片裡看到市場潛力

唱片店的成功，卻讓布蘭森看到音樂行業的巨大潛力。他抵押所有資產，買下了一個莊園，作為錄音棚出租。維珍因簽下了邁克·奧德菲爾德，出版了他的個人專輯《管鐘》，連續兩個月位居排行榜冠軍，最後賣出了 1,300 萬張，成為歐美唱片史上的經典，讓布蘭森挖到「第一桶金」。接著，布蘭森簽下了流行樂隊「性手槍」、「人民聯盟」、「簡單頭腦」，以及歌手菲爾·柯林斯，和喬治男孩等。這些樂隊和歌手後來陸續竄紅，尤其是喬治男孩一個人，就佔了他們 1983 年營收的 40%。後來，布蘭森又創辦了維珍出版公司和維珍影視公司。

維珍航空改變格局

維珍集團真正引人矚目，是在 1984 年成立「維珍航空」時。從娛樂界進軍既無經驗、門檻又高的航空業，布蘭森的行為被當時企業界視為自殺行為。但是，經過布蘭森和維珍航空的員工們的奮戰，維珍終於克服萬難，首航成功，從此改變了維珍集團的企業格局。

熱氣球大冒險

布蘭森瘋狂的行徑何只一端，有一回著名熱氣球專家佩爾找到了他，問他願不願意一起進行熱氣球冒險，布蘭森立即同意加入。幾次操作失敗後，熱氣球失去了控制，布蘭森和佩爾被迫從半空中跳向結冰的大西洋。所幸，他們碰上了巡邏的英國海軍。後來，在首次飛越大西洋成功後，布蘭森和佩爾又計劃從日本飛越太平洋到美國，第一次因為天氣不佳放棄了，第二次他們降落在加拿大暴風雪的森林中。

死裡逃生後，布蘭森和佩爾居然又開始準備環球航行。首次環球航行因為熱氣球被電線纏住，落在了阿爾及利亞的沙漠中，他倆成為民兵俘虜。第二次環球航行他們從摩洛哥出發，飛過了利比亞、土耳其、烏茲別克等國後，於 1998 年 12 月 23 日進入中國領空。但是他們的飛行路線比中國政府預先允許的路線偏北了 150 哩，他們接到了中國政府的無線警告。布蘭森急中生智，透過英國首相幫忙，中國政府終於網開一面，允許熱氣球繼續飛行。讓布蘭森驚訝的是，當他的熱氣球離開中國海岸時，他收到一封電報，維珍航空將成為唯一可以從英格蘭直航上海的航空公司。

樂趣是成功的祕密

布蘭森認為「樂趣」是自己從事商業與維珍集團成功的祕密。樂趣讓布蘭森保持著創業的激情，全身心地投入工作，抓住一次次好的創意，不斷地克服困難，帶領維珍一次次進入陌生領域，並獲得成功。

TEST 14

說明： 第 1 至 5 題，每題一個空格。請依文意在文章後所提供的 (A) 到
(F) 選項中分別選出最適當者。

Carnegie Hall, the famous concert hall in New York
City, has undergone another restoration. ___1___

Carnegie Hall owes its existence to Andrew Carnegie,
the wealthy owner of a steel company in the late 1800s.
The hall was completed in 1891 and quickly gained fame
as an excellent arts hall where accomplished musicians
performed. ___2___ During the Great Depression, when
few people could afford to attend performances, the
directors sold part of the building to commercial
businesses. ___3___ A renovation in 1946 seriously
damaged the acoustical quality of the hall when the
makers of the film *Carnegie Hall* dug a hole in the dome
of the ceiling to allow for lights and air vents. ___4___

In 1960, a group of real estate developers planned to
demolish Carnegie Hall and build a high-rise office
building on the site. ___5___ The movement was
successful, and the concert hall is now owned by the city.

In the current restoration, builders restored the outer walls to their original appearance and closed the coffee shop. Carnegie Hall has never sounded better, and its prospects for the future have never looked more promising.

(A) It was later covered with short curtains and a fake ceiling, but the hall never sounded the same afterwards.

(B) Because of it, Carnegie Hall once again has the quality of sound that it had when it was first built.

(C) The city government had endeavored to restore the walls and the acoustic dome damaged in an earthquake.

(D) Despite its reputation, however, the concert hall suffered from several harmful renovations over the years.

(E) Consequently, a coffee shop was opened in one corner of the building, for which the builders replaced the brick and terra cotta walls with windowpanes.

(F) This threat triggered public support for Carnegie Hall and encouraged the City of New York to buy the property.

TEST 14 詳解

Carnegie Hall, *the famous concert hall in New York City*, has undergone another restoration. [1](B) *Because of it*, Carnegie Hall *once again* has the quality *of sound that* it had *when* it was first built.

紐約著名的卡內基音樂廳，已經進行了另一次的整修。正因爲如此，卡內基音樂廳再次擁有它最初建好時的音質。

* Carnegie〔kɑrˈnɛgɪ〕 n. 卡內基
　hall[2]〔hɔl〕 n. 大廳；會堂　　concert[3]〔ˈkɑnsɝt〕 adj. 音樂會用的
　undergo[6]〔ˌʌndɚˈgo〕 v. 經歷　　restoration[6]〔ˌrɛstəˈreʃən〕 n. 修復
　quality[2]〔ˈkwɑlətɪ〕 n. 品質；特質　　*quality of sound* 音質

Carnegie Hall owes its existence *to Andrew Carnegie, the wealthy owner of a steel company in the late 1800s.* The hall was completed *in 1891 and quickly* gained fame *as an excellent arts hall where accomplished musicians performed.*

卡內基音樂廳的存在，要歸功於 19 世紀末，一位富有的鋼鐵公司老闆安德魯・卡內基。音樂廳於 1891 年完工，很快就以優秀的藝術殿堂而聞名，技巧高超的音樂家都會在這裡表演。

* owe[3]〔o〕 v. 把…歸功於 < to >　　existence[3]〔ɪgˈzɪstəns〕 n. 存在
　Andrew Carnegie〔ˈændru kɑrˈnɛgɪ〕 n. 安德魯・卡內基【1835-1919，美國鋼鐵工業及慈善家】

wealthy[3]〔'wɛlθɪ〕 *adj.* 富有的　　owner[3]〔'onɚ〕 *n.* 擁有者

steel[2]〔stil〕 *adj.* 鋼鐵的　 *n.* 鋼鐵　　late[1]〔let〕 *adj.* 末期的

the 1800s 十九世紀　　complete[2]〔kəm'plit〕 *v.* 完成

gain[2]〔gen〕 *v.* 獲得　　fame[4]〔fem〕 *n.* 名聲

excellent[2]〔'ɛkslənt〕 *adj.* 優秀的

arts[1]〔arts〕 *adj.* 藝術的；美術的　　***arts hall*** 藝術館；藝術殿堂

accomplished[4]〔ə'kamplɪʃt〕 *adj.* 技術高超的

musician[2]〔mju'zɪʃən〕 *n.* 音樂家　　perform[3]〔pɚ'fɔrm〕 *v.* 表演

[2]**(D)** *Despite its reputation, however,* the concert hall suffered from

several harmful renovations *over the years.*

然而，儘管音樂廳有好的名聲，但多年來它卻遭受了幾次有害的裝修。

　　* despite[4]〔dɪ'spaɪt〕 *prep.* 儘管　　reputation[4]〔ˌrɛpjə'teʃən〕 *n.* 名聲

　　suffer from 受…之苦　　harmful[3]〔'harmfəl〕 *adj.* 有害的

　　renovation〔ˌrɛnə'veʃən〕 *n.* 裝修；翻新　　***over the years*** 多年來

During the Great Depression, ***when*** *few people could afford to attend*

performances, the directors sold part *of the building to commercial*

businesses.

在經濟大蕭條時期，很少人能負擔得起觀賞表演的費用，所以主管們就
把建築物的一部分，賣給了商業公司。

　　* depression[4]〔dɪ'prɛʃən〕 *n.* 不景氣

　　the Great Depression 大蕭條【1929-1933 年起於美國的經濟大衰退】

　　afford[3]〔ə'fɔrd〕 *v.* 負擔得起　　attend[2]〔ə'tɛnd〕 *v.* 出席；參加

performance[3] (pə'fɔrməns) *n.* 表演
director[2] (də'rɛktə) *n.* 主管；主任
commercial[3] (kə'mɝʃəl) *adj.* 商業的
business[2] ('bɪznɪs) *n.* 企業；公司

[3](E) *Consequently*, a coffee shop was opened *in one corner of the building, for **which** the builders replaced the brick **and** terra cotta walls with windowpanes.*

結果，建築物的一個角落裡開了一家咖啡店，為此，建造者用窗玻璃取代了磚頭和紅土牆。

* consequently[4] ('kɑnsə,kwɛntlɪ) *adv.* 因此；結果
   builder ('bɪldə) *n.* 建造者　　replace[3] (rɪ'ples) *v.* 取代
   brick[2] (brɪk) *n.* 磚頭
   terra cotta ('tɛrə'kɑtə) *n.* 紅土；赤陶土；陶俑【義大利文「烤過的
       土」，從拉丁文而來，是以黏土為原料，上釉或者是不上釉。赤陶土
       最常被用在花瓶、水道、屋瓦，還有建築工程的外部裝飾】
   windowpane ('wɪndo,pen) *n.* 窗玻璃

A renovation *in 1946 seriously* damaged the acoustical quality *of the hall* **when** *the makers of the film Carnegie Hall dug a hole in the dome of the ceiling to allow for lights **and** air vents.*

1946 年的裝修工程，嚴重損害了音樂廳的音響品質，當時《卡內基音樂廳》的電影製作人，考慮到光線和通風，在天花板的圓頂上挖了一個洞。

* acoustical〔ə'kustɪkl̩〕*adj.* 聽覺的；音響的
film[2]〔fɪlm〕*n.* 電影　　dig[1]〔dɪg〕*v.* 挖
hole[1]〔hol〕*n.* 洞　　dome[6]〔dom〕*n.* 圓頂
ceiling[2]〔'silɪŋ〕*n.* 天花板　　***allow for*** 考慮到
vent〔vɛnt〕*n.* 通風口

[4](A) It was *later* covered *with short curtains **and** a fake ceiling, **but***

the hall *never* sounded the same *afterwards*.
後來用短布簾和假的天花板覆蓋這個洞，但在那之後，音樂廳的音響品質聽起來已經不一樣了。

* later[2]〔'letɚ〕*adv.* 後來　　cover[2]〔'kʌvɚ〕*v.* 覆蓋
curtain[2]〔'kɝtn̩〕*n.* 窗簾；帷幕　　fake[3]〔'fek〕*adj.* 假的
afterwards[3]〔'æftɚwɚdz〕*adv.* 後來；之後

In 1960, a group of real estate developers planned to demolish

Carnegie Hall ***and*** build a high-rise office building *on the site*.
1960 年，一群房地產開發商打算拆除卡內基音樂廳，並在原址建造一棟高層辦公大樓。

* estate[5]〔ə'stet〕*n.* 地產　　***real estate*** 不動產；房地產
developer[2]〔dɪ'vɛləpɚ〕*n.* 開發業者
demolish〔də'malɪʃ〕*v.* 拆除（= *tear down* = *pull down*）
high-rise〔'haɪ'raɪz〕*adj.* 高層的
office building 辦公大樓　　site[4]〔saɪt〕*n.* 地點

5(F) This threat triggered public support *for Carnegie Hall **and*** encouraged the City of New York *to buy the property.* The movement was successful, ***and*** the concert hall is *now* owned *by the city*.

這個威脅激發了大眾對卡內基音樂廳的支持，並鼓勵紐約市府購買下該地產。這場運動是成功的，音樂廳現在為市府所有。

* threat[3] 〔θrɛt〕 *n.* 威脅　　trigger[6] 〔'trɪgɚ〕 *v.* 引發
public[1] 〔'pʌblɪk〕 *adj.* 大眾的　　support[2] 〔sə'port〕 *v.* 支持
encourage[2] 〔ɪn'kɝɪdʒ〕 *v.* 鼓勵　property[3] 〔'prapɚtɪ〕 *n.* 財產；地產
movement[1] 〔'muvmənt〕 *n.* （政治性、社會性之）運動

In the current restoration, builders restored the outer walls *to their original appearance **and*** closed the coffee shop. Carnegie Hall has *never* sounded better, ***and*** its prospects *for the future* have *never* looked *more* promising.

以目前的修復來說，建造者恢復外牆的原貌，並且關閉咖啡店。卡內基音樂廳從來沒有聽起來如此好過，而且它未來的前景從未如此光明過。

* current[3] 〔'kɝənt〕 *adj.* 現在的；目前的
restore[4] 〔rɪ'stor〕 *v.* 恢復；重建　　outer[3] 〔'autɚ〕 *adj.* 外面的
original[3] 〔ə'rɪdʒənl̩〕 *adj.* 最初的；原本的
appearance[2] 〔ə'pɪrəns〕 *n.* 外觀；樣子
prospect[5] 〔'praspɛkt〕 *n.* 希望；前景
promising[2] 〔'pramɪsɪŋ〕 *adj.* 有希望的

TEST 15

說明： 第 1 至 5 題，每題一個空格。請依文意在文章後所提供的 (A) 到
(F) 選項中分別選出最適當者。

____1____: in the online game Farmville players plant
strawberries and trees, milk cows and build farm
buildings. Farmville is open to members of the social
network Facebook and has developed in record time into
a mass phenomenon.

Just under 75 million virtual farmers from all over
the world make up Farmville's membership. ____2____.

____3____. Zynga also offers a game called Fishville
that allows you to build your own aquarium.

The virtual world of online gaming is a source of
money in the real world. In Farmville, for example,
players can earn experience points and online money for
free through diligence, which allows them to buy seeds
and farm animals. ____4____. But popular and sought-after
game elements such as barns and houses can be gotten
faster if you put real money into a Farmville account with
a credit card or PayPal.

      __5__. German data protectionists have warned against attempts by the game's owners to gather information on players. Some of Farmville's players have also reported unauthorized withdrawals from their bank accounts.

(A) Along with Farmville, other social network-based games have also experienced a boom

(B) The American Internet firm Zynga is behind Farmville and has said it was amazed at the speed with which the game took off

(C) However, not everything is rosy in the world of Farmville

(D) It sounds harmless and quite peaceful

(E) To do that the farmer must regularly check his fields or else crops will die

(F) If someone withdraws money from your account without your permission, report it to Zynga

TEST 15 詳解

[1](D) It sounds harmless **and** quite peaceful: *in the online game*
Farmville players plant strawberries **and** trees, milk cows **and** build
farm buildings.

這聽起來無害而且相當寧靜：在線上遊戲開心農場裡，玩家會種植
草莓和樹、擠牛奶，和蓋農場建築物。

* harmless[3] 〔'hɑrləs 〕 *adj.* 無害的
  peaceful[2] 〔'pisfəl 〕 *adj.* 平靜的；寧靜的
  online 〔'ɑn,laɪn 〕 *adj.* 線上的；網路上的
  Farmville 〔'fɑrm,vɪl 〕 *n.* 開心農場【一個由線上遊戲公司 Zynga 所
  提供的即時 (real-time) 農場模擬 (simulation) 遊戲。只要是
  Facebook 會員就可申請】　　strawberry[2] 〔'strɔ,bɛrɪ 〕 *n.* 草莓
  milk[1] 〔 mɪlk 〕 *v.* 擠 (奶)　　cow[1] 〔 kaʊ 〕 *n.* 母牛

Farmville is open *to members of the social network Facebook **and*** has
developed *in record time into a mass phenomenon.*

開心農場對社群網路臉書的成員開放，並且以創紀錄的速度，發展成一
個大眾化的現象。

* member[2] 〔'mɛmbɚ 〕 *n.* 成員　　social[2] 〔'soʃəl 〕 *adj.* 社會的；社交的
  network[3] 〔'nɛt,wɝk 〕 *n.* 網路
  develop[2] 〔 dɪ'vɛləp 〕 *v.* 發展　　record[2] 〔'rɛkɚd 〕 *adj.* 破記錄的
  in record time 迅速地；以創紀錄的速度
  mass[2] 〔 mæs 〕 *adj.* 大眾的；影響許多人的
  phenomenon[4] 〔 fə'nɑmə,nɑn 〕 *n.* 現象【複數形為 phenomena】

Just under 75 million virtual farmers *from all over the world* make up Farmville's membership. [2](B) The American Internet firm *Zynga* is behind Farmville ***and*** has said *it is amazed at the speed with which the game took off*.

來自世界各地將近 7,500 萬個虛擬農民，組成了開心農場的全體會員。在開心農場幕後的，就是美國網路公司星佳，他們表示，對於遊戲突然大受歡迎的速度感到驚訝。

* virtual[6]〔ˋvɝtʃuəl〕*adj.* 虛擬的　　***all over the world***　世界各地
make up　組成　　　membership[3]〔ˋmɛmbɚˏʃɪp〕*n.* 會員數；全體會員
Internet[4]〔ˋɪɪntɚˏnɛt〕*n.* 網際網路　　firm[2]〔fɝm〕*n.* 公司
Zynga〔ˋzɪngə〕*n.* 星佳【美國社交遊戲公司，於 2007 年 6 月在舊金山
　　成立】　　amaze[3]〔əˋmez〕*v.* 使驚訝　　speed[2]〔spid〕*n.* 速度
take off　（觀念、產品等）突然大受歡迎；（產品銷售量）急升

[3](A) *Along with Farmville*, other social network-based games have *also* experienced a boom. Zynga *also* offers a game ⌈called *Fishville **that** allows you to build your own aquarium*.

和開心農場一樣，其他以社群網路為基礎的遊戲，也經歷了榮景。星佳還提供了一個名為開心水族箱的遊戲，讓你打造自己的水族館。

* ***along with***　與…一起；在…以外
　　-based 表「以…為基地或特徵」，例如：London-based（總部在
　　　倫敦的）、oil-based（油性的）、computer-based（運用電腦的）。
　　experience[2]〔ɪkˋspɪrɪəns〕*v.* 經歷　　boom[5]〔bum〕*n.* 興隆
　　offer[2]〔ˋɔfɚ〕*v.* 提供　　allow[1]〔əˋlau〕*v.* 允許；讓
　　aquarium[3]〔əˋkwɛrɪəm〕*n.* 水族箱；水族館

The virtual world *of online gaming* is a source *of money in the*

real world. In Farmville, for example, players can earn experience

points *and* online money *for free through diligence,* **which** *allows*

them to buy seeds **and** *farm animals.* [4](**E**) *To do that* the farmer must

regularly check his fields *or else* crops will die.

　　線上遊戲的虛擬世界，是現實世界的金錢來源。例如，在開心農場裡，玩家可以藉由辛勤工作，免費賺得經驗值和線上金錢，讓他們可以購買種子和農場動物。要做到這一點，農民必須定期查看自己的田地，否則農作物將會死亡。

* gaming[1] 〔'gemɪŋ〕 *n.* 玩電腦遊戲　　source[2] 〔sors〕 *n.* 來源
earn[2] 〔ɝn〕 *v.* 賺　　**experience point** 經驗值 (= *XP*)
for free 免費　　diligence[4] 〔'dɪlədʒəns〕 *n.* 勤勉
seed[1] 〔sid〕 *n.* 種子　　regularly[2] 〔'rɛgjələˌlɪ〕 *adv.* 定期地
field[2] 〔fild〕 *n.* 田野　　*or else* 否則；不然
crop[2] 〔krɑp〕 *n.* 農作物

But popular **and** sought-after game elements *such as barns* **and**

houses can be gotten *faster* **if** *you put real money into a Farmville*

account with a credit card **or** *PayPal.*

但是，如果想更快得到搶手的遊戲要素（如穀倉和房屋），就要使用信用卡或 PayPal，將眞實金錢存入開心農場帳戶。

* sought-after〔'sɔt,æftɚ〕*adj.* 搶手的；很受歡迎的
element[2]〔'ɛləmənt〕*n.* 要素
such as 像是　　barn[3]〔barn〕*n.* 穀倉
account[3]〔ə'kaʊnt〕*n.* 帳戶　　***credit card*** 信用卡
PayPal 是一家總部在美國加州的電子商務（e-commerce）公司。它提供用戶之間線上轉移資金的服務，避免了傳統的郵寄支票或者匯款的方法。現在 PayPal 爲 e-Bay 全權擁有的子公司（subsidiary）。

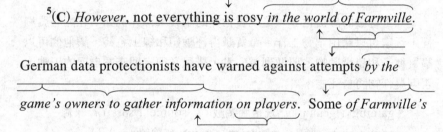

[5](C) *However,* not everything is rosy *in the world of Farmville.*
German data protectionists have warned against attempts *by the game's owners to gather information on players.* Some *of Farmville's players* have *also* reported unauthorized withdrawals *from their bank accounts.*

　　然而，在開心農場的世界裡，並非一切都是美好的。德國的數據保護主義者警告遊戲的擁有者，不要企圖收集玩家的資訊。有些開心農場的玩家也聲稱，他們的銀行帳戶有未經授權的提款。

* rosy〔'rozɪ〕*adj.* 玫瑰色的；美好的　　data[2]〔'detə〕*n. pl.* 資料
protectionist[2]〔prə'tɛkʃənɪst〕*n.* 保護主義者
warn against 告誡防範　　attempt[3]〔ə'tɛmpt〕*n.* 企圖
gather[2]〔'gæðɚ〕*v.* 收集　　on[1]〔an〕*prep.* 關於（= *about*[1]）
report[1]〔rɪ'port〕*v.* 報告；聲稱
unauthorized[6]〔ʌn'ɔθə,raɪzd〕*adj.* 未經授權的
withdrawal[4]〔wɪð'drɔəl〕*n.* 提取；提款

TEST 16

說明： 第 1 至 5 題，每題一個空格。請依文意在文章後所提供的 (A) 到 (F) 選項中分別選出最適當者。

Many people associate the Nobel Prizes with public recognition and financial reward for achievement reached by genius. ___1___ For example, William Shockley, the Nobel winner in physics in 1958 for inventing the transistor, was refused admission to a long-term genius study as a child due to his unremarkable IQ score. Luis Alvarez, another Nobel winner for his work on elementary particles, had been excluded from the same research program. ___2___ In 1928, Louis Terman, a Stanford University professor, pioneered the use of IQ tests to identify geniuses, defined by him as those with an IQ greater than 140. None of the children in the study has ever won a Nobel Prize.

___3___ Einstein once said if a new idea isn't considered absurd at first, it will go nowhere. It takes extraordinary nerve to make seemingly foolish thoughts successful and widely accepted.

Moreover, having a high IQ is no guarantee of financial security in life. ___4___ Einstein is reputed to have lost most of his Nobel money on bad investments. You don't usually find geniuses as CEOs either. Many are socially inept and not great people managers. ___5___ In the 1990s, Bell Labs found its most productive and valued electrical engineers were not the geniuses it employed, but those who were cooperative, persuasive and had the ability to build consensus.

(A) But it doesn't necessarily work that way.

(B) No wonder genius is 10% inspiration and 90% perspiration.

(C) One theory suggests that geniuses are endowed with unusual enthusiasm for risk taking.

(D) As kids, they must have lacked something like the ability to write tests and score high marks.

(E) Geniuses are notoriously poor managers of money, likely because their focus in life is elsewhere.

(F) Sometimes genius doesn't actually contribute toward success in the working world.

TEST 16 詳解

Many people associate the Nobel Prizes with public recognition *and* financial reward *for achievement reached by genius.* [1](A) *But* it doesn*'t necessarily* work *that way.*

　　許多人把諾貝爾獎和因天才達到成就，所得到公眾的認可和財務獎勵聯想在一起。但事實不一定是那樣。

* *associate A with B* 將 A 與 B 聯想在一起

Nobel Prizes 諾貝爾獎【是根據瑞典化學家阿爾弗雷德・諾貝爾的遺囑所設立的獎項。諾貝爾一生沒有結婚，所以沒有妻子、兒女，死前連親兄弟也去世了。但他發明炸藥，取得眾多的科研成果，成功地開辦了許多工廠，積聚了巨大的財富。在即將辭世之際，諾貝爾立下了遺囑：「請將我的財產變做基金，每年用這個基金的利息作為獎金，獎勵那些在前一年為人類做出卓越貢獻的人。」根據他的遺囑，從 1901 年開始，具有國際性的諾貝爾獎創立了】

recognition[4] ﹝ˌrɛkəgˋnɪʃən﹞ *n.* 認同；認出；承認

financial[4] ﹝fəˋnænʃəl﹞ *adj.* 財務的　　reward[4] ﹝rɪˋwɔrd﹞ *n.* 獎賞

achievement[3] ﹝əˋtʃivmənt﹞ *n.* 成就　　genius[4] ﹝ˋdʒinɪəs﹞ *n.* 天才

necessarily[2] ﹝ˌnɛsəˋsɛrɪlɪ﹞ *adv.* 必要地　　*not necessarily* 不一定

For example, William Shockley, *the Nobel winner in physics in 1958 for inventing the transistor*, was refused admission *to a long-term genius study as a child due to his unremarkable IQ score.*

例如，1958年發明電晶體的諾貝爾物理學獎得主威廉‧肖克利，小時候的智商因爲不出色，而被拒絕加入一項長期的天才研究。

* physics[4] (ˊfɪzɪks) *n.* 物理學　　invent[2] (ɪnˊvɛnt) *v.* 發明
transistor (trænˊzɪstə) *n.* 電晶體　　refuse[2] (rɪˊfjuz) *v.* 拒絕
admission[2] (ədˊmɪʃən) *n.* 允許進入　　***long-term*** *adj.* 長期的
due to 由於　　unremarkable[2] (ˏʌnrɪˊmɑrkəbḷ) *adj.* 不出色的
IQ 智商 (= *Intelligence Quotient*)　　score[2] (skor) *n.* 分數

Luis Alvarez, *another Nobel winner for his work on elementary*

particles, had been excluded *from the same research program.*

[2](D) *As kids*, they must have lacked something *like the ability to*

*write tests **and score high marks**.*

另一位因爲基本粒子研究而獲獎的諾貝爾得主，路易斯‧阿爾瓦雷斯，也被排除在同一研究課程之外。他們小時候，一定缺乏像是做考題和得高分的能力。

* elementary[4] (ˏɛləˊmɛntərɪ) *adj.* 基本的
particle[5] (ˊpɑrtɪkḷ) *n.* 微粒　　***elementary particle*** 基本粒子
exclude[5] (ɪkˊsklud) *v.* 排除 < *from* >
research[4] (rɪˊsɝtʃ ,ˊrisɝtʃ) *v. n.* 研究
program[3] (ˊprogræm) *n.* 課程　　lack[1] (læk) *v.* 缺乏
ability[2] (əˊbɪlətɪ) *n.* 能力　　score[2] (skor) *v.* 得分
mark[2] (mɑrk) *n.* 記號；分數

In 1928, Louis Terman, *a Stanford University professor*, pioneered

the use *of IQ tests* *to identify geniuses, defined by him as those with an*

IQ greater than 140. None *of the children in the study* has *ever* won

a Nobel Prize.

1928 年，史丹佛大學教授路易斯・特曼，率先使用智商測試來辨識天才，根據他的定義，就是那些智商高於 140 的人。那些在該研究中的孩子，沒有一個人得過諾貝爾獎。

* professor[4] 〔 prəˋfɛsɚ 〕 *n.* 教授　　pioneer[4] 〔ˏpaɪəˋnɪr 〕 *v.* 成爲先驅
   identify[4] 〔 aɪˋdɛntəˏfaɪ 〕 *v.* 確認；辨認
   define[3] 〔 dɪˋfaɪn 〕 *v.* 下定義

[3](C) One theory suggests *that geniuses are endowed with unusual*

enthusiasm for risk taking. Einstein *once* said *if a new idea isn't*

considered absurd at first, it will go *nowhere*. It takes extraordinary

nerve *to make seemingly foolish thoughts successful **and** widely*

accepted.

　　有一種理論認爲，天才具有異乎尋常的冒險熱情。愛因斯坦曾經說過，如果一個新想法一開始不被認爲是荒謬的，那將不會成功。使看似愚蠢的想法成功和被廣泛接受，需要非常的勇氣。

* theory[3] 〔ˋθɪərɪ 〕 *n.* 理論　　suggest[3] 〔 sə(g)ˋdʒɛst 〕 *v.* 建議；暗示
   endow 〔 ɪnˋdaʊ 〕 *v.* 賦予　　***be endowed with*** 被賦予；具有

enthusiasm[4] 〔 ɪn'θjuzɪˌæzəm 〕 *n.* 熱忱

risk[3] 〔 rɪsk 〕 *n.* 風險

consider[2] 〔 kən'sɪdə 〕 *v.* 認為；考慮

absurd[5] 〔 əb'sɝd 〕 *adj.* 荒唐的；可笑的

go nowhere 不成功

extraordinary[4] 〔 ɪk'strɔdnˌɛrɪ 〕 *adj.* 異常的

nerve[3] 〔 nɝv 〕 *n.* 膽量；神經　　seemingly 〔'simɪŋlɪ 〕 *adv.* 表面上

foolish[2] 〔'fulɪʃ 〕 *adj.* 愚蠢的　　thought[1] 〔 θɔt 〕 *n.* 思想

successful[2] 〔 sək'sɛsfəl 〕 *adj.* 成功的

widely[1] 〔'waɪdlɪ 〕 *adv.* 廣泛地

accepted[2] 〔 ək'sɛptɪd 〕 *adj.* 被接受的

---

absurd *adj.*
　荒唐的；可笑的
= ridiculous
= ludicrous
= foolish
= silly

Moreover, having a high IQ is no guarantee *of financial security*

in life. [4](E) Geniuses are *notoriously* poor managers *of money, likely*

because their focus in life is elsewhere. Einstein is reputed to have

lost most *of his Nobel money on bad investments.*

　　而且，擁有高智商並不能保證人生中財務上的安全。天才是臭名遠播糟糕的金錢管理者，可能是因為他們的人生焦點是在其他地方。愛因斯坦據說因失敗的投資，而失去大部分諾貝爾獎的獎金。

* guarantee[4] 〔ˌgærən'ti 〕 *n.* 保證　　security[3] 〔 sɪ'kjurətɪ 〕 *n.* 安全
notoriously[6] 〔 no'torɪəslɪ 〕 *adv.* 惡名昭彰地
manager[3] 〔'mænɪdʒə 〕 *n.* 管理者　　likely[1] 〔'laɪklɪ 〕 *adv.* 可能地
focus[2] 〔'fokəs 〕 *n.* 焦點
reputed 〔 rɪ'pjutɪd 〕 *adj.* 據稱的；普遍認為的
investment[4] 〔 ɪn'vɛstmənt 〕 *n.* 投資

You don't *usually* find geniuses as CEOs *either*. Many are *socially*

inept and not great people managers. [5](F) *Sometimes* genius doesn't

actually contribute toward success *in the working world.*

你通常也不會發現天才能當上總裁。許多天才不擅於社交，而且不會管
理人員。有時候天才在工作的世界裡是不會成功的。

> * *CEO* 總裁（= *chief executive officer*）
> socially[2]（'soʃəlɪ）*adv.* 社交方面地
> inept（ɪn'ɛpt）*adj.* 不擅長的　　contribute[4]（kən'trɪbjut）*v.* 貢獻
> *contribute toward/to* 促成；成為～之因

In the 1990s, Bell Labs found its *most* productive *and* valued

electrical engineers were not the geniuses *it employed*, *but* those *who*

were cooperative, persuasive *and* had the ability to build consensus.

在 1990 年代，貝爾實驗室發現其最有生產力和最有價值的電機工程
師，不是雇用的天才，而是那些能合作、有說服力、有能力達成共識的
人。

> * *Bell Labs* 貝爾實驗室【美國 AT&T 電信公司的研究開發部門】
> productive[4]（prə'dʌktɪv）*adj.* 有生產力的
> valued[2]（'væljud）*adj.* 有價值的
> *electrical engineer* 電機工程師　　employ[3]（ɪm'plɔɪ）*v.* 雇用
> cooperative[4]（ko'apə,retɪv）*adj.* 合作的
> persuasive[4]（pə'swesɪv）*adj.* 有說服力的
> consensus[6]（kən'sɛnsəs）*n.* 共識

TEST 17

說明： 第1至5題，每題一個空格。請依文意在文章後所提供的(A)到
(F) 選項中分別選出最適當者。

Taking vitamins and minerals on a regular basis is common
in many Western countries. Lately, more and more people in
Taiwan have been getting into the habit of taking vitamins for
the sake of their health. ___1___ It has led both experts and
vitamin fans to reconsider the necessity of taking vitamins.

___2___ In fact, one report indicates that taking
antioxidants may even increase the risk of death by up to 16
percent. Still another study points out that smokers who take
potent vitamin E capsules for more than ten years are at
slightly greater risk of lung cancer than those who don't.
Researchers have found that excessive vitamin A consumption
can increase the risk of certain cancers and may also cause
birth defects and decreased bone density.

___3___ Consumers should be aware that vitamins
and other non-prescription health supplements are sold by
companies that tend to overstate the health benefits of their
products and are not subject to strict government controls.
Vitamin C, one of the most commonly taken vitamins, has

long been considered an effective measure to prevent the common cold. However, studies have proven it to be effective only for high-performance athletes, rather than regular people.
____4____ Those who don't have a balanced and healthy diet may benefit from a simple multi-vitamin, but overdoing it may have the opposite effect of what was intended. ____5____

(A) However, recent studies have shown that excessive vitamin use may have some negative side effects.

(B) Furthermore, the overuse of vitamins, especially in conjunction with prescription medication, is potentially dangerous.

(C) Most people think that over-the-counter vitamins are natural and safe since they can be purchased without a prescription.

(D) Experts all seem to agree that eating a healthy diet low in salt and fat is the best way to avoid disease and live a long life.

(E) Vitamin B6 is a water-soluble vitamin that is naturally present in many foods.

(F) Therefore, with these recent findings in mind, you may want to think twice before taking health supplements.

TEST 17 詳解

Taking vitamins **and** minerals *on a regular basis* is common *in many Western countries.* *Lately,* more **and** more people *in Taiwan* have been getting into the habit *of taking vitamins for the sake of their health.*

定期服用維他命和礦物質，在西方國家很常見。最近越來越多的台灣人為了健康的緣故，也逐漸養成服用維他命的習慣。

* vitamin³ 〔ˈvaɪtəmɪn〕 *n.* 維他命　　mineral⁴ 〔ˈmɪnərəl〕 *n.* 礦物質
regular² 〔ˈrɛgjələ〕 *adj.* 規律的　　basis² 〔ˈbesɪs〕 *n.* 基礎
on a regular basis 定期地 (= *regularly*)
common² 〔ˈkɑmən〕 *adj.* 常見的　　lately⁴ 〔ˈletlɪ〕 *adv.* 最近
get into the habit of… 養成…的習慣

> get out of/shake off/abandon/drop a habit　戒除習慣
> get into/acquire/develop/form a habit　養成習慣

for the sake of… 為了…的緣故

¹**(A)** *However,* recent studies have shown **that** *excessive vitamin use may have some negative side effects.* It has led both experts **and** vitamin fans *to reconsider the necessity of taking vitamins.*

然而，最近的研究顯示，過量維他命使用可能會有一些副作用。這讓專家和維他命粉絲重新考慮服用維他命的必要性。

* excessive[6] (ɪkˈsɛsɪv) *adj.* 過度的
  negative[2] (ˈnɛgətɪv) *adj.* 負面的
  side effect 副作用　　expert[2] (ˈɛkspɝt) *n.* 專家
  fan[3] (fæn) *n.* 熱衷者；（影、歌、球）迷
  reconsider (ˌrikənˈsɪdə) *v.* 重新考慮
  necessity[3] (nəˈsɛsətɪ) *n.* 必要；需要

[2](C) Most people think *that over-the-counter vitamins are natural and safe since they can be purchased without a prescription.* In fact, one report indicates *that taking antioxidants may even increase the risk of death by up to 16 percent.*

大多數人認爲非處方用藥的維他命是天然、安全的，因爲它們可以在沒有醫生處方的情況下購買。事實上，一份報告指出，服用抗氧化劑，甚至可能使死亡風險最多增加 16%。

* over-the-counter *adj.* 非處方藥的【又稱爲成藥，指的是未經處方而可以從藥店購買得到的藥品，與處方藥相對。這些藥品臨床應用時間較長、藥效確定、藥物不良反應較少，患者不須過多的專業知識，僅憑藥品說明書和標籤就可以安全使用】
  natural[2] (ˈnætʃərəl) *adj.* 自然的
  safe[1] (sef) *adj.* 安全的
  purchase[5] (ˈpɝtʃəs) *v.* 購買 (= *buy*)
  prescription[6] (prɪˈskrɪpʃən) *n.* 處方
  indicate[2] (ˈɪndəˌket) *v.* 指出

antioxidant〔͵æntɪˈɑksədənt〕 *n.* 抗氧化劑

increase[2]〔ɪnˈkris〕*v.* 增加　　***up to*** 高達；多達

Still another study points out ***that*** *smokers* ***who*** *take potent vitamin E*

capsules for more than ten years are at *slightly* greater risk *of lung*

cancer ***than*** *those* ***who*** *don't.*

還有一項研究指出，服用強效維他命 E 膠囊超過 10 年的吸煙者，肺癌的風險稍高於不吸煙者。

* ***point out*** 指出　　　potent〔ˈpotn̩t〕*adj.* 強效的
 capsule[6]〔ˈkæps!̩〕*n.* 膠囊　　slightly[4]〔ˈslaɪtlɪ〕*adv.* 輕微地
 at risk of⋯ 冒⋯的風險　　***lung cancer*** 肺癌

Researchers have found ***that*** *excessive vitamin A consumption can*

increase the risk of certain cancers ***and*** *may also cause birth defects*

and *decreased bone density.*

研究人員發現，維他命 A 服用過量會增加某些癌症的風險，也可能導致出生缺陷和骨質密度降低。

* researcher[4]〔rɪˈsɝtʃɚ〕*n.* 研究員
 consumption[6]〔kənˈsʌmpʃən〕*n.* 消耗
 certain[1]〔ˈsɝtn̩〕*adj.* 某一；某些
 defect[6]〔ˈdifɛkt〕*n.* 缺陷；缺點
 density[6]〔ˈdɛnsətɪ〕*n.* 密度

³ **(B)** *Furthermore,* the overuse *of vitamins, especially in*

conjunction with prescription medication, is *potentially* dangerous.

Consumers should be aware *that* vitamins *and* other non-prescription

health supplements are sold by companies *that* tend to overstate the

health benefits of their products **and** *are not subject to strict*

government controls.

　　此外，過量使用維他命，特別是與處方藥一起使用，可能會有危
險。消費者應該知道，販賣維他命和其他非處方保健品的公司，傾向於
誇大其產品對健康的益處，而不受政府嚴格控制。

* furthermore⁴〔'fɜðə‚mor〕*adv.* 此外
　overuse〔'ovə'juz〕*n.* 過度使用
　especially²〔ə'spɛʃəlɪ〕*adv.* 特別地
　conjunction⁴〔kən'dʒʌŋkʃən〕*n.* 連接
　in conjunction with 與～一起
　medication⁶〔‚mɛdɪ'keʃən〕*n.* 藥物治療；藥物
　potentially⁵〔pə'tɛnʃəlɪ〕*adv.* 可能地
　consumer⁴〔kən'sjumə〕*n.* 消費者
　be aware that… 意識到…

> be aware/conscious of + N.
> be aware/conscious that + S. + V….
> 　知道…；察覺到…

　non-prescription〔‚nɑnprɪ'skrɪpʃən〕*adj.* 非處方藥的
　supplement⁶〔'sʌpləmənt〕*n.* 補給品

tend to V. 容易…；傾向於　　overstate〔'ovə'stet〕v. 誇張
benefit[3]〔'bɛnəfɪt〕n. 利益；好處
be subject to… 受…支配；受…影響
strict[2]〔strɪkt〕adj. 嚴格的

Vitamin C, *one of the most commonly taken vitamins*, has *long* been

considered an effective measure *to prevent the common cold.*

However, studies have proven it to be effective *only for*

high-performance athletes, **rather than** regular people.

維他命 C 是最常被服用的維他命之一，長期以來被認為是預防普通感
冒的有效措施。然而，研究證明，它只對優異運動員有效，而不是對
一般人。

* commonly[1]〔'kɑmənlɪ〕adv. 通常地
consider[2]〔kən'sɪdə〕v. 認為
effective[2]〔ɪ'fɛktɪv〕adj. 有效的
measure[2]〔'mɛʒə〕n. 措施；手段
prevent[2]〔prɪ'vɛnt〕v. 預防　　prove[1]〔pruv〕v. 證明
high-performance〔ˌhaɪpə'fɔrməns〕adj. 高性能的；優異的
athlete[3]〔'æθlit〕n. 運動員　　**rather than…** 而非

[4]**(D)** Experts all seem to agree **that** *eating a healthy diet low in salt*

and *fat is the best way to avoid disease* **and** *live a long life.* Those

who *don't have a balanced and healthy diet* may benefit *from a simple* *multi-vitamin, **but** overdoing it may have the opposite effect of **what**

was intended.*

專家們似乎都同意，吃低鹽和低脂肪的健康飲食，是避免疾病和長壽的
最好方法。那些沒有均衡和健康飲食的人，可能會受益於簡單的綜合維
他命，但過度使用可能會產生與預期相反的效果。

* diet³ (ˈdaɪət) *n.* 飲食　　avoid² (əˈvɔɪd) *v.* 避免
  balanced³ (ˈbælənst) *adj.* 均衡的
  multi-vitamin (ˌmʌltəˈvaɪtəmɪn) *n.* 綜合維他命
  overdo⁵ (ˌovəˈdu) *v.* 做得過分
  opposite³ (ˈɑpəzɪt) *adj.* 相反的
  effect² (ɪˈfɛkt) *n.* 作用；影響
  intend⁴ (ɪnˈtɛnd) *v.* 打算；意圖

⁵**(F)** *Therefore, with these recent findings in mind, you may want to*

think twice before taking health supplements.

因此，考慮到最近的這些發現，在服用保健品之前，你可能要三思。

* recent² (ˈrisn̩t) *adj.* 最近的　　findings (ˈfaɪndɪŋz) *n.* 發現物
  think twice 三思；重新考慮

TEST 18

說明： 第 1 至 5 題，每題一個空格。請依文意在文章後所提供的 (A) 到
(F) 選項中分別選出最適當者。

Holding onto resentment is like swallowing poison and
hoping the other person will die. Resentment doesn't hurt
the person you're angry at; instead, it hurts you. You can't
feel resentment and gratitude at the same time. ___1___ So
would you rather hold onto your self-righteous resentment or
fill your heart with forgiveness and gratitude?

My friend Belle recently told me about her own
experience with resentment. She once worked for a large
metropolitan newspaper, where she found the corporate
culture extremely frustrating. ___2___ Their past success
had blinded them to the need for change. As the years went
by, Belle grew more frustrated, and finally she left the
company. ___3___ She carried them with her.

She decided to write about her feelings at the newspaper
and purge herself of the negative baggage. What she wrote
turned out to be a whole book! She called it A Peacock in the
Land of Penguins. She was "the peacock" and those

newspaper executives were "the stupid penguins." However, after the publication of the book, she didn't find a bit of peace. She came to realize that there had been nothing personal in the way they treated her. ___4___ She was the one who had made it personal. Then she invited her former boss to dinner and made her apology for being so resentful. She finally felt free of the resentment that had been eating her up. ___5___ It can take a long time and a lot of reflection to be able to see the situation with some emotional maturity, as Belle's story illustrates.

(A) Trading resentments for gratitude isn't always easy.

(B) One will always drive out the other.

(C) But she found that she hadn't left her resentment, frustration, and anger behind when she resigned.

(D) The company was a hundred years old, steeped in tradition and bureaucracy.

(E) They had just been doing what they thought best for the company.

(F) She never wanted to be a penguin, as being a peacock suited her fine.

TEST 18 詳解

Holding onto resentment is like swallowing poison *and* hoping the other person will die. Resentment doesn't hurt the person *you're angry at*; *instead*, it hurts you.

緊抓著憤恨不放，就像是吞下毒藥卻希望對方會死。憤恨不會傷害讓你生氣的人；相反地，它會傷害你。

* ***hold onto*** 抓住
  resentment⁵ (rɪˋzɛntmənt) *n.* 憤恨
  swallow² (ˋswɑlo) *v.* 吞下
  poison² (ˋpɔɪzn̩) *n.* 毒藥

You can't feel resentment *and* gratitude *at the same time.* ¹(**B**) One will *always* drive out the other. So would you *rather* hold onto your self-righteous resentment *or* fill your heart *with forgiveness and gratitude*?

你無法同時感受到憤恨和感激。一個總是會驅走另一個。所以，你寧願堅持著自以爲是的憤恨，或是讓寬恕和感激充滿你的心？

* gratitude⁴ (ˋɡrætəˏtjud) *n.* 感激   ***drive out*** 驅趕
  would rather 寧願
  self-righteous (ˋsɛlfˋraɪtʃəs) *adj.* 自以爲是的
  forgiveness² (fəˋɡɪvnɪs) *n.* 寬恕；饒恕

My friend Belle *recently* told me about her own experience *with resentment*. She *once* worked for a large metropolitan newspaper, *where she found the corporate culture extremely frustrating.*

我的朋友貝兒最近告訴我，她自己的憤恨經歷。她曾經在一家大都會報社工作，她發現那裡的企業文化非常令人挫敗。

* metropolitan⁶〔,mɛtrə'pɑlətn̩〕*adj.* 大都市的
newspaper¹〔'njuz,pepɚ〕*n.* 報社
corporate⁶〔'kɔrpərɪt〕*adj.* 公司的；企業的
culture²〔'kʌltʃɚ〕*n.* 文化　　extremely³〔ɪk'strimlɪ〕*adv.* 非常
frustrating³〔'frʌstretɪŋ〕*adj.* 令人挫敗的

²**(D)** The company was a hundred years old, *steeped in tradition and bureaucracy*. Their past success had blinded them *to the need for change.*

這家公司已有百年歷史，充滿傳統和官僚作風。他們過去的成功使他們不知道需要改變。

* steep³〔stip〕*v.* 浸泡；浸透
be steeped in sth. 充滿（某物）
tradition²〔trə'dɪʃən〕*n.* 傳統
bureaucracy⁶〔bjʊ'rɑkrəsɪ〕*n.* 官僚制度
blind²〔blaɪnd〕*v.* 使盲目；使失去判斷力
blind sb. ***to*** sth. 使某人對某事失去判斷力或察覺力

bureau *n.* 局；科；處
bureaucrat *n.* 官僚
bureaucratic *adj.* 官僚的
bureaucracy *n.* 官僚制度

As the years went by, Belle grew *more* frustrated, ***and** finally* she left the company. [3](C) ***But*** she found ***that** she hadn't left her resentment, frustration, **and** anger behind **when she resigned.*** She carried them *with her*.

隨著時間過去，貝兒變得更加沮喪，而且最後她離開了公司。但是她發現她的憤恨、挫敗和憤怒並沒有在辭職時離開她。她背負著他們。

> * **go by** （指時間）過去；消逝
> ***leave behind*** 把…拋在後面
> frustration[4] 〔frʌsˈtreʃən〕 *n.* 挫折；挫敗；失望
> resign[4] 〔rɪˈzaɪn〕 *v.* 辭職

She decided to write about her feelings *at the newspaper **and** purge herself of the negative baggage.* ***What** she wrote* turned out to be a whole book! She called it *A Peacock in the Land of Penguins.* She was "the peacock" ***and*** those newspaper executives were "the stupid penguins."

她決定寫下自己對報社的感受，來清除自己的負面包袱。她所寫的東西結果成了一整本書！她把書名定為「企鵝國度裡的孔雀」。她是「孔雀」，而那些報社的主管是「愚蠢的企鵝」。

> * purge 〔pɝdʒ〕 *v.* 清除（有害的東西）< *of* >
> negative[2] 〔ˈnɛgətɪv〕 *adj.* 負面的
> baggage[3] 〔ˈbægɪdʒ〕 *n.* 精神包袱
> ***turn out to be*** 結果是…

peacock[5] 〔'pi,kɑk 〕 *n.* 孔雀
penguin[2] 〔'pɛngwɪn 〕 *n.* 企鵝
executive[5] 〔 ɪg'zɛkjutɪv 〕 *n.* 主管

> execute *v.* 執行;處死
> execution *n.* 執行;處死
> executive *n.* 主管　*adj.* 執行的

However, *after the publication of the book*, she didn't find a bit of

peace. She came to realize *that* there had been nothing personal in

the way they treated her. [4](E) They had *just* been doing *what* they

thought best for the company. She was the one *who* had made it

personal.

然而,在這本書出版後,她並沒有找到一絲和平。她逐漸了解到,他們
對待她的方式並不是針對她個人的。他們只是做了他們認為最適合公司
的方式。是她讓它變成是針對她個人。

* publication[4] 〔,pʌblɪ'keʃən 〕 *n.* 出版　　bit[1] 〔 bɪt 〕 *n.* 一點點
  peace[2] 〔 pis 〕 *n.* (心的) 平靜;寧靜
  come to realize 逐漸了解到
  personal[2] 〔'pɝsn̩l 〕 *adj.* 針對個人的
  treat[5,2] 〔 tret 〕 *v.* 對待

Then she invited her former boss *to dinner **and*** made her apology *for*

being so resentful. She *finally* felt free of the resentment *that* had

been eating her up.

然後，她邀請她的前老闆吃晚餐，並且爲她如此不滿而道歉。她終於擺脫了一直吞噬她的憤恨。

> * invite[2] (ɪn'vaɪt) v. 邀請
> former[2] ('fɔrmɚ) adj. 以前的；前任的
> boss[1] (bɔs) n. 老闆　　apology[4] (ə'pɑlədʒɪ) n. 道歉
> resentful[5] (rɪ'zɛntfəl) adj. 氣憤的　　***eat up*** 吞噬
> free[1] (fri) adj. 自由的；免於～的

[5]**(A)** Trading resentments *for gratitude* isn't *always* easy. It can take a long time ***and*** a lot of reflection *to be able to see the situation with some emotional maturity,* **as Belle's story illustrates.**

以怨恨交換感激未必是容易的。正如貝兒的故事所說明的，能以一定的情感成熟度去了解情況，可能需要很長時間和許多反省。

> * trade[2] (tred) v. 交換 < *for* >　　***not always*** 未必；不一定
> ***take a long time*** 花很長的時間
> reflection[4] (rɪ'flɛkʃən) n. 反省
> situation[3] (,sɪtʃu'eʃən) n. 情況
> emotional[4] (ɪ'moʃənḷ) adj. 感情的
> maturity[4] (mə'tʃʊrətɪ) n. 成熟
> illustrate[4] ('ɪləstret) v. (用圖解或實例) 說明

TEST 19

說明： 第 1 至 5 題，每題一個空格。請依文意在文章後所提供的 (A) 到 (F) 選項中分別選出最適當者。

There are good reasons why we study geography. Indeed, geography is interesting and can be studied and enjoyed. ___1___

First, it helps us understand the forms and features of the landscapes and the human imprint on the physical environment. ___2___

Second, we are living in a world of increasingly rapid transport and new means of communication. Distances are becoming less in the sense that the travelling time is being constantly reduced. ___3___ People living in different parts of the earth are becoming more closely linked together. Thus, it is important that we know as much as possible about the places and people in other parts of the world.

Third, we must remember that anything that happens anywhere in the world may have and often does have influences on the whole world. ___4___ No countries can live these days in complete isolation and shut their eyes to what is going on in the world around them.

Fourth, geography is even more important for such countries like Britain. These countries live by what they can make in factories and export. Simply and brutally put, they must "export or die." ___5___ On the other hand, these raw materials and their food need to be paid for by exports. It is important, then, to know how other people live, what their wants are, what kinds of markets they offer, and what raw materials they have for sale. Thus, we should study geography.

(A) Through this understanding we can learn how to make the best use of the land and its resources for our own benefit.

(B) A knowledge of geography will help him to avoid making tragic mistakes.

(C) In other words, the world is getting smaller.

(D) However, other than that, it has many useful and practical advantages.

(E) They cannot produce their manufactured goods without the raw materials they import.

(F) For example, a war in the Middle East, a famine in Africa, and an economic recession in the United States all affect the area we live in.

TEST 19 詳解

There are good reasons ***why** we study geography. Indeed,*
geography is interesting ***and** can be studied **and** enjoyed.

[1](**D**) *However, other than that, it has many useful **and** practical*
advantages.

　　我們學習地理的理由很充分。事實上，地理是有趣的，而且可以研究和樂在其中的。但是，除此之外，它具有許多有用和實用的優點。

* geography[2] (dʒɪˈɑgrəfɪ) *n.* 地理；地理學
other than 除了～之外　　practical[3] (ˈpræktɪkḷ) *adj.* 實際的
advantage[3] (ədˈvæntɪdʒ) *n.* 優點

*First, it helps us understand the forms **and** features of the*
*landscapes **and** the human imprint on the physical environment.*

[2](**A**) *Through this understanding we can learn **how** to make the best*
*use of the land **and** its resources for our own benefit.*

　　第一，它有助於我們了解景觀的形成和特徵，以及人類在這片自然環境中的痕跡。通過這種了解，我們可以學習如何充分利用土地及其資源，為我們自己謀福利。

* form[2] (fɔrm) *n.* 形成　　feature[3] (ˈfitʃə) *n.* 特色
landscape[4] (ˈlændskep) *n.* 風景；景觀
imprint (ˈɪmprɪnt) *n.* 痕跡；持久影響
physical[4] (ˈfɪzɪkḷ) *adj.* 自然的；物理的

environment[2] 〔 ɪnˈvaɪrənmənt 〕 *n.* 環境
make the best use of 充分利用　　resource[3] 〔 rɪˈsors 〕 *n.* 資源
benefit[3] 〔ˈbɛnəfɪt 〕 *n.* 利益；好處

Second, we are living in a world of increasingly rapid transport

and *new means of communication.* Distances are becoming less *in*

*the sense **that** the travelling time is being constantly reduced.*

　　第二，我們生活在一個交通運輸越來越快速，擁有新的溝通方式的世界裡。就旅行時間逐漸減少的意義來說，距離變得越來越短。

* increasingly[2] 〔 ɪnˈkrisɪŋlɪ 〕 *adv.* 逐漸增加地
  rapid[2] 〔ˈræpɪd 〕 *adj.* 快速的
  transport[3] 〔ˈtrænsport 〕 *n.* 交通運輸系統
  means[2] 〔 minz 〕 *n.* 方法；手段 (= *way*)
  communication[4] 〔 kə,mjunəˈkeʃən 〕 *n.* 溝通
  distance[2] 〔ˈdɪstəns 〕 *n.* 距離　　***in the sense*** 就…意義而言
  constantly[3] 〔ˈkɑnstəntlɪ 〕 *adv.* 不斷地
  reduce[3] 〔 rɪˈdjus 〕 *v.* 減少

[3]**(C)** *In other words*, the world is getting smaller. People *living in*

different parts of the earth are becoming *more closely* linked *together*.

　　換句話說，世界正在變小。生活在地球不同地區的人們，逐漸更加緊密地連結在一起。

* ***in other words*** 換句話說
closely[1] 〔'kloslı〕 *adv.* 接近地；緊密地
link[2] 〔lıŋk〕 *v.* 連結

Thus, it is important ***that*** *we know as much as possible about the*

*places **and** people in other parts of the world.*

換句話說，世界正在變小。生活在地球不同地區的人們，逐漸更加緊密地連結在一起。因此，我們必須盡可能多地了解世界其他部分的地方和人民。

* ***as⋯as possible*** 盡可能地⋯

Third, we must remember ***that*** *anything **that** happens anywhere in*

*the world may have **and** often does have influences on the whole world.*

[4](F) *For example*, a war *in the Middle East*, a famine *in Africa*, ***and*** an

economic recession *in the United States* all affect the area *we live in.*

　　第三，我們必須記得，世界上任何地方發生的任何事情，對全世界來說都可能有且經常的確有影響。例如，中東的一場戰爭，非洲的一場飢荒，以及美國的經濟衰退，都影響到我們生活的地區。

* influence[2] 〔'ınfluəns〕 *n.* 影響 < *on* >
　the Middle East 中東地區
　famine[6] 〔'fæmın〕 *n.* 飢荒　　Africa〔'æfrıkə〕 *n.* 非洲
　economic[4] 〔,ikə'nɑmık〕 *adj.* 經濟的
　recession[6] 〔rı'sɛʃən〕 *n.* 不景氣　　affect[3] 〔ə'fɛkt〕 *v.* 影響

No countries can live *these days in complete isolation **and*** shut their

eyes *to **what** is going on in the world around them.*

現在沒有一個國家能夠完全與世隔絕，而且忽視他們周遭世界所發生的事。

> * ***these days*** 現在；最近
> complete² 〔 kəm'plit 〕 *adj.* 完全的
> isolation⁴ 〔 ‚aɪsl̩'eʃən 〕 *n.* 隔離　　　shut¹ 〔 ʃʌt 〕 *v.* 關閉
> ***shut** one's eyes to sth.* 忽視某事
> ***be going on*** 發生

Fourth, geography is *even more* important *for such countries like*

Britain. These countries live *by **what** they can make in factories **and***

*export. Simply **and** brutally put,* they must "export *or* die."

　　第四，地理對於像英國這樣的國家更為重要。這些國家靠工廠生產的產品和出口來生活。簡單而殘酷地說，它們必須「出口，不然就會死亡」。

> * fourth¹ 〔 forθ 〕 *adv.* 第四　　　Britain 〔 'brɪtn̩ 〕 *n.* 英國
> factory¹ 〔 'fæktrɪ 〕 *n.* 工廠
> export³ 〔 ɪks'port 〕 *v.* 輸出；出口
> simply² 〔 'sɪmplɪ 〕 *adv.* 簡單地
> brutally⁴ 〔 'brutl̩ɪ 〕 *adv.* 殘忍地；無情地
> put¹ 〔 put 〕 *v.* 說；表達

[5] **(E)** They cannot produce their manufactured goods *without the raw materials they import.* *On the other hand*, these raw materials *and* their food need to be paid for *by exports.*

沒有進口的原料就不能生產製成商品。另一方面,這些原料和他們食品需要透過出口來支付。

* produce[2] (prə'djus) v. 生產;製造
  manufacture[4] (‚mænjə'fæktʃæ) v. 製造
  goods[4] (gʊdz) n. pl. 商品　　raw[3] (rɔ) adj. 生的;未加工的
  material[2.6] (mə'tɪrɪəl) n. 原料;材料
  raw material 原物料　　*pay for* 支付
  import[3] (ɪm'port) v. 進口

It is important, *then,* *to know **how** other people live, **what** their wants are, **what** kinds of markets they offer, **and what** raw materials they have for sale.* *Thus*, we should study geography.

所以,去了解其他人如何生活、他們想要什麼、他們提供了什麼樣的市場,以及他們出售什麼原料,是非常重要的。因此,我們應該學習地理。

* market[1] ('mɑrkɪt) n. 市場　　offer[2] ('ɔfæ) v. 提供
  for sale 出售　　thus[1] (ðʌs) adv. 因此;所以

TEST 20

說明： 第1至5題，每題一個空格。請依文意在文章後所提供的(A)到
(F) 選項中分別選出最適當者。

A Swedish entrepreneur is trying to market and sell a
biodegradable plastic bag that acts as a single-use toilet
for urban slums in the developing world. Once used, the
bag can be knotted and buried, and a layer of urea crystals
breaks down the waste into fertilizer while killing off
disease-producing pathogens found in feces. ___1___ "Not
only is it sanitary," said Mr. Wilhelmson, who has patented
the bag, "They can reuse this to grow crops."

___2___ He also found that slum dwellers there
collected their excrement in a plastic bag and disposed of it
by flinging it, calling it a "flyaway toilet" or a "helicopter
toilet." ___3___ He plans to sell it for about 2 or 3 cents—
comparable to the cost of an ordinary plastic bag.

___4___ It is a public health crisis: open defecation can
contaminate drinking water. As a result, an estimated 1.5
million children worldwide die yearly from diarrhea. To
improve this, the United Nations has a goal to reduce by
half the number of people without access to toilets by 2015.

However, Therese Dooley, senior adviser on sanitation and hygiene for Unicef, said that inculcating sanitation habits was no easy task. ___5___ In addition, while "the private sector can play a major role, it will never get to the bottom of the pyramid." Therefore, a sizable population, poor and uneducated, will still be left without toilets.

(A) In his research, Wilhelmson found that urban slums in Kenya, despite being densely populated, had open spaces where waste could be buried.

(B) The bag, called the Peepoo, is the brainchild of Anders Wilhelmson, an architect and professor in Stockholm.

(C) This inspired Mr. Wilhelmson to design the Peepoo, an environmentally friendly alternative that he is confident will turn a profit.

(D) Farmers have protested the research, citing massive damage to their crops.

(E) For one thing, it will take a large amount of behavior change.

(F) In the developing world, an estimated 2.6 billion people do not have access to a toilet, according to United Nations figures.

TEST 20 詳解

A Swedish entrepreneur is trying to market *and* sell a biodegradable plastic bag *that acts as a single-use toilet for urban slums in the developing world.* *Once used,* the bag can be knotted *and* buried, *and* a layer *of urea crystals* breaks down the waste *into fertilizer while killing off disease-producing pathogens found in feces.*

一位瑞典企業家正試圖行銷和出售一種可生物分解的塑膠袋，用來作為開發中國家都市貧民窟的一次性廁所。這種袋子一旦被使用後，可以被打結掩埋，並且有一層尿素晶體將排泄物分解成肥料，同時除掉糞便中發現的製造疾病的病原體。

* Swedish〔'swidɪʃ〕*adj.* 瑞典的
  entrepreneur〔ˌɑntrəprə'nɝ〕*n.* 企業家
  market[1]〔'mɑrkɪt〕*v.*（在市場上）銷售
  biodegradable〔ˌbaɪodɪ'gredəbḷ〕*adj.* 可生物分解的
  plastic[3]〔'plæstɪk〕*adj.* 塑膠的　　***act as*** 做為；擔任
  toilet[2]〔'tɔɪlɪt〕*n.* 廁所　　urban[4]〔'ɝbən〕*adj.* 都市的
  slum[6]〔slʌm〕*n.* 貧民窟
  developing[2]〔dɪ'vɛləpɪŋ〕*adj.* 發展中的
  knot[3]〔nat〕*v.* 打結　　bury[3]〔'bɛrɪ〕*v.* 埋；埋藏
  layer[5]〔'leɚ〕*n.* 層　　urea〔'jurɪə〕*n.* 尿素
  crystal[5]〔'krɪstḷ〕*n.* 結晶；晶體　　***break down*** 瓦解；分解
  waste[1]〔west〕*n.* 排泄物　　fertilizer[5]〔'fɝtḷˌaɪzɚ〕*n.* 肥料
  kill off 破壞某事物；除掉　　disease[3]〔dɪ'ziz〕*n.* 疾病
  pathogen〔'pæθədʒən〕*n.* 病原體　　feces〔'fisiz〕*n.* 糞便

1(B) The bag, *called the Peepoo*, is the brainchild *of Anders*

*Wilhelmson, an architect **and** professor in Stockholm.* "**Not only** is

it sanitary," said Mr. Wilhelmson, **who** *has patented the bag*, "They

can reuse this *to grow crops*."

這款名為 Peepoo 的袋子，是斯德哥爾摩的建築師兼教授安德斯·威漢森的創意。威漢森先生已取得這個袋子的專利，他說：「它不僅衛生，還可以再利用去種植作物。」

* brainchild〔'bren,tʃaɪld〕*n.*（某人的）創作；獨創的觀念
  architect[5]〔'ɑrkə,tɛkt〕*n.* 建築師
  professor[4]〔prə'fɛsə〕*n.* 教授
  sanitary〔'sænə,tɛrɪ〕*adj.* 公共衛生的；衛生上的
  patent[5]〔'pætn̩t〕*v.* 取得…的專利

2(A) *In his research*, Wilhelmson found **that** *urban slums in*

*Kenya, despite being densely populated, had open spaces **where***

waste could be buried.

　　威漢森在他的研究中發現，儘管肯亞的都市貧民窟人口密集，但還是有可以埋葬廢物的空地。

* research[4]〔'risɜtʃ〕*v.* 研究
  Kenya〔'kɛnjə〕*n.* 肯亞【東非國家】
  despite[4]〔dɪ'spaɪt〕*prep.* 儘管　　densely[4]〔'dɛnslɪ〕*adv.* 濃密地
  densely populated *adj.* 人口稠密的

He *also* found ***that*** *slum dwellers there collected their excrement in a*

plastic bag ***and*** *disposed of it by flinging it, calling it a "flyaway toilet"*

or *a "helicopter toilet."*

他還發現，那裡的貧民窟居民把他們的排泄物收集在塑膠袋裡，處理掉它時用扔的，所以稱之為「飛越式廁所」或「直升機廁所」。

* dweller[5] (ˈdwɛlɚ) *n.* 居民　　collect[2] (kəˈlɛkt) *v.* 收集
  excrement (ˈɛkskrɪmənt) *n.* 排泄物 (= *feces*)
  dispose[5] (dɪˈspoz) *v.* 處置　　***dispose of*** 處理掉；丟掉
  fling[6] (flɪŋ) *v.* 扔；抛　　flyaway (ˈflaɪəˌwe) *adj.* 飛越的
  helicopter[4] (ˈhɛlɪˌkɑptɚ) *n.* 直昇機

[3](C) This inspired Mr. Wilhelmson *to design the Peepoo, an*

environmentally friendly alternative ***that*** *he is confident will turn a*

profit. He plans to sell it *for about 2* ***or*** *3 cents—comparable to the*

cost of an ordinary plastic bag.

這給了威漢森先生靈感，設計出一種符合環保的選擇 Peepoo，他有信心會賺錢。他計劃要賣它約 2 或 3 美分——相當於一個普通的塑膠袋的成本。

* inspire[4] (ɪnˈspaɪr) *v.* 激勵；給予靈感
  design[2] (dɪˈzaɪn) *v. n.* 設計
  environmentally[3] (ɪnˌvaɪrənˈmɛntļɪ) *adv.* 環境地
  friendly[2] (ˈfrɛndlɪ) *adj.* 友善的
  environmentally friendly 符合環保的

alternative[6] 〔 ɔl'tɜnətɪv 〕 *n.* 可選擇的事物；替代物
confident[3] 〔'kɑnfədənt 〕 *adj.* 有信心的
profit[3] 〔'prɑfɪt 〕 *n.* 利潤　***turn a profit*** 獲得利潤
comparable[6] 〔'kɑmpərəbl̩ 〕 *adj.* 可比較的 < to >
cost[1] 〔 kɔst 〕 *n.* 費用；成本　ordinary[2] 〔'ɔrdn̩,ɛrɪ 〕 *adj.* 普通的

[4](F) *In the developing world*, an estimated 2.6 billion people do not have access *to a toilet, according to United Nations figures.* It is a public health crisis: open defecation can contaminate drinking water.

根據聯合國的數字顯示，開發中國家估計有 26 億人沒有廁所可以使用。這是一場公共衛生的危機：露天排便會污染飲用水。

* estimate[4] 〔'ɛstə,met 〕 *v.* 估計　billion[2] 〔'bɪljən 〕 *n.* 十億
access[4] 〔'æksɛs 〕 *n.* 接近或使用權
have access to 有權使用　***the United Nations*** 聯合國
figure[2] 〔'fɪgjɚ 〕 *n.* 數字　public[1] 〔'pʌblɪk 〕 *adj.* 公共的
health[1] 〔 hɛlθ 〕 *n.* 健康；衛生　crisis[2] 〔'kraɪsɪs 〕 *n.* 危機
defecation 〔,dɛfə'keʃən 〕 *n.* 排便
contaminate[5] 〔 kən'tæmə,net 〕 *v.* 污染
drinking water 飲用水

As a result, an estimated 1.5 million children *worldwide* die *yearly from diarrhea.* *To improve this*, the United Nations has a goal *to reduce by half the number of people without access to toilets by 2015.*

因此，全世界估計每年有 150 萬兒童因腹瀉而死亡。為了改善這一狀況，聯合國的目標是到 2015 年之前，將無法使用到廁所的人數減少一半。

* ***as a result*** 結果；因此
  worldwide〔'wɜld,waɪd〕*adv.* 在全世界
  diarrhea〔,daɪə'riə〕*n.* 腹瀉　　improve[2]〔ɪm'pruv〕*v.* 改善
  goal[2]〔gol〕*n.* 目標　　reduce[3]〔rɪ'djus〕*v.* 減少

However, Therese Dooley, *senior adviser on sanitation **and***

hygiene for Unicef, said ***that** inculcating sanitation habits was no*

easy task.

然而，聯合國兒童基金會的資深衛生顧問泰瑞斯・杜利說，灌輸公共衛生和個人衛生的習慣並非易事。

* senior[4]〔'sinjɚ〕*adj.* 年長的；資深的
  adviser[3]〔əd'vaɪzɚ〕*n.* 顧問
  sanitation[6]〔,sænə'teʃən〕*n.*（公共）衛生
  hygiene[6]〔'haɪdʒin〕*n.*（個人）衛生
  Unicef〔'junɪsɛf〕*n.* 聯合國兒童基金會（= *United Nations
    International Children's Fund*）
  inculcate〔ɪn'kʌlket〕*v.* 灌輸（觀念）

[5](E) *For one thing*, it will take a large amount *of behavior change.*

*In addition, **while** "the private sector can play a major role, it will*

never get to the bottom of the pyramid."

首先，這將需要大量的行為改變。此外，杜利說：「雖然私部門可以起主要作用，但永遠無法到達金字塔的底端。」

> * *for one thing* 首先　　*a large amount of* 大量的
> behavior[4] 〔 bɪ'hevjɚ 〕 n. 行為
> *in addition* 此外　　while[1] ('hwaɪl) conj. 雖然
> private[2] ('praɪvɪt) adj. 私人的
> sector[6] ('sɛktɚ) n. 部門
> *private sector* 私營機構；私部門
> major[3] ('medʒɚ) adj. 主要的　　role[2] ('rol) n. 角色
> *play a major role* 扮演主要的角色；起主要作用
> *get to* 到達　　bottom[1] ('batəm) n. 底部
> pyramid[5] ('pɪrəmɪd) n. 金字塔

Therefore, a sizable population, poor *and* uneducated, will *still* be left without toilets.

因此，相當多貧窮和沒有受過教育的人，仍然是沒有廁所可用的。

> * sizable ('saɪzəbl̩) adj. 相當大的
> population[2] (,papjə'leʃən) n. 人口
> uneducated (ʌn'ɛdʒu,ketɪd) adj. 未受教育的；無知的
> leave[1] (liv) v. 使處於 (某種狀態)

TEST 21

說明：　第 1 至 5 題，每題一個空格。請依文意在文章後所提供的 (A) 到
(F) 選項中分別選出最適當者。

　　Feeling guilty about checking personal e-mail, chatting
with coworkers or addressing other minor distractions
throughout your workday?

　　According to a professor at the University of Illinois,
brief diversions may help people concentrate and improve
their performance on more important tasks, said Alejandro
Lleras in a report on the topic for the journal *Cognition*.

　　According to Lleras' study, ＿＿1＿＿. "When you are
distracted, it doesn't mean you aren't paying attention,"
Lleras said. Priests who meditate for hours don't concentrate
solely on breathing or one object, he said. "It's not that they
don't get distracted but that they're very good at dealing with
the distractions and releasing themselves from them," Lleras
said. "Good meditators will get distracted and get back to
their main focus very quickly."

　　Lleras based his theory on the idea that ＿＿2＿＿. If you
stare at one penny and place another coin 10 inches away, the
penny in your peripheral vision will eventually disappear. If
you blink or move, the second penny reappears as ＿＿3＿＿.

The same can be true of the thought process. Sustained attention to a thought can cause it to disappear. If you are given something else to think about, ___4___.

To prove his theory, Lleras had 84 students focus on various numbers flashing on a computer for an hour. One group received no breaks or distractions. Other groups were told to memorize numbers and wait for those numbers to pop up on the screen. The groups that received diversions sustained their concentration; ___5___.

"It's unrealistic to expect people to focus at high levels for a long period of time," Lleras said. "It's important to create an environment where it's OK to take small breaks."

(A) other participants' attention spans reduced gradually after 20 minutes

(B) the change jolts the brain

(C) attention span is the amount of time that one can concentrate on a task without being distracted

(D) attention is like a gas tank that refills during short breaks from the task at hand

(E) the original thought will seem fresh when you return to it

(F) our senses become used to stimulus

TEST 21 詳解

Feeling guilty about checking personal e-mail, chatting *with coworkers or* addressing other minor distractions *throughout your workday*?

查看個人電子郵件、與同事聊天，或是整個工作日都在處理其他使你分心的小事，你會感到內疚嗎？

* guilty[4]（'gɪltɪ）*adj.* 有罪的　　personal[2]（'pɝsn̩l）*adj.* 個人的
  chat[3]（tʃæt）*v.* 聊天 < *with* >　　coworker（'ko,wɝkɚ）*n.* 同事
  address[1]（ə'drɛs）*v.* 處理；辦理
  minor[3]（'maɪnɚ）*adj.* 較小的；較少的
  distraction[6]（dɪ'strækʃən）*n.* 分心；使人分心的事物
  throughout[2]（θru'aʊt）*prep.* 遍及
  workday（'wɝk,de）*n.* 工作日；平日

According to a professor at the University of Illinois, brief diversions may help people concentrate *and* improve their performance *on more important tasks*, said Alejandro Lleras *in a report on the topic for the journal Cognition.*

根據美國伊利諾州立大學一位教授的說法，簡短的轉移可能會幫助人們專心，並提高他們在更重要的工作上的表現，阿雷漢多‧雷拉斯在認知期刊中的一篇報告中表示。

* ***according to*** 根據　professor[4] 〔 prə'fɛsə 〕 *n.* 教授
Illinois 〔 ͵ɪlə'nɔɪ 〕 *n.* 美國伊利諾州　brief[2] 〔 brif 〕 *adj.* 簡短的
diversion[6] 〔 də'vɝʒən, daɪ-, -ʃən 〕 *n.* 轉移
concentrate[4] 〔'kɑnsṇ͵tret 〕 *v.* 專心；集中 < *on* >
improve[2] 〔 ɪm'pruv 〕 *v.* 改善
performance[3] 〔 pə'fɔrməns 〕 *n.* 表現
task[2] 〔 tæsk 〕 *n.* 工作；任務　report[1] 〔 rɪ'port 〕 *n.* 報導；報告
topic[2] 〔'tɑpɪk 〕 *n.* 主題　journal[3] 〔'dʒɝnḷ 〕 *n.* 期刊
cognition 〔 kɑg'nɪʃən 〕 *n.* 認知；知識

According to Lleras' study, [1](**D**) attention is like a gas tank *that*

refills during short breaks from the task at hand. "***When** you are*

distracted, it doesn't mean *you aren't paying attention*," Lleras said.

　　根據雷拉斯的研究，從手邊工作得到短暫休息的期間，注意力就像
是油箱再加滿一樣。「當你分心時，並不意味著你沒有注意，」雷拉斯
說。

* attention[2] 〔 ə'tɛnʃən 〕 *n.* 注意力
tank[2] 〔 tæŋk 〕 *n.* 油箱；坦克車
gas tank 油箱　refill 〔 ri'fɪl 〕 *v.* 再裝滿；再灌滿
at hand 在手邊　distract[6] 〔 dɪ'strækt 〕 *v.* 使分心

Priests *who meditate for hours* don't concentrate *solely* on breathing

or one object, he said. "It's ***not that** they don't get distracted **but***

***that** they're very good at dealing with the distractions **and** releasing* *themselves from them*," Lleras said. "Good meditators will get

distracted **and** get back to their main focus *very quickly*."

冥想幾個小時的牧師，不僅僅只專注在呼吸或者一個物件，雷拉斯說：
「這並不是說他們不會分心，但是他們非常擅長處理分心，並從中釋放
自己。好的冥想者會分心，然後很快地回到他們的主要焦點。」

* priest³〔prist〕n.（基督教）牧師；（天主教）神父
meditate⁶〔'mɛdə,tet〕v. 冥想　　solely⁵〔'sollɪ〕adv. 僅僅
breathe³〔brið〕v. 呼吸　　object²〔'abdʒɪkt〕n. 物體
be good at 擅長　　**deal with** 處理
release³〔rɪ'lis〕v. 釋放　　meditator⁶〔'mɛdə,tetɚ〕n. 冥想者
get back to 回到…；恢復工作
main²〔men〕adj. 主要的　　focus²〔'fokəs〕n. 焦點

Lleras based his theory *on the idea **that** ²*(F) *our senses become*

used to stimulus. *If you stare at one penny **and** place another coin*

10 inches away, the penny *in your peripheral vision* will *eventually*

disappear. *If you blink **or** move*, the second penny reappears *as*

³(B) *the change jolts the brain*.

雷拉斯的理論建立在我們的感官習慣於刺激的這個想法之上。如果
你盯著一分硬幣，把另一枚硬幣放在10英吋遠的地方，那麼在邊緣視野
的那一分硬幣最後便會消失。如果你眨眼或移動，第二枚一分硬幣會再
出現，因為這個變化刺激到大腦。

* ***base…on…*** 建立…在…之上　　theory[3] 〔'θɪərɪ 〕 *n.* 理論

be/become used to N/V-ing 習慣於

stimulus[6] 〔'stɪmjələs 〕 *n.* 刺激（物）

stare[3] 〔 stɛr 〕 *v.* 凝視 < *at* >　　penny[3] 〔'pɛnɪ 〕 *n.* 一分硬幣

peripheral 〔 pə'rɪfərəl 〕 *adj.* 周圍的；邊緣的

vision[3] 〔'vɪʒən 〕 *n.* 視力　　eventually[4] 〔 ɪ'vɛntʃuəlɪ 〕 *adv.* 最後

disappear[2] 〔,dɪsə'pɪr 〕 *v.* 消失　　blink[4] 〔 blɪŋk 〕 *v.* 眨眼

reappear 〔,riə'pɪr 〕 *v.* 再出現；重新顯露

jolt 〔 dʒolt 〕 *v.* 劇烈搖晃；打擊

The same can be true of the thought process. Sustained
attention *to a thought* can cause it *to disappear*. ***If you are given***
something else to think about, [4]**(E) the original thought will seem**
fresh ***when you return to it***.

　　思維過程也是如此。持續注意力在一種思維上會導致它消失。如果
你有其他的想法，當你回到原來的想法時它似乎還是很鮮明。

* ***be true of*** 適用於　　thought[1] 〔 θɔt 〕 *n.* 思想；想法

process[3] 〔'prɑsɛs 〕 *n.* 過程　　sustained[5] 〔 sə'stend 〕 *adj.* 持續的

original[3] 〔 ə'rɪdʒənḷ 〕 *adj.* 最初的；原本的

fresh[1] 〔 frɛʃ 〕 *adj.* 新鮮的；鮮明的

To prove his theory, Lleras had 84 students focus on various
numbers *flashing on a computer for an hour*. One group received no
breaks *or* distractions.

　　爲了證明他的理論，雷拉斯讓84名學生專注於在電腦上閃爍的各種數字，時間一小時。一個小組沒有任何休息或分心。

> * prove[1] 〔 pruv 〕 v. 證明　　various[3] 〔ˈvɛrɪəs〕 adj. 各式各樣的
> flash[2] 〔 flæʃ 〕 v. 閃爍

Other groups were told to memorize numbers ***and*** wait for those numbers *to pop up on the screen.* The groups ***that*** *received diversions* sustained their concentration; [5]**(A) other participants'** attention spans reduced *gradually after 20 minutes*.

其他小組被告知要記住數字並等待在螢幕上彈出這些數字。有事情可分心的小組專注力持續；其他參與者注意力集中的時間20分鐘後漸漸減少。

> * memorize[2] 〔ˈmɛməˌraɪz〕 v. 背誦　　***pop up*** 突然出現
> screen[2] 〔 skrin 〕 n. 螢幕　　span[6] 〔 spæn 〕 n. 持續的時間；期間
> gradually[3] 〔ˈgrædʒʊəlɪ〕 adv. 逐漸地

"It's unrealistic *to expect people to focus at high levels for a long period of time*," Lleras said. "It's important *to create an environment **where** it's OK to take small breaks*."

雷拉斯說：「期望人們長時間高度專心是不切實際的。創造一個可以輕鬆休息的環境是很重要的。」

> * unrealistic[4] 〔ˌriəˈlɪstɪk〕 adj. 寫實的　　level[1] 〔ˈlɛvl̩〕 n. 高度；程度

TEST 22

說明： 第1至5題，每題一個空格。請依文意在文章後所提供的(A)到
(F) 選項中分別選出最適當者。

Obesity in pets has become an increasingly serious problem in the US, despite the warnings in the press and in the vet clinic. __1__ To deal with this issue, make your pets take in fewer calories. First, record all of the food and treats that your pet gets. Reducing the number of treats your pet gets, or replacing high calorie treats with low-cal options may be all it takes to help melt the weight away. If your pet is not overindulged with treats, a reduction in the amount of food that you are feeding it can be the first step to cutting calories. __2__ Weigh your pet in two weeks to see how the weight loss is coming. A 2% loss per week is ideal.

__3__ For dogs, an extra trip around the block every night will do both dogs and owners some good. Swimming is great exercise for overweight dogs that already suffer from painful joints. Cats are a bit more challenging. __4__ Just two short sessions of play each day can give your cat more exercise than it has probably gotten in a long time.

Another option is changing to the light or weight loss variety of food in the brand that you are feeding. Most pet foods offer a variety that helps your pet lose weight and achieve a healthy body condition. ___5___ Your vet can help you set goals and will monitor your pet's weight loss for you. Do the right thing for your pet's health and get that extra weight off now!

(A) It's harder to restrict a cat's diet because it likes to hunt its own food.

(B) Overweight pets are more likely to suffer from diabetes, heart problems, and painful arthritis.

(C) However, there are many different types of toys that are designed to encourage play (exercise) for cats.

(D) If you are following the package recommendations, decrease the amount by 25%.

(E) Talk to your veterinarian prior to beginning a weight loss program for your pet.

(F) In addition to decreasing calorie intake, set a workout plan for them.

TEST 22 詳解

Obesity *in pets* has become an *increasingly* serious problem *in the US*, *despite the warnings in the press **and** in the vet clinic.*

雖然新聞和獸醫診所都有警告，但寵物肥胖已成爲美國越來越嚴重的問題。

* obesity (o'bisətɪ) *n.* 肥胖
increasingly[2] (ɪn'krisɪŋlɪ) *adv.* 越來越
despite[4] (dɪ'spaɪt) *prep.* 儘管
warning[3] ('wɔrnɪŋ) *n.* 警告　　press[2] (prɛs) *n.* 新聞界
veterinarian[6] (ˌvɛtrə'nɛrɪən) *n.* 獸醫 (= *vet*)
clinic[3] ('klɪnɪk) *n.* 診所

[1](**B**) Overweight pets are *more* likely to suffer from diabetes, heart problems, ***and*** painful arthritis. *To deal with this issue*, make your pets take in fewer calories.

體重過重的寵物更容易罹患糖尿病、心臟問題和令人疼痛的關節炎。爲了應付這個問題，請讓你的寵物攝取少一點卡路里。

* overweight ('ovə,wet) *adj.* 體重過重的
suffer from 遭受…困擾；罹患
diabetes[6] (,daɪə'bitɪs) *n.* 糖尿病
painful[2] ('penfəl) *adj.* 疼痛的；痛苦的
arthritis (ɑr'θraɪtɪs) *n.* 關節炎　　***deal with*** 處理；應付
issue[5] ('ɪʃu , 'ɪʃju) *n.* 議題；問題　　***take in*** 攝取
calorie[4] ('kælərɪ) *n.* 卡路里

First, record all *of the food **and** treats **that** your pet gets*. Reducing

the number of treats *your pet gets* , *or* replacing high calorie treats

with low-cal options may be all it takes *to help melt the weight away*.

首先，記錄你的寵物得到的所有食物和零食。減少你的寵物得到零食的
數量，或用低卡路里的選擇替代高熱量的零食，可能是幫助體重慢慢減
輕最要緊的事。

* record[2] 〔 rɪˋkɔrd 〕 v. 記錄　　treat[2] 〔 trit 〕 n. 請客；零食
  replace[3] 〔 rɪˋples 〕 v. 取代 < *with* >
  option[6] 〔 ˋɑpʃən 〕 n. 選擇
  melt away 融化；慢慢消失

If your pet is not overindulged with treats, a reduction *in the amount*

*of food **that** you are feeding it* can be the first step *to cutting calories*.

[2](D) *If you are following the package recommendations*, decrease the

amount *by 25%*.

如果你的寵物沒有對零食過度放縱，減少你餵食的攝入量可能是減少卡
路里的第一步。如果您遵循包裝上的建議，請將餵食量減少 25%。

* overindulge 〔 ͵ovɚɪnˋdʌldʒ 〕 v. 放縱
  【indulge[5] 〔 ɪnˋdʌldʒ 〕 v. 使沈迷】
  reduction[4] 〔 rɪˋdʌkʃən 〕 n. 減少
  amount[2] 〔 əˋmaʊnt 〕 n. 數量

package[2] (ˈpækɪdʒ) *n.* 包裹;包裝
recommendation[6] (ˌrɛkəmɛnˈdeʃən) *n.* 推薦;建議
decrease[4] (dɪˈkris) *v.* 減少

Weigh your pet *in two weeks to see **how** the weight loss is coming.*

A 2% loss *per week* is ideal.

兩個星期內幫你的寵物量體重,看看減重的情形如何。理想狀況是每週
減少體重的 2%。

[3](**F**) *In addition to decreasing calorie intake*, set a workout plan

for them. For dogs, an extra trip *around the block every night* will do

both dogs **and** owners some good. Swimming is great exercise *for*

*overweight dogs **that** already suffer from painful joints.*

　　除了減少卡路里攝入量之外,還要為他們制定運動計劃。對狗來
說,每晚在街區周圍多走一趟,這對狗和主人都有益。對於體重過重,
而且已經遭受關節疼痛之苦的狗,游泳是很好的運動。

* ***in addition to*** 除了…之外(還有)
  intake (ˈɪnˌtek) *n.* 攝取量　　set[1] (sɛt) *v.* 設定;制定
  workout (ˈwɝkˌaut) *n.* 運動
  extra[2] (ˈɛkstrə) *adj.* 額外的　　trip[1] (trɪp) *n.* 旅行;走一趟
  block[1] (blɑk) *n.* 街區　　***do good*** 有益
  owner[2] (ˈonɚ) *n.* 擁有者;主人
  joint[2] (dʒɔɪnt) *n.* 關節

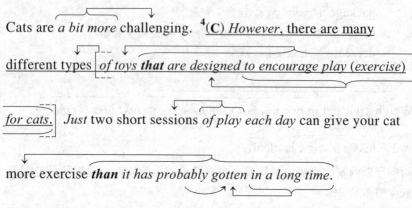

Cats are *a bit more* challenging.　[4](C) *However,* there are many different types *of toys **that** are designed to encourage play (exercise) for cats.* *Just* two short sessions *of play each day* can give your cat more exercise ***than*** *it has probably gotten in a long time.*

貓就比較有點挑戰性了。然而，有許多不同類型的玩具，是設計成鼓勵貓玩（運動）的。每天兩次短時間的玩遊戲比一次長時間，可以讓你的貓運動得更多。

* * ***a bit*** 有點　　challenging[2]〔ˈtʃælɪndʒɪŋ〕*adj.* 有挑戰性的
  type[2]〔taɪp〕*n.* 類型　　design[2]〔dɪˈzaɪn〕*v. n.* 設計
  encourage[2]〔ɪnˈkɝɪdʒ〕*v.* 鼓勵
  session[6]〔ˈsɛʃən〕*n.* 一段時間

Another option is changing to the light ***or*** weight loss variety of food *in the brand **that** you are feeding.* Most pet foods offer a variety ***that*** *helps your pet lose weight **and** achieve a healthy body condition.*

另一種選擇是改餵食物品牌中是輕食或減重的類型。大多數寵物食品的品牌，都有一種能提供幫助你的寵物減肥，並達到健康的身體狀況。

* variety[3] 〔 vəˈraɪətɪ 〕 *n.* 多樣性；種類
brand[2] 〔 brænd 〕 *n.* 品牌
achieve[3] 〔 əˈtʃiv 〕 *v.* 達到
condition[3] 〔 kənˈdɪʃən 〕 *n.* 情況

[5](E) Talk to your veterinarian *prior to beginning a weight loss*

program for your pet. Your vet can help you set goals *and* will

monitor your pet's weight loss *for you.* Do the right thing *for your*

pet's health and get that extra weight off *now!*

在爲寵物開始減肥計劃之前，請先與獸醫談談。你的獸醫可以幫助你設
定目標，並會爲你監控寵物的體重減輕。爲了寵物的健康做正確的事
情，現在就讓額外的體重消失吧！

* *prior to* 在…之前（= *before*）
goal[2] 〔 gol 〕 *n.* 目標　　*set a goal* 設定目標
monitor[4] 〔ˈmɑnətɚ〕 *v.* 監測；監視；監控
health[1] 〔 hɛlθ 〕 *n.* 健康　　*get…off* 除掉

TEST 23

說明： 第 1 至 5 題，每題一個空格。請依文意在文章後所提供的(A) 到
(F) 選項中分別選出最適當者。

Confucius and his students went on a trip to a majestic
waterfall. As they topped a rise and were able to see the
waterfall, they gasped collectively, because at the bottom of
it they saw a man in the churning water, being spun around
and whipped this way and that by the terrifying currents.
____1____

But they lost sight of the man as they descended the
hillside, so they broke through the forest, a short distance
downstream from the waterfall. ____2____ Instead, they saw
him swimming casually away from the waterfall and singing
loudly, evidently having a great time. They were
dumbfounded.

When he got out of the river, Confucius went to speak
with him: "Sir, how can it be that you were not harmed by the
waterfall? Are there some special skills that you possess?"

"No," the man replied. ____3____ That's how I started with
it, developed a habit out of it, and derived lifelong

enjoyment from it. When the powerful torrents twist around me, I turn with them. If a strong current drives me down, I dive alongside it. I am fully aware that when we get to the riverbed, the current will reverse course and provide a strong lift upward. And when this occurs, I am already anticipating it, so I rise together with it. I was born in this area and grew up playing with these powerful currents, so I have always felt comfortable with them. Whatever success I have with water is simply a natural result of my lifelong habit. ___4___ To me, it is just the way life is." Confucius thanked him and smiled. ___5___

(A) I simply follow the nature of the water.

(B) They ran as fast as they could in order to save him.

(C) He was enlightened as to what he and his disciples could talk about on their trip home.

(D) They expected to see the man's lifeless body in the river.

(E) He expressed the well-known principle, *"Do not do to others what you do not want done to yourself."*

(F) To be quite frank, I have no idea why this approach works so well.

TEST 23 詳解

Confucius **and** his students went on a trip *to a majestic waterfall*.

孔子和他的學生前往一處雄偉的瀑布。

* Confucius[2] ﹝kən'fjuʃəs﹞ *n.* 孔子
  go on a trip to⋯ 去⋯旅行；前往⋯
  majestic[5] ﹝mə'dʒɛstɪk﹞ *adj.* 雄偉的
  waterfall[2] ﹝'wɔtɚˌfɔl﹞ *n.* 瀑布

As they topped a rise **and** *were able to see the waterfall*, they gasped collectively, **because** *at the bottom of it they saw a man in the churning water, being spun around* **and** *whipped this way and that by the terrifying currents.* [1] **(B)** They ran *as fast as they could in order to save him.*

當他們登上小山丘，能看見瀑布時，他們全都屏息，因為他們看到有一個人在瀑布的底部，在翻攪的水中轉來轉去，被那可怕的水流任意地攪動著。他們儘可能快跑去救他。

* top[1] ﹝tɑp﹞ *v.* 登上
  rise[1] ﹝raɪz﹞ *n.* 上坡路；山丘
  gasp[5] ﹝gæsp﹞ *v.* 驚嘆；屏息
  collectively[6] ﹝kə'lɛktɪvlɪ﹞ *adv.* 共同地；集體地

gasp	*v.* 驚歎
grasp	*v.* 緊抓；領略
grab	*v.* 抓取
grip	*v.* 緊握

bottom[1] (ˈbatəm) *n.* 底部　　churn (tʃɜn) *v.* 翻騰
spin[3] (spɪn) *v.* 旋轉【三態變化：spin–spun–spun】
whip[3] (hwɪp) *v.* 攪動　　***this way and that*** 任意地
terrifying[4] (ˈtɛrə͵faɪɪŋ) *adj.* 可怕的　　current[3] (ˈkɜənt) *n.* 水流
as ~ as one can 儘可能地~ (= *as ~ as possible*)

But they lost sight of the man ***as*** *they descended the hillside,* ***so***

they broke through the forest, *a short distance downstream from the*

waterfall.

　　但當他們下山時，他們沒看見那個人，於是他們穿過了瀑布下游不
遠處的森林。

　　* ***lose sight of*** 看不見　　descend[6] (dɪˈsɛnd) *v.* 走下；下降
　　hillside (ˈhɪl͵saɪd) *n.* 山坡　　***break through*** 穿過
　　forest[1] (ˈfɔrɪst) *n.* 森林　　distance[2] (ˈdɪstəns) *n.* 距離
　　downstream (ˈdaʊnˈstrim) *adv.* 在下游

[2](**D**) They expected to see the man's lifeless body *in the river.*

Instead, they saw him swimming *casually away from the waterfall*

and singing *loudly, evidently having a great time.*　They were

dumbfounded.

他們預想會在河裡看到這個人的屍體。相反地，他們看見他若無其事地
從瀑布裡游了出來，還大聲地唱歌，顯然很開心。他們傻眼了。

* lifeless〔'laɪflɪs〕*adj.* 無生命的
casually[3]〔'kæʒʊəlɪ〕*adv.* 若無其事地
evidently[4]〔'ɛvədəntlɪ〕*adv.* 顯然
have a great time 很開心
dumbfounded〔,dʌm'faʊndɪd〕*adj.* 目瞪口呆的

When *he got out of the river*, Confucius went to speak with him:

"Sir, how can it be ***that*** *you were not harmed by the waterfall*? Are

there some special skills ***that*** *you possess*?"

　　當他離開河邊的時候，孔子就跟他說：「先生，你怎麼可能不被瀑布傷害呢？你擁有一些特殊技能嗎？」

* ***get out of*** 從…出去；離開
how can it be that + S. + V… 怎麼能
skill[1]〔skɪl〕*n.* 技巧；技能
possess[4]〔pə'zɛs〕*v.* 擁有

"No," the man replied. "[3](A) I *simply* follow the nature *of the water.* That's ***how*** *I started with it, developed a habit out of it,* ***and*** *derived lifelong enjoyment from it.*

　　「沒有，」那個人回答。「我只是跟隨水的性質。我就是這樣開始的，養成了一種習慣，從中獲得終身的樂趣。

* nature[1]〔'netʃɚ〕*n.* 自然；本質　　derive[6]〔də'raɪv〕*v.* 得到
lifelong[5]〔'laɪf,lɔŋ〕*adj.* 終身的
enjoyment[2]〔ɪn'dʒɔɪmənt〕*n.* 樂趣

When the powerful torrents twist around me, I turn *with them*. *If a strong current drives me down*, I dive *alongside it*. I am *fully* aware *that when we get to the riverbed*, the current will reverse course *and* provide a strong lift *upward*. *And when this occurs*, I am *already* anticipating it, *so* I rise *together with it*.

當強而有力的急流在我周圍旋轉時，我隨著一起轉。如果強大的水流驅使我向下，我就會一起潛。我完全知道當我們到達河床時，水流將會逆轉並提供強勁向上的力量。發生這種情況時，我已經預料到了，所以我就跟著水流上升了。

* powerful[2] ('pauɚfəl) adj. 強有力的   torrent[5] ('tɔrənt) n. 急流
  twist[3] (twɪst) v. 扭轉   dive[3] (daɪv) v. 潛水
  alongside[6] (ə'lɔŋ'saɪd) prep. 在…旁邊
  be aware that 知道
  riverbed ('rɪvɚ,bɛd) n. 河床
  reverse[5] (rɪ'vɝs) v. 反轉
  course[1] (kors) n. 過程
  lift[1] (lɪft) n. 舉起   upward[5] ('ʌp,wɚd) adv. 向上
  occur[2] (ə'kɝ) v. 發生
  anticipate[6] (æn'tɪsə,pet) v. 預期

  | reverse v. 迴轉；倒帶 |
  | diverse adj. 不同的 |
  | universe n. 宇宙 |
  | adverse adj. 不利的 |

I was born *in this area **and*** grew up *playing with these powerful currents*, *so* I have *always* felt comfortable *with them*. **Whatever** *success I have with water* is *simply* a natural result *of my lifelong*

habit. [4](F) *To be quite frank*, I have no idea **why** *this approach*

works so well. *To me*, it is *just* the way life is."

我在這個地區出生,和這些強大的水流一起玩長大的,所以我一直覺得和它們為伍很舒服。無論我與水有什麼成就,都只是我終身習慣的自然結果。坦白說,我不知道為什麼這種方法運作得很好。對我來說,生活就是這樣。」

> * natural[2] ('nætʃərəl) *adj.* 自然的;天生的
> result[2] (rɪ'zʌlt) *n.* 結果　　frank[2] (fræŋk) *adj.* 坦白的
> **have no idea** 不知道　　approach[3] (ə'protʃ) *n.* 方法
> work[1] (wɝk) *v.* 運作;有效

Confucius thanked him **and** smiled. [5](C) He was enlightened *as to*

what he **and** *his disciples could talk about on their trip home*.

孔子微笑感謝他。他被啟蒙了,他和他的弟子在回家的路上可以談論了。

> * enlighten[6] (ɪn'laɪtn̩) *v.* 啟蒙　　**as to** 關於;有關
> disciple[5] (dɪ'saɪpl̩) *n.* 弟子

TEST 24

說明： 第 1 至 5 題，每題一個空格。請依文意在文章後所提供的 (A) 到
(F) 選項中分別選出最適當者。

K2 is the second-highest mountain on Earth after
Mount Everest, with a peak elevation of 8,611 meters.
____1____

K2 is known as the Savage Mountain due to the
difficulty of ascent and its high fatality rate, second only
to that of Annapurna. ____2____ The name K2 is derived
from the notation used by a European survey team in
1856. Thomas Montgomerie was the member of the
team who designated it "K2" for being the second
highest peak in the Karakoram range. ____3____ In the
early 1900's, modern transportation did not exist: It took
fourteen days just to reach the foot of the mountain.
After five serious and costly attempts, the team reached
6,525 meters—despite the lack of modern climbing
equipment or weatherproof fabrics. ____4____

K2 is believed by many to be the world's most difficult and dangerous climb. Even now, with more advanced equipment, many bold climbers who dare to challenge this peak still fail and die in the mountains.

___5___

(A) The failures were attributed to a combination of sickness, questionable physical training, personality conflicts, and poor weather conditions.

(B) The first serious attempt to climb K2 was undertaken in 1902 by Oscar Eckenstein and Aleister Crowley, via the Northeast Ridge.

(C) As of July 2010, only 302 people have completed the ascent, compared with over 2,700 individuals who have ascended the more popular target of Everest.

(D) For every four people who have reached the summit, one has died trying.

(E) It is located on the border between the Autonomous County of Xinjiang in China and Gilgit in Pakistan.

(F) Besides, volunteers must face rugged rocky terrain as well as snow and ice and hazardous slopes.

TEST 24 詳解

K2 is the second-highest mountain *on Earth after Mount Everest,* *with a peak elevation of 8,611 meters.* [1](E) It is located *on the* *border between the Autonomous County of Xinjiang in China and* *Gilgit in Pakistan.*

K2 僅次於珠穆朗瑪峰，是地球上第二高的山峰，山頂海拔 8,611 公尺。它位於中國新疆自治區和巴基斯坦吉爾吉特的邊界上。

* ***Mount Everest*** 珠穆朗瑪峰【又叫做聖母峰。為地球第一高峰，屬於喜馬拉雅山脈，位於中國西藏自治區與尼泊爾的邊界上】

peak[3] (pik) *n.* 高峰；山頂　　elevation (ˌɛlə'veʃən) *n.* 海拔
be located 位於　　border[3] ('bɔrdə) *n.* 邊界
autonomous[2] (ɔ'tɑnəməs) *adj.* 自治的；自治權的；自主的
county[2] ('kaʊntɪ) *n.* 縣；郡
Pakistan (ˌpækɪ'stæn) *n.* 巴基斯坦

K2 is known as the Savage Mountain *due to the difficulty of* *ascent **and** its high fatality rate, second only to **that** of Annapurna.* [2](D) *For every four people **who** have reached the summit,* one has died *trying.*

　　K2 被稱爲野蠻山，因爲上坡段攀登困難，以及它僅次於安納布爾納峰群的高死亡率。每四個到達頂峰的人，就有一人在試圖登頂而死亡。

> * ***be known as*** 被稱爲　　savage[5] 〔'sævɪdʒ〕*adj.* 野蠻的
> ***due to*** 由於　　ascent〔ə'sɛnt〕*n.* 上升；登高
> fatality[4]〔fə'tælətɪ〕*n.* 死亡　　rate[3]〔ret〕*n.* 速率；比率
> Annapurna 安納布爾納【位於喜馬拉雅山脈、尼泊爾中北部境內，
> 　　海拔 8,091 公尺，是世界第十高峰。安納布爾納山巒長 55 公里（34
> 　　英里），包括一座 8,000 公尺以上的山峰、十三座 7,000 公尺以上、
> 　　十六多座 6,000 公尺以上】
> summit[3]〔'sʌmɪt〕*n.* 山頂；顛峰

The name K2 is derived from the notation *used by a European survey team in 1856.* Thomas Montgomerie was the member *of the team who designated it "K2" for being the second highest peak in the Karakoram range.*

K2 的名稱來自於 1856 年歐洲勘察小組所使用的批註。托馬斯‧蒙哥馬利是該隊的成員，他將這座喀喇昆崙山脈的第二高峰標示爲 K2。

> * ***be derived from*** 來自於
> notation〔no'teʃən〕*n.* 註釋；批註；記錄
> European〔͵jurə'piən〕*adj.* 歐洲的
> survey[3]〔'sɜve〕*n.* 勘察；調查
> designate[6]〔'dɛzɪg͵net〕*v.* 標示；指定

be derived from 源自
= derive from
= originate from
= arise from
= stem from
= come from

range[2] 〔 rendʒ 〕 *n.* 山脈

Karakoram range 喀喇昆崙山脈【中亞細亞大山脈，從阿富汗最
　　東部向東南延伸約 480 公里（300 哩）。為世界上高山和高緯度之
　　外最長的冰川最集中的地方。塔吉克、中國、巴基斯坦、阿富汗
　　和印度的邊界全都輻輳於這一山系，賦予這一僻遠的地區巨大的
　　地緣政治意義】

[3](B) The first serious attempt *to climb K2* was undertaken *in 1902*

by Oscar Eckenstein **and** *Aleister Crowley, via the Northeast Ridge.*
第一次認真嘗試攀登 K2 的是奧斯卡・艾肯斯坦和阿萊斯特・克羅利，
他們於 1902 年經由東北山脊進行攀登。

* serious[2] 〔 'sɪrɪəs 〕 *adj.* 認真的
　attempt[3] 〔 ə'tɛmpt 〕 *n.* 企圖；嘗試
　undertake[6] 〔 ˌʌndɚ'tek 〕 *v.* 進行；從事
　ridge[5] 〔 rɪdʒ 〕 *n.* 山脊　　via[5] 〔 'vaɪə 〕 *prep.* 經由

In the early 1900's, modern transportation did not exist: It took

fourteen days *just to reach the foot of the mountain.*

在二十世紀初期，現代化交通系統並不存在：光是到達山腳下就花了十
四天。

* modern[2] 〔 'madən 〕 *adj.* 現代化的
　transportation[4] 〔 ˌtrænspɚ'teʃən 〕 *n.* 運輸；交通（系統）
　exist[2] 〔 ɪg'zɪst 〕 *v.* 存在　　reach[1] 〔 ritʃ 〕 *v.* 到達

*After five serious **and** costly attempts*, the team reached 6,525 meters—

*despite the lack of modern climbing equipment **or** weatherproof fabrics.*

經過五次認眞而昂貴的嘗試之後，登山隊到達海拔 6,525 公尺處——儘管缺乏現代的登山裝備或是防風雨的布料。

* costly² 〔'kɔstlɪ 〕*adj.* 昂貴的　　despite⁴ 〔 dɪ'spaɪt 〕*prep.* 儘管
  lack¹ 〔 læk 〕*n.* 缺乏　　equipment⁴ 〔 ɪ'kwɪpmənt 〕*n.* 設備
  weatherproof 〔'wɛðə‚pruf 〕*adj.* 防風雨的
  fabric⁵ 〔'fæbrɪk 〕*n.* 布料

⁴(A) The failures were attributed to a combination *of sickness,*

*questionable physical training, personality conflicts, **and** poor*

weather conditions.

攀登失敗的原因結合了疾病、可疑的體育訓練、人格衝突，和惡劣的天候狀況等因素。

* failure² 〔'feljə 〕*n.* 失敗
  attribute 〔 ə'trɪbjut 〕*v.* 歸因於 < *to* >
  combination⁴ 〔‚kɑmbə'neʃən 〕*n.* 結合
  questionable 〔'kwɛstʃənəbḷ 〕*adj.* 可疑的；不確定的
  physical⁴ 〔'fɪzɪkḷ 〕*adj.* 身體的
  training¹ 〔'trenɪŋ 〕*n.* 訓練
  personality³ 〔‚pɝsṇ'ælətɪ 〕*n.* 個性
  conflict² 〔'kɑnflɪkt 〕*n.* 衝突
  condition³ 〔 kən'dɪʃən 〕*n.* 情況

K2 is believed *by many* to be the world's *most* difficult *and*

dangerous climb. *Even now*, *with more advanced equipment*, many

bold climbers *who dare to challenge this peak still* fail *and* die *in the*

mountains.

攀登 K2 被許多人認爲是世界上最艱難和最危險的。即使是現在，有更先進的設備，敢於挑戰這座高峰的許多大膽登山者，仍然挑戰失敗而死在山裡。

* advanced[3] 〔əd'vænst〕 *adj.* 進步的　　bold[3] 〔bold〕 *adj.* 大膽的
dare[3] 〔dɛr〕 *v.* 敢　　challenge[3] 〔'tʃælɪndʒ〕 *v.* 挑戰

[5](**C**) *As of July 2010, only* 302 people have completed the ascent,

*compared with over 2,700 individuals **who** have ascended the more*

popular target of Everest.

截至 2010 年 7 月，相比於較受歡迎的目標——珠穆朗瑪峰，已經超過 2,700 人完成攻頂，K2 只有 302 人完成。

* *as of* 到~時候爲止　　complete[2] 〔kəm'plit〕 *v.* 完成
compared with 相較於~　　individual[3] 〔,ɪndə'vɪdʒuəl〕 *n.* 個人
ascend[5] 〔ə'sɛnd〕 *v.* 上升；攀登 (= *climb*)
target[2] 〔'tɑrgɪt〕 *n.* 目標

TEST 25

說明： 第 1 至 5 題，每題一個空格。請依文意在文章後所提供的 (A) 到 (F) 選項中分別選出最適當者。

Long long ago, in a faraway place lived a nice old dollmaker. He had spent all his life creating dolls of all sorts, making all the little girls in the world happy. He had kept up with the trends of the world and made dolls that say "mama", that cry, that stand up by themselves, and that even wink at you. But the dollmaker was very wise. ___1___ So, with special resolve in his heart, he made his most beautiful creation. He gave her long brown hair with curls, which he personally felt was the most beautiful hairstyle. He gave her the bluest of blue eyes, ___2___.

This special doll was given long legs with which she could dance, run and play. He gave her beautiful hands to work and serve with and teach all the other dolls. Her fingers were long and slender. ___3___ She had a beautiful face and he planned this so that she could see the beauty in others. He dressed her in a gown, and ___4___ and set her gently in front of a large mirror.

"What do you think, little doll?" he asked. "Are
you not the most beautiful doll in the world?" The
doll looked through her long lashes, full of excited
anticipation.   5   "Oh dollmaker, I hate brown hair
and I have always longed for green eyes. These are not
the colors I'd have chosen for myself. And look how long
my legs are! How large my feet are! How unfashionable
they will seem to the world. My gown is really very
ordinary. Oh dollmaker, I am not a beautiful doll at all!"

(A) into which he put the promises of eternity and into
     which one could gaze forever

(B) He knew that his time for special contribution was
     growing short.

(C) Suddenly her pretty face clouded up, and then she
     stormed,

(D) With these, the old man hoped she would comfort
     those around her.

(E) he knew his doll would be able to give the most
     joy to the one who owned her

(F) on the last day when she was completed, he lifted
     her up with great care

TEST 25 詳解

Long long ago, *in a faraway place* lived a nice old dollmaker.

He had spent all his life *creating dolls of all sorts*, *making all the little girls in the world happy*.

很久很久以前，在一個遙遠的地方，住著一個很會製作娃娃的老人。他一生都在創造各式各樣的娃娃，讓世界上所有的小女孩都開心。

* faraway〔ˈfɑrəˌwe〕*adj.* 遙遠的　　create[2]〔krɪˈet〕*v.* 創造
  sort[2]〔sɔrt〕*n.* 種類　　　*of all sorts* 各種的

He had kept up with the trends *of the world* **and** made dolls **that** say "mama", **that** cry, **that** stand up by themselves, **and that** even wink at you.

他一直以來都有跟上世界潮流，做出了會叫「媽媽」、會哭、會自己站立，甚至會對著你眨眼睛的娃娃。

* *keep up with* 跟上；維持　　trend[3]〔trɛnd〕*n.* 趨勢
  by oneself 獨力；靠自己　　wink[3]〔wɪŋk〕*v.* 眨眼

But the dollmaker was *very* wise. [1](B) He knew **that** *his time for special contribution* was growing short.

但是娃娃製作者非常聰明。他知道他能做出特殊貢獻的時間越來越短。

* wise[2] 〔waɪz〕*adj.* 聰明的；有智慧的
contribution[4] 〔ˌkɑntrəˈbjuʃən〕*n.* 貢獻　　grow[1] 〔gro〕*v.* 變得

So, *with special resolve in his heart*, he made his *most* beautiful
creation.　He gave her long brown hair with curls, ***which he***
personally felt was the most beautiful hairstyle.

所以，他心中有了特別的決定，要做出他最美的創作。他給了她長棕捲
髮，這是他個人覺得最美的髮型。

* resolve[4] 〔rɪˈzɑlv〕*n.* 決心；決定
creation[4] 〔krɪˈeʃən〕*n.* 創造；創作品　　curl[4] 〔kɝl〕*n.* 鬈髮
personally[2] 〔ˈpɝsn̩ḷ〕*adv.* 個人地　　hairstyle[5] 〔ˈhɛrˌstaɪl〕*n.* 髮型

He gave her the bluest of blue eyes, [2](A) *into **which** he put the*
*promises of eternity **and** into **which** one could gaze forever.*

他給她最藍的眼睛，他把永恆的承諾放在裡面，人們可以永遠凝視。

* promise[2] 〔ˈprɑmɪs〕*n.* 承諾　　eternity[6] 〔ɪˈtɝnətɪ〕*n.* 永恆
gaze[4] 〔gez〕*v.* 凝視　　forever[4] 〔fəˈɛvɚ〕*adv.* 永遠地

This special doll was given long legs *with **which** she could*
*dance, run **and** play.*　He gave her beautiful hands *to work **and** serve*
*with **and** teach all the other dolls.*　Her fingers were long ***and*** slender.

　　這個特別的娃娃被賦予可以跳舞、跑步和玩耍的長腿。他給了她美麗的雙手去工作、服務和教所有其他的娃娃。她的手指又長又纖細。

　　* serve¹ 〔 sɜv 〕 *v.* 服務
　　　slender² 〔'slɛndɚ〕 *adj.* 修長的；苗條的

³(**D**) *With these*, the old man hoped *she would comfort those around her.* She had a beautiful face *and* he planned this *so that* she could *see the beauty in others.*

有了這些，老人希望她會安慰到她周圍的人。她有一張美麗的臉龐，而他計劃這樣為的是讓她能看到別人的美麗。

　　* comfort³ 〔'kʌmfɚt〕 *v.* 安慰　　*so that* 為的是；以便

He dressed her *in a gown*, *and* ⁴(**F**) *on the last day **when** she was completed*, he lifted her *up with great care* *and* set her *gently in front of a large mirror.*

他幫她穿上禮服，而且在完成她的最後一天，他非常謹慎地舉起她，輕柔地把她放在一面大鏡子前面。

　　* dress² 〔 drɛs 〕 *v.* 使穿衣　　　gown³ 〔 gaʊn 〕 *n.* 禮服
　　　complete² 〔 kəm'plit 〕 *v.* 完成
　　　lift up 舉起；抱起　　　*with care* 小心地（= *carefully*）
　　　set¹ 〔 sɛt 〕 *v.* 放置　　　gently² 〔'dʒɛntlɪ〕 *adj.* 溫柔地
　　　mirror² 〔'mɪrɚ〕 *n.* 鏡子

"What do you think, little doll?" he asked. "Are you not the *most* beautiful doll *in the world*?" The doll looked through her long lashes *full of excited anticipation*.

「小娃娃，妳覺得怎麼樣？」他問。「妳不是世界上最漂亮的洋娃娃嗎？」洋娃娃透過她的長長的睫毛看著，充滿激動的期待。

* lash[5] 〔 læʃ 〕 *n.* 睫毛　　anticipation[6] 〔 æn͵tɪsə'peʃən 〕 *n.* 期待

5(C) *Suddenly* her pretty face clouded up, *and then* she stormed, "Oh dollmaker, I hate brown hair *and* I have *always* longed for green eyes. These are not the colors *I'd have chosen for myself.* And look *how* long my legs are! *How* large my feet are! *How* unfashionable they will seem *to the world.* My gown is *really very* ordinary. Oh dollmaker, I am not a beautiful doll *at all*!"

突然，她漂亮的臉龐蒙上了一層陰影，而且接著暴怒說：「喔，娃娃製作者，我討厭棕色頭髮，而我一直渴望有綠眼睛。這些不是我自己選擇的顏色。看看我的腿是多麼地長！我的腳好大！這在世上看起來多麼不合時宜。我的禮服真的很普通。喔，娃娃製作者，我根本不是一個漂亮的娃娃！」

* suddenly[2] 〔'sʌdn̩lɪ 〕 *adv.* 突然
  cloud[1] 〔 klaʊd 〕 *v.* 使陰暗；使模糊 < *up* >
  storm[2] 〔 stɔrm 〕 *v.* 暴怒；怒罵　　*long for* 渴望
  unfashionable[3] 〔 ʌn'fæʃənəbl̩ 〕 *adj.* 不流行的
  ordinary[2] 〔'ɔrdn̩͵ɛrɪ 〕 *adj.* 普通的
  not…at all 根本不是；一點也不…

TEST 26

說明： 第1至5題，每題一個空格。請依文意在文章後所提供的(A)到
(F) 選項中分別選出最適當者。

We often hear children wish they could grow up
soon, and old people wish they could be children again.
___1___ To be a happy person, one must enjoy what
each age brings him without wasting time on useless and
endless regrets.

In childhood, life is never difficult. Whatever a
child does, he is always fed, taken care of, and loved.
Never again in his life will he be given so much without
having to do anything in return. Besides, life is always
presenting novel things. ___2___ But childhood has its
pains. He needs to get permission even for a sleepover.
___3___ As a consequence, his life is not totally perfect.

As time goes by, the young man starts to work for his
clothes, food, and lodging. ___4___ He can no longer
expect others to look after him all the time. However,
depending completely on himself, he is thus free from all
the strict disciplines of school and parents. Also, he can

get the happiness of seeing himself make steady progress in his career and of taking his own position in society.

Most people think of old age as the worst life stage, but an old man is not necessarily unhappy. Indeed, life is deficient in energy and passion. ___5___ Best of all, he has lived through the battle of life safely and reached a time when he can lie back and rest. When he looks back on his life, the satisfaction is beyond words.

(A) It is time he took full responsibility for himself.

(B) Being constantly told what to do and what not to do, he is not allowed to do whatever he wishes.

(C) It must be kept in mind that each life stage has its pros and cons.

(D) Moreover, the more obstacles one encounters on his life path, the stronger he gets.

(E) Yet accumulated wisdom is an invaluable treasure.

(F) Shining stars in the sky, heavy rain in the afternoon, and a trip to the forest, can all bring great pleasure.

TEST 26 詳解

We *often* hear children wish *they could grow up soon*, *and* old people wish *they could be children again.* **[1](C) It must be kept in mind *that* each life stage has its pros *and* cons.**

我們經常聽到孩子們希望他們能很快長大,老人希望他們能再次成為孩子。必須記住,每個生命階段都有其優點和缺點。

* *keep in mind* 記住　　stage[2] (stedʒ) *n.* 舞台;階段
  pros and cons 優點和缺點

To be a happy person, one must enjoy **what** each age brings him without wasting time on useless *and* endless regrets.

要成為一個快樂的人,就必須享受每個年紀所帶給他的,不浪費時間在無用且無盡的後悔。

* useless ('juslɪs) *adj.* 無用的;無價值的
  endless ('ɛndlɪs) *adj.* 無盡的;不斷的
  regret[3] (rɪ'grɛt) *v. n.* 後悔

In childhood, life is *never* difficult. **Whatever** a child does, he is always fed, taken care of, *and* loved. *Never again in his life* will he be given so much *without having to do anything in return*.

　　童年時，人生從來都不難。無論孩子做什麼，他總是被餵飽、被照顧和被愛。在他的人生中再也不會得到這麼多的東西，而不需要做任何事情作為交換。

> * feed¹〔fid〕v. 餵【三態變化：feed–fed–fed】
> ***take care of*** 照顧；留意　　***in return*** 回報；交換

Besides, life is *always* presenting novel things.　²**(F)** Shining stars *in the sky*, heavy rain *in the afternoon*, **and** a trip *to the forest*, can all bring great pleasure.

此外，生活總是呈現新奇的東西。天空中閃爍的星星、下午的大雨以及森林之旅，都可以帶來大大的樂趣。

> * present²〔prɪ'zɛnt〕v. 呈現　　novel²〔'nɑvl̩〕adj. 新奇的
> shining¹〔'ʃaɪnɪŋ〕adj. 閃爍的
> forest¹〔'fɔrɪst〕n. 森林
> pleasure²〔'plɛʒɚ〕n. 樂趣

But childhood has its pains.　He needs to get permission *even for a sleepover*.　³**(B)** *Being constantly told **what** to do **and what** not to do,* he is not allowed to do ***whatever** he wishes.*　*As a consequence*, his life is not *totally* perfect.

但童年有它的痛苦。他甚至在外面過夜都必須得到許可。不斷被告知要做什麼和不該做什麼，他不被允許做任何他想做的事情。因此，他的生活並不是完全完美的。

* **childhood**[3] (ˈtʃaɪld,hʊd) *n.* 童年　　**pain**[2] (pen) *n.* 痛苦
permission[3] (pəˈmɪʃən) *n.* 許可
sleepover (ˈslip,ovɚ) *n.* 在別人家過夜
constantly[3] (ˈkɑnstəntlɪ) *adv.* 不斷地　　**allow**[1] (əˈlaʊ) *v.* 允許
consequence[4] (ˈkɑnsə,kwɛns) *n.* 後果
as a consequence 因此；所以　　**totally**[1] (ˈtotḷɪ) *adv.* 完全地
perfect[2] (ˈpɝfɪkt) *adj.* 完美的

As time goes by, the young man starts to work *for his clothes,*
food, **and** *lodging.* [4](A) It is time *he took full responsibility for himself.*
He can *no longer* expect others to look after him *all the time.*

　　隨著時間過去，年輕人開始為自己的衣服、食物和住宿而工作。是
他自己承擔全部責任的時候了。他不能再期望別人一直照顧他。

* *go by* （指時間）過去；消逝　　**lodging**[5] (ˈlɑdʒɪŋ) *n.* 住宿
responsibility[3] (rɪ,spɑnsəˈbɪlətɪ) *n.* 責任
take responsibilty for 為…承擔責任
no longer 不再　　**expect**[2] (ɪkˈspɛkt) *v.* 期待
look after 照顧　　*all the time* 一直

look after 照顧
= see after
= care for
= take care of

However, depending completely on himself, he is *thus* free from all
the strict disciplines *of school* **and** *parents. Also,* he can get the
happiness *of seeing himself make steady progress in his career* **and**
of taking his own position in society.

但是完全地靠自己，他也因此擺脫了學校和家長的嚴格管制。同樣地，看到自己在事業上穩定進步，在社會上佔有一席之地，他也得到了幸福。

* depend² (dɪ'pɛnd) v. 依賴 < on >
  completely² (kəm'plitlɪ) adv. 完全地　　thus¹ (ðʌs) adv. 因此
  be free from 沒有；免於　　strict² (strɪkt) adj. 嚴格的
  discipline⁴ ('dɪsəplɪn) n. 法律；管制
  steady³ ('stɛdɪ) adj. 穩定的　　progress² ('prɑgrɛs) n. 進步
  make progress in ~ 在 ~ 方面有進步
  career⁴ (kə'rɪr) n. 職業；事業　　position¹ (pə'zɪʃən) n. 位置
  society² (sə'saɪətɪ) n. 社會

Most people think of old age as the worst life stage, **but** an old

man is *not necessarily* unhappy. *Indeed*, life is deficient *in energy*

and passion. ⁵(**E**) *Yet* accumulated wisdom is an invaluable treasure.

雖然大多數人認爲老年是最糟糕的人生階段，但老人不一定是不快樂的。的確，生命在能量和激情上是不足的。但累積的智慧是個無價的寶藏。

* **think of A as B** 認爲 A 是 B
  necessarily² ('nɛsə,sɛrəlɪ) adv. 必定
  not necessarily 未必；不一定
  indeed³ (ɪn'did) adv. 的確；真正地
  deficient⁶ (dɪ'fɪʃənt) adj. 不足的；缺乏的
  energy² ('ɛnədʒɪ) n. 活力；精力　　passion³ ('pæʃən) n. 熱情
  accumulated⁶ (ə'kjumjə,letɪd) adj. 累積的
  wisdom³ ('wɪzdəm) n. 智慧
  invaluable⁶ (ɪn'væljəbḷ) adj. 珍貴的；無價的
  treasure² ('trɛʒə) n. 寶藏

Best of all, he has lived *through the battle of life safely* *and* reached a

time *when he can lie back* *and rest*. *When he looks back on his life,*

the satisfaction is beyond words.

最好的是，他已經平安度過生命的戰役，到了可以躺下休息的時候。當
他回顧自己的人生時，那滿足是無以言表的。

* ***best of all*** 最好的是
* ***live through*** 經歷過…
* battle² ﹝ˈbætḷ﹞ *n.* 戰役　　reach¹ ﹝ritʃ﹞ *v.* 到達
* ***lie back*** 休息；放鬆　　rest¹ ﹝rɛst﹞ *v. n.* 休息
* ***look back on*** 回頭看；回顧
* satisfaction⁴ ﹝ˌsætɪsˈfækʃən﹞ *n.* 滿足
* beyond² ﹝bɪˈjɑnd﹞ *prep.* 超過
* word¹ ﹝wɝd﹞ *n.* 言語；話
* ***beyond words*** 無法用語言表達

TEST 27

In the movie Dead Poets Society, Robin Williams plays an outrageous teacher in a boys' school. ___1___ Unlike Mr. Williams, who encourages students to question authority, teachers I have known are mild and conventional. Based on their years of teaching, I will divide them into three types: paranoid teachers who have been newly recruited, enthusiastic teachers who have taught for less than 10 years, and idle teachers who will soon retire.

Firstly, the most dreaded form of teacher is the paranoid "new grad." ___2___ Therefore, in order to prove their worth, this group of teachers often assigns a lot of homework and teaches at great speed despite the fact that students may not be able to digest the materials they eagerly offer.

The second group of teachers has taught students for less than 10 years. Unlike new teachers who are anxious about their popularity, this group of teachers still has the enthusiasm of their youth but also the confidence that comes with experience to create an exciting educational experience for their students. ___3___

Lastly, just as milk and food have an expiration date, the final group of teachers is now simply counting their time, waiting for their pension to take effect. In spite of their idleness, there is no doubt that "senior" instructors possess a wealth of knowledge that is unmatched by any other type of teacher I have encountered. ___4___ Class time often passes at a snail's pace as a teacher sits lifelessly at his/her desk reading decades-old notes.

___5___ From my observation of my teachers, I hope that I can adopt the best traits of each group and avoid the teaching methods students hate.

(A) However, they are also too bitter and dull to share their wisdom.

(B) Now I am still a student, but soon I will be on the "other side of the desk."

(C) In their minds, the students, the parents and the administrators are all watching their performance.

(D) In one scene, he jumps on the podium, ordering his students to rip out all of the pages in the introduction of their new textbook.

(E) In addition to their lectures, activities like debates, experiments, and field trips all add an extra dimension to each student's schooling.

(F) Graduation is the pinnacle of our academic careers.

TEST 27 詳解

In the movie Dead Poets Society, Robin Williams plays an
outrageous teacher *in a boys' school.*

在電影《春風化雨》中，羅賓‧威廉斯扮演了一位在一所男子學校裡無法無天的老師。

* outrageous[6] 〔aʊt'redʒəs〕 *adj.* 無法無天的

[1]**(D)** *In one scene*, he jumps *on the podium, ordering his students to*
rip out all of the pages in the introduction of their new textbook.

在一幕中，他跳上講台，命令學生撕掉他們新課本中的所有引言的頁面。

* scene[1] 〔sin〕 *n.* 場景；一幕　　*jump on* 跳上
  podium 〔'podɪəm〕 *n.* 講台　　order[1] 〔'ɔrdə〕 *v.* 命令
  rip out 拆掉；撕下
  introduction[3] 〔,ɪntrə'dʌkʃən〕 *n.* 引言；序言
  textbook[2] 〔'tɛkst,bʊk〕 *n.* 教科書

*Unlike Mr. Williams, **who** encourages students to question authority,*
teachers *I have known* are mild *and* conventional.

與鼓勵學生質疑權威的威廉斯先生不同，我所認識的教師是溫和而傳統的。

* encourage[2] 〔ɪn'kɝɪdʒ〕 *v.* 鼓勵

question¹ (ˈkwɛstʃən) v. 質問；質疑
authority⁴ (əˈθɔrətɪ) n. 權威；權力　　mild⁴ (maɪld) adj. 溫和的
conventional⁴ (kənˈvɛnʃənḷ) adj. 傳統的；老套的

Based on their years of teaching, I will divide them *into three types*:

*paranoid teachers **who** have been newly recruited, enthusiastic*

*teachers **who** have taught for less than 10 years, **and** idle teachers*

***who** will soon retire.*

根據他們教學多少年，我將他們分為三類：新招聘的偏執教師、教書不
到十年的熱心教師、即將退休的閒散教師。

　*　**based on** 根據　　divide² (dəˈvaɪd) v. 劃分
　　divide into 把…分成；劃分
　　paranoid (ˈpærəˌnɔɪd) adj. 偏執的　　recruit⁶ (rɪˈkrut) v. 招募
　　enthusiastic⁵ (ɪnˌθjuzɪˈæstɪk) adj. 熱心的
　　idle⁴ (ˈaɪdḷ) adj. 懶惰的；閒散的　　retire⁴ (rɪˈtaɪr) v. 退休

Firstly, the *most* dreaded form *of teacher* is the paranoid "new

grad." ²(C) *In their minds*, the students, the parents **and** the

administrators are all watching their performance.

　　首先，最可怕的教師類型是偏執的「菜鳥畢業生」。在他們的心目
中，學生、家長以及行政人員都在看著他們的表現。

　*　dreaded⁴ (ˈdrɛdɪd) adj. 可怕的

grad〔græd〕*n.* 畢業生（= *graduate*[3]）
administrator[6]〔əd'mɪnə͵stretɚ〕*n.* 行政人員
performance[3]〔pɚ'fɔrməns〕*n.* 表現

Therefore, in order to prove their worth, this group *of teachers often*

assigns a lot of homework *and* teaches *at great speed despite the fact*

that students may not be able to digest the materials they eagerly offer.

因此，爲了證明自己的價值，這類教師經常會分配很多作業，並且以很快的速度教學，儘管學生可能無法消化他們熱切提供的資料。

* *in order to V* 爲了　　prove[1]〔pruv〕*v.* 證明
worth[2]〔wɝθ〕*n.* 價值　　assign[4]〔ə'saɪn〕*v.* 指定；分派
despite[4]〔dɪ'spaɪt〕*prep.* 儘管　　*be able to V* 能夠
digest[4]〔daɪ'dʒɛst〕*v.* 消化　　material[2]〔mə'tɪrɪəl〕*n.* 材料
eagerly[3]〔'igɚlɪ〕*adj.* 渴望地；熱切地　　offer[2]〔'ɔfɚ〕*v. n.* 提供

The second group of teachers has taught students *for less than*

10 years. *Unlike new teachers* **who** *are anxious about their*

popularity, this group of teachers *still* has the enthusiasm *of their*

youth **but** *also* the confidence *that comes with experience to create*

an exciting educational experience for their students.

　　第二類教師教學不到十年。與渴望受歡迎的新老師不同的是，這類老師仍然有著青春的熱情，也因經驗而有信心，為學生創造令人興奮的教育經驗。

> * anxious[4]〔'æŋkʃəs〕*adj.* 渴望的 < about >
> popularity[4]〔ˌpɑpjə'lærətɪ〕*n.* 受歡迎
> enthusiasm[4]〔ɪn'θjuzɪˌæzəm〕*n.* 熱忱　　youth[2]〔juθ〕*n.* 年輕
> confidence[4]〔'kɑnfədəns〕*n.* 信心
> experience[2]〔ɪk'spɪrɪəns〕*n.* 經驗　　create[2]〔krɪ'et〕*v.* 創造
> educational[3]〔ˌɛdʒə'keʃənḷ〕*adj.* 教育的

[3]**(E)** *In addition to their lectures*, activities *like debates, experiments,*
***and** field trips* all add an extra dimension *to each student's schooling.*

除了講課之外，像辯論、實驗和戶外教學等活動，都為每個學生的學校教育增添額外的面向。

> * ***in addition to*** 除了…之外　　lecture[4]〔'lɛktʃə〕*n.* 演講；講課
> activity[3]〔æk'tɪvətɪ〕*n.* 活動　　debate[2]〔dɪ'bet〕*n.* 辯論
> experiment[3]〔ɪk'spɛrəmənt〕*n.* 實驗　　***field trip*** 戶外教學
> dimension[2]〔də'mɛnʃən〕*n.* 面向　　***add** A **to** B* 把 A 加入 B 中
> extra[2]〔'ɛkstrə〕*adj.* 額外的
> schooling〔'skulɪŋ〕*adj.* 學校教育；培養

*Lastly, just **as** milk **and** food have an expiration date*, the final
group of teachers is *now simply* counting their time, *waiting for*
their pension to take effect.

　　最後，就像牛奶和食物有到期日一樣，最後一類教師只是在倒數他們的時間，等待他們的退休金生效。

* expiration[6] 〔͵ɛkspə'reʃən〕 *n.* 期滿
  expiration date 到期日；有效期限
  pension[6] 〔'pɛnʃən〕 *n.* 退休金　　***take effect*** 有效；生效

In spite of their idleness, there is no doubt ***that*** *"senior" instructors*

possess a wealth of knowledge | ***that** is unmatched by any other type of*

teacher I have encountered.

儘管他們很懶惰，毫無疑問地，資深講師擁有豐富的知識，而這點是我
遇過的任何其他類型的教師無法比擬的。

* ***in spite of*** 儘管 (= *despite*)　　doubt[2] 〔daʊt〕 *v. n.* 懷疑
  no dount 無疑地　　senior[4] 〔'sinjɚ〕 *adj.* 年長的；資深的
  instructor[4] 〔ɪn'strʌktɚ〕 *n.* 講師　　possess[4] 〔pə'zɛs〕 *v.* 擁有
  wealth[3] 〔wɛlθ〕 *n.* 財富；豐富　　***a wealth of*** 豐富的
  knowledge[2] 〔'nɑlɪdʒ〕 *n.* 知識
  unmatched 〔ʌn'mætʃt〕 *adj.* 無比的；無與倫比的
  encounter[4] 〔ɪn'kaʊntɚ〕 *v.* 遭遇

[4](A) *However*, they are *also too* bitter ***and*** dull *to share their wisdom.*

Class time *often* passes *at a snail's pace **as** a teacher sits lifelessly at*

his/her desk reading decades-old notes.

然而，他們也太苦澀太沈悶，而無法分享他們的智慧。課堂的時間經常
隨著老師毫無生氣地坐在桌前，讀著陳年老舊的筆記，緩慢的流逝。

* ***too…to + V*** 太…而不能～　　bitter[2] 〔'bɪtə 〕 *adj.* 苦的

dull[2] 〔 dʌl 〕 *adj.* 遲鈍的；沉悶的　　wisdom[3] 〔'wɪzdəm 〕 *n.* 智慧

snail[2] 〔 snel 〕 *n.* 蝸牛　　pace[4] 〔 pes 〕 *n.* 步調

at a snail's pace 極緩慢地

lifelessly[2] 〔'laɪflɪslɪ 〕 *adv.* 無生氣地

[5]**(B)** *Now* I am *still* a student, ***but*** *soon* I will be on the "other side *of the desk*." *From my observation of my teachers*, I hope ***that*** I can adopt the best traits of each group ***and*** avoid the teaching methods students hate.

　　現在我還是個學生，但是很快我就會在「桌子的另一邊」。從我觀察的老師中，我希望能夠採用每種老師的最佳特質，而且避免學生討厭的教學方法。

* observation[4] 〔ˌɑbzə'veʃən 〕 *n.* 觀察　　adopt[3] 〔 ə'dɑpt 〕 *v.* 採用

trait[6] 〔 tret 〕 *n.* 特點　　avoid[2] 〔 ə'vɔɪd 〕 *v.* 避免

method[2] 〔'mɛθəd 〕 *n.* 方法　　hate[1] 〔 het 〕 *v.* 討厭；痛恨

【補充資料】

　　「春風化雨」（Dead Poets Society）是 1989 年彼得·威爾（Peter Weir）所執導的電影。本片講述在一個傳統學校的老師，用反傳統的方法來教導學生們詩歌、文學、生活的故事。電影不僅是男主角羅賓·威廉斯（Robin Williams）的經典之作，同時也是講述師生關係的優秀電影。以下是電影中的經典台詞：

Carpe Diem.　Seize the day.　Make your lives extraordinary!
把握當下，讓你的生命不凡！

TEST 28

說明：第1至5題，每題一個空格。請依文意在文章後所提供的 (A) 到 (F) 選項中分別選出最適當者。

A young man was getting ready to graduate from college. For a long time he had admired a beautiful sports car in a dealer's showroom, and knowing his father could well afford it, he told his father that was all he wanted.

As graduation day approached, the young man awaited signs that his father had purchased the car. ___1___ His father told him how proud he was to have such a fine son, and told him how much he loved him. He handed his son a beautifully wrapped gift box. Curious, and somewhat disappointed, the young man opened the box and found a lovely, leather-bound Bible, with his name on it. He raised his voice to his father angrily and said, "With all your money, you give me a Bible?" and stormed out of the house.

___2___ He had a beautiful house and a wonderful family. One day, he realized his father was getting old and thought perhaps he should see him. He had not seen him since that graduation day. Before he could make arrangements, he received a telegram telling him his father had passed away, and willed all of his possessions to his son. ___3___ When he arrived at his father's house, sudden sadness and regret filled his heart. He began to search through his father's important papers and saw the still gift-wrapped Bible, just as he had left it years ago. ___4___ His father had carefully underlined a verse, "And if ye, being evil, know how to give good gifts to your children, how much more shall your Heavenly Father which is in Heaven, give to those who ask Him?"

As he read on, a car key suddenly dropped from the back of the Bible. It had a tag with the dealer's name, the same dealer who had the sports car he had desired. ___5___

(A) Many years passed and the young man was very successful in business.

(B) In tears, he opened the Bible and began to turn the pages.

(C) The worst thing that happened to him was to have an ungrateful son that could not maintain the family fortune.

(D) He needed to go home immediately and take care of things.

(E) Finally, on the morning of his graduation, his father called him into his private study.

(F) On the tag was the date of his graduation.

TEST 28 詳解

A young man was getting ready *to graduate from college.*
For a long time he had admired a beautiful sports car *in a dealer's*
showroom, **and** *knowing his father could well afford it,* he told his
father *that was all he wanted.*

一個年輕人正準備從大學畢業。他長久以來一直很欣賞一位經銷商的展示間裡一輛很漂亮的跑車，而他知道他的父親負擔得起，就告訴他的父親，那就是他想要的。

* ***get ready*** 準備好　　graduate[3] (ˈgrædʒu͵et) v. 畢業
college[3] (ˈkɑlɪdʒ) n. 大學；學院
admire[3] (ədˈmaɪr) v. 欣賞；讚嘆　　***sports car*** 跑車
dealer[3] (ˈdilɚ) n. 商人　　showroom (ˈʃo͵rum) n. 展示間
afford[3] (əˈfɔrd) v. 負擔得起

As *graduation day approached,* the young man awaited signs
that his father had purchased the car.

隨著畢業日的接近，年輕人等待著他父親購買那輛車的跡象。

* graduation[4] (͵grædʒuˈeʃən) n. 畢業
approach[3] (əˈprotʃ) v. 接近
await[4] (əˈwet) v. 等待 (= *wait for*)
sign[2] (saɪn) n. 跡象；前兆 < *that* >
purchase[5] (ˈpɝtʃəs) v. 購買

[1](E) *Finally, on the morning of his graduation*, his father called him into his private study. His father told him *how proud he was to have such a fine son*, *and* told him *how much he loved him*. He handed his son a *beautifully* wrapped gift box.

最後，在他畢業的那天早上，他父親把他叫進他的私人書房。他的父親告訴他，他有多驕傲有他這樣的一個好兒子，而且告訴他他有多愛他。他遞給兒子一個包裝美麗的禮盒。

* private[2] (ˈpraɪvɪt) *adj.* 私人的　　study[1] (ˈstʌdɪ) *n.* 書房
proud[2] (praʊd) *adj.* 驕傲的；自豪的
hand[1] (hænd) *v.* 面交；給；傳遞　　wrap[3] (ræp) *v.* 包裝

Curious, and somewhat disappointed, the young man opened the box *and* found a lovely, leather-bound Bible, *with his name on it*.

好奇而且有些失望，年輕人打開了盒子，發現一本美麗的、皮面的聖經，上面有他的名字。

* curious[2] (ˈkjʊrɪəs) *adj.* 好奇的
somewhat[3] (ˈsʌm,hwɑt) *adv.* 稍微；有點
disappointed[3] (,dɪsəˈpɔɪntɪd) *adj.* 失望的
lovely[2] (ˈlʌvlɪ) *adj.* 可愛的；美麗的
leather-bound (ˈlɛðɚˈbaʊnd) *adj.* 皮面的
Bible[3] (ˈbaɪbl̩) *n.* 聖經

He raised his voice to his father angrily ***and*** said, *"With all your*

money, you give me a Bible?" ***and*** stormed *out of the house*.

他對著父親生氣地提高聲量說：「你那麼有錢，才送我一本聖經？」然
後衝出屋外。

> * raise[1] 〔 rez 〕 *v.* 提高；舉起　　voice[1] 〔 vɔɪs 〕 *n.* 聲音；音量
> angrily[1] 〔 'æŋgrɪlɪ 〕 *adv.* 生氣地　　***with all*** 儘管；雖然
> storm[2] 〔 stɔrm 〕 *v.* 猛衝

[2](A) Many years passed ***and*** the young man was *very* successful

in business. He had a beautiful house ***and*** a wonderful family.

One day, he realized his father was getting old ***and*** thought *perhaps*

he should see him. He had not seen him *since that graduation day.*

　　許多年過去了，這個年輕人的生意非常成功。他有漂亮的房子和美
好的家庭。有一天，他意識到他的父親越來越老了，想著也許他應該去
見他。從畢業那天以後，他就沒有見過他了。

> * realize[2] 〔 'rɪəˌlaɪz 〕 *v.* 了解；領悟

Before he could make arrangements, he received a telegram *telling*

him his father had passed away, ***and*** willed all of his possessions to

his son.

在他可以做出安排之前,他收到一封電報告訴他,他的父親已經去世了,他的遺囑中將所有的財產都贈與他的兒子。

* arrangement[2] ﹙ əˈrendʒmənt ﹚ *n.* 安排;排列
  receive[1] ﹙ rɪˈsiv ﹚ *v.* 收到
  telegram[4] ﹙ˈtɛləˌgræm ﹚ *n.* 電報
  pass away 去世
  will[1] ﹙ wɪl ﹚ *n.* 遺囑　*v.* 立遺囑贈與
  possession[4] ﹙ pəˈzɛʃən ﹚ *n.* 財產

pass away　去世
pass by　經過
pass down　傳下來
pass on　傳遞
pass out　昏倒

[3](**D**) He needed to go home *immediately **and*** take care of things.

When he arrived at his father's house, sudden sadness ***and*** regret

filled his heart.

他需要立即回家處理事情。當他到達父親的家時,突然的悲傷和後悔充滿了他的內心。

* immediately[3] ﹙ ɪˈmidɪɪtlɪ ﹚ *adv.* 立刻　　***take care of*** 處理
  arrive[2] ﹙ əˈraɪv ﹚ *v.* 到達　　sudden[2] ﹙ˈsʌdn̩ ﹚ *adj.* 突然的
  regret[3] ﹙ rɪˈgrɛt ﹚ *v. n.* 後悔

He began to search *through his father's important papers **and*** saw

the *still* gift-wrapped Bible, *just **as** he had left it years ago*.

他開始搜尋他父親的重要文件,並看到了那本仍然被包成禮物的聖經,就像他幾年前離開時一樣。

* search[2] ﹙ sɝtʃ ﹚ *v.* 搜尋
  gift-wrapped ﹙ˈgɪftˈræpt ﹚ *adj.* 被包成禮物的

[4] **(B)** *In tears*, he opened the Bible *and* began to turn the pages.　His father had *carefully* underlined a verse, "***And if*** *ye, being evil, know* ***how*** *to give good gifts to your children,* ***how*** *much more shall your Heavenly Father* **which** *is in Heaven*, give to those ***who*** *ask Him*?"

含著眼淚，他打開聖經，然後開始翻頁。他的父親小心地將一段韻文劃了底線：「你們雖然不好，尚且知道把好東西給你們兒女，更何況是你們在天上的父，豈不是會把更好的東西給有求於祂的人嗎？」

　　* tear[2] 〔 tɪr 〕 *n.* 眼淚　　underline[5] 〔ˌʌndɚˋlaɪn 〕 *v.* 在…畫底線
　　verse[3] 〔 vɝs 〕 *n.* 韻文；詩句　　evil[3] 〔ˋivḷ 〕 *adj.* 邪惡的
　　heavenly[5] 〔ˋhɛvənlɪ 〕 *adj.* 天堂的；天空的
　　Heavenly Father 天父　　heaven[3] 〔ˋhɛvən 〕 *n.* 天堂

As he read on, a car key *suddenly* dropped *from the back of the Bible*.　It had a tag *with the dealer's name*, the same dealer *who had the sports car he had desired*.　[5] **(F)** *On the tag* was the date *of his graduation*.

　　當他繼續讀下去，一把車鑰匙突然從聖經背面掉下來。上面有著經銷商名字的標籤，就是那位有他夢寐以求跑車的經銷商。標籤上的日期正是他畢業那天。

　　* ***read on*** 繼續讀；讀下去　　drop[2] 〔 drɑp 〕 *v.* 掉落
　　tag[3] 〔 tæg 〕 *n.* 標籤；貼紙　　desire[2] 〔 dɪˋzaɪr 〕 *v.* 渴望

TEST 29

說明: 第1至5題,每題一個空格。請依文意在文章後所提供的(A)到 (F) 選項中分別選出最適當者。

"Look at fatso!"

Freshmen in high school can be cruel, and we certainly were to a young man named Matt who was in my class. ____1____ He was at least fifty pounds overweight. He felt the pain of being the last one picked to play basketball, baseball or football. Matt will always remember the endless pranks that were played on him—trashing his locker, piling library books on his desk and spraying him with icy streams of water in the shower after gym class. One day he sat near me in gym class. Someone pushed him and he fell on me and banged my foot quite badly. The kid who pushed him said Matt did it. With the whole class watching, I was put on the spot to either shrug it off or pick a fight with Matt. ____2____

I shouted, "C'mon, Matt, let's fight!" He said he didn't want to. But peer pressure forced him into the conflict whether he liked it or not. He came toward me with his fists in the air. With one punch I bloodied his nose and the class went wild. ____3____ He saw that we were fighting and he sent us out to the oval running track.

He followed us with a smile on his face and said, "I want you two guys to go out there and run that mile holding each other's hands." The room erupted into a roar of laughter. The two of us were embarrassed beyond belief, but Matt and I went out to the track and ran our mile—hand-in-hand.

At some point during the course of our run, I remember looking over at him, with blood still trickling from his nose and his weight slowing him down. __4__ We both looked at each other and began to laugh. Going around that track, hand-in-hand, I no longer saw Matt as fat or dumb. It was amazing what I learned when I was forced to go hand-in-hand with someone for only one mile. __5__

(A) I chose to fight in order to keep my image intact.

(B) The gym teacher decided to ground those who bullied the chubby kid.

(C) For the rest of my life I never so much as raised a hand against another person.

(D) We mimicked him, teased him and taunted him about his size.

(E) It struck me that here was a person, not all that different from myself.

(F) Just then the gym teacher walked into the room.

TEST 29　詳解

"Look at fatso!"

Freshmen *in high school* can be cruel, ***and*** we *certainly* were *to*

*a young man named Matt **who** was in my class.*

「看！胖子！」

高中新生可能是很殘忍的，對我班上一個叫麥特的年輕人來說，我們確實是。

* fatso〔ˋfætso〕*n.* 胖子　　freshman[4]〔ˋfrɛʃmən〕*n.* 新生
cruel[2]〔ˋkruəl〕*adj.* 殘酷的
certainly[1]〔ˋsɝtn̩lɪ〕*adv.* 當然；確實地

[1](D) We mimicked him, teased him ***and*** taunted him *about his size.*

He was *at least* fifty pounds overweight. He felt the pain *of being*

*the last one picked to play basketball, baseball **or** football.*

我們模仿他、捉弄他、嘲弄他的體型。他體重超重至少 50 磅。他感到打籃球、棒球或美式足球，都是最後一個被挑中的痛苦，。

* mimic[6]〔ˋmɪmɪk〕*v.* 模仿　　tease[3]〔tiz〕*v.* 捉弄
taunt[5]〔tɔnt〕*v.* 嘲弄　　***at least*** 至少
pound[2]〔paʊnd〕*n.* 磅【重量單位】
overweight〔ˋovɚˏwet〕*adj.* 過重的
pain[2]〔pen〕*n.* 痛苦；疼痛　　pick[2]〔pɪk〕*v.* 挑選

Matt will *always* remember the endless pranks *that were played on*

him—trashing his locker, piling library books on his desk and

spraying him with icy streams of water in the shower after gym class.

麥特會一直記得那些對他無止盡的惡作劇——搗毀他的置物櫃、在他的
桌上堆放圖書館的書、體育課之後在淋浴間向他噴冰水。

* endless〔'ɛndlɪs〕*adj.* 不斷的；無休止的
  prank〔præŋk〕*n.* 胡鬧；惡作劇
  play a prank on sb. 對某人惡作劇
  trash³〔træʃ〕*v.* 搗毀；破壞　　locker⁴〔'lɑkɚ〕*n.* 置物櫃
  pile²〔'paɪl〕*v.* 堆積　　spray³〔spre〕*v.* 噴灑
  icy³〔'aɪsɪ〕*adj.* 冰冷的；結冰的
  stream²〔strim〕*n.* 溪流；水流　　gym³〔dʒɪm〕*n.* 體育

One day he sat *near me in gym class.* Someone pushed him *and* he

fell on me *and* banged my foot *quite badly.* The kid *who pushed him*

said Matt did it.

有一天，他體育課坐在我附近。有人推他，他倒向我，狠狠地撞到我的
腳。推他的孩子說是麥特做的。

* bang³〔bæŋ〕*v.* 重擊；猛撞
  quite¹〔kwaɪt〕*adv.* 非常地；相當地
  badly³〔'bædlɪ〕*adv.* 嚴重地

With the whole class watching, I was put on the spot *to either shrug it off **or** pick a fight with Matt.* ²(A) I chose to fight *in order to keep my image intact.*

因為全班看著，我當場的處境是，要就不當一回事，要不就是與麥特打一架。為了保持我的形象不受損，我選擇了打架。

* whole[1] 〔 hol 〕 *adj.* 全部的；整個的
  put[1] 〔 pʊt 〕 *v.* 使處於（某種狀態）
  spot[2] 〔 spɑt 〕 *n.* 地點；立場；處境
  either…or… 不是…就是…
  shrug[4] 〔 ʃrʌg 〕 *v.* 聳肩　　***shrug off*** 對…不當回事
  pick a fight with *sb.* 向某人尋釁格鬥
  image[3] 〔 'ɪmɪdʒ 〕 *n.* 形象
  intact[6] 〔 ɪn'tækt 〕 *adj.* 完整的；未受損的

I shouted, "*C'mon, Matt, let's fight!*" He said *he didn't want to.* ***But*** peer pressure forced him *into the conflict **whether** he liked it **or** not.* He came *toward me with his fists in the air.* *With one punch* I bloodied his nose ***and*** the class went wild.

我大喊：「來吧，麥特，來打吧！」他說他不想，但同儕壓力迫使他無論喜歡與否，都得打這一架。他向我走來，拳頭舉起來，我一拳就把他的鼻子打流血，全班都瘋了。

* shout[1] 〔 ʃaʊt 〕 *v.* 吼叫　　peer[4] 〔 pɪr 〕 *n.* 同儕
  pressure[3] 〔'prɛʃɚ 〕 *n.* 壓力　　***peer pressure*** 同儕壓力
  force[1] 〔 fors 〕 *v.* 強迫　　conflict[2] 〔'kɑnflɪkt 〕 *n.* 衝突

fist³〔fɪst〕*n.* 拳頭　　***in the air*** 在空中

punch³〔pʌntʃ〕*n.* 重擊　　blood¹〔blʌd〕*v.* 使流血

go wild 瘋狂

³**(F)** *Just then* the gym teacher walked *into the room.* He saw ***that*** *we were fighting **and** he sent us out to the oval running track.*

就在那時，體育老師走進室內。他看到我們正在打架，把我們叫去外面的橢圓形跑道。

* oval⁴〔'ovl̩〕*adj.* 橢圓形的　　track²〔træk〕*n.* 跑道

　running track 跑道

He followed us *with a smile on his face **and** said, "I want you two guys to go out there **and** run that mile holding each other's hands."* The room erupted into a roar *of laughter.*

他臉上帶著笑容跟著我們，接著說：「我要你們兩個人出去，牽著彼此的手跑一哩。」室內爆出一陣大笑聲。

* erupt⁵〔ɪ'rʌpt〕*v.* 爆發　　roar³〔ror〕*n.* 吼叫聲；大笑聲

　a roar of laughter 一陣笑聲

The two *of us* were embarrassed *beyond belief*, ***but*** Matt ***and*** I went out to the track ***and*** ran our mile—*hand-in-hand.*

雖然麥特和我都感到難以置信地尷尬，但是我們還是到了跑道上，手牽手跑完了我們的一哩。

* embarrassed[4] ﹝ ɪmˋbærəst ﹞ *adj.* 感到尷尬的
beyond belief 難以置信的　　**hand-in-hand** 手牽手

At some point during the course of our run, I remember looking

over at him, *with blood still trickling from his nose **and** his weight*

slowing him down.

在我們跑步過程中的某個時刻，我記得我轉過去看他，血還在緩緩地從他的鼻子流出來，他的體重使他速度變慢。

* point[1] ﹝ pɔɪnt ﹞ *n.* 點；時刻　　course[1] ﹝ kɔrs ﹞ *n.* 路線；過程
look over at 轉過去看著　　trickle ﹝ˋtrɪkḷ﹞ *v.* 細細地流；流淌
weight[1] ﹝ wet ﹞ *n.* 重量　·　**slow down** 減速

[4](E) It struck me *that here was a person, not all that different from*

myself. We both looked at each other **and** began to laugh.　*Going*

around that track, *hand-in-hand*, I *no longer* saw Matt as fat **or** dumb.

我突然想到這是一個人，一個和我並沒有完全不同的人。我們倆看著對方開始笑了起來。手牽著手一起跑那條跑道，我不再把麥特看作是肥胖或是愚蠢。

* strike[2] ﹝ straɪk ﹞ *v.* 使 (某人) 忽然想到
【三態變化：strike–struck–struck 或 stricken】

no longer 不再　　***see A as B*** 視 A 為 B

dumb² 〔 dʌm 〕 *adj.* 愚蠢的

It was amazing ***what** I learned* ***when** I was forced to go hand-in-hand with someone for only one mile.* ⁵(**C**) *For the rest of my life* I *never so much **as** raised a hand against another person.*

當我被迫與一個人手牽手一起跑僅僅一哩時，很神奇的我學到了東西。

在我接下來的人生中，我甚至再也沒有打過別人了。

* amazing³ 〔 ə'mezɪŋ 〕 *n.* 令人驚訝的；驚人的；神奇的
  not so much as 甚至連～也沒有
  raise a hand against sb. 打某人

TEST 30

說明： 第1至5題，每題一個空格。請依文意在文章後所提供的(A)到
(F) 選項中分別選出最適當者。

There are many different levels of awareness in
dreams. Some appear as just a misty scene of vague
images where we seem to be nothing more than an
outside observer. ___1___ In these dreams, the dreamer
is fully aware that what he or she is seeing is a dream.
The dreamer has complete control over his or her actions
and can sometimes even change the surroundings or
people in the dream at will. ___2___ The secret is to ask
ourselves often (even in our dreams!) if we are awake or
if what we see around us might actually be a dream.

___3___ If we pay attention to them, dreams can
teach us much about ourselves and they can provide us
with very useful insight or creative inspiration. Since
the average person spends over 20 years of his or her
life asleep, it seems like a waste not to spend this time
enjoying dreams and exploring the incredible worlds to
which they allow us to travel.

___4___ Most people wake up and immediately start thinking of what they have to do that day. This often prevents us from remembering any dreams at all.

___5___ Focus your thoughts on what you were just dreaming and you'll be surprised how much you can remember with a little practice. If you are already good at remembering your dreams, try challenging yourself to remember them in even more detail. What sounds, smells, tastes and feelings did you experience?

(A) Do you remember many of your dreams?

(B) Experts say that with practice, all of us are capable of having lucid dreams.

(C) At the other end of the spectrum is what is called lucid dreaming.

(D) Instead, remaining lying in bed with your eyes closed for a few minutes after you start to wake up.

(E) There is no doubt that the world of dreams is a boundless universe where we have no limitations.

(F) Some dreams may scare us awake.

TEST 30 詳解

There are many different levels *of awareness in dreams*. Some

appear as *just* a misty scene *of vague images **where** we seem to be*

*nothing more **than** an outside observer.*

在夢中的意識有許多不同的等級。有些似乎就像是充滿模糊影像的場景，我們似乎就只是在外面的觀察者。

* level[3] ﹝'lɛvl̩﹞ *n.* 程度；等級
  awareness[3] ﹝ə'wɛrnɪs﹞ *n.* 意識
  appear[1] ﹝ə'pɪr﹞ *v.* 似乎；看起來
  misty[3] ﹝'mɪstɪ﹞ *adj.* 籠罩著煙霧的；模糊的【mist[3] *n.* 薄霧】
  scene[1] ﹝sin﹞ *n.* 景色；場景　　vague[5] ﹝veg﹞ *adj.* 模糊的
  image[3] ﹝'ɪmɪdʒ﹞ *n.* 形象；影像　　seem[1] ﹝sim﹞ *v.* 似乎
  nothing more than 只是（= *only*）
  outside[1] ﹝'aʊt,saɪd﹞ *adj.* 外面的；局外人的
  observer[5] ﹝əb'zɝvɚ﹞ *n.* 觀察者

[1](C) *At the other end of the spectrum* is ***what** is called* lucid dreaming.

In these dreams, the dreamer is *fully* aware ***that what*** he ***or*** she is

seeing is a dream. The dreamer has complete control *over his **or** her*

*actions **and*** can *sometimes even* change the surroundings ***or*** people

in the dream at will.

在夢的光譜的另一端（*和這種夢相反的*），就是所謂的清醒夢。在這些夢當中，做夢的人完全知道自己所看見的是夢。做夢的人能完全控制自己的行動，有時甚至能任意改變夢中的環境或人。

* end[1] 〔εnd 〕*n.* 一頭；一端　　spectrum[6] 〔'spεktrəm 〕*n.* 光譜
what is called 所謂的（ *= what we call = so-called* ）
lucid 〔'lusɪd 〕*adj.* 頭腦清晰的；清醒的
lucid dreaming 清醒夢
At the other end of the spectrum is what is called lucid dreaming.
*= **The opposite of this*** is what is called lucid dreaming.
dreamer[1] 〔'drimɚ 〕*n.* 做夢的人
fully[1] 〔'fʊlɪ 〕*adv.* 十分地；完全地
aware[3] 〔ə'wεr 〕*adj.* 知道的；察覺到的
complete[2] 〔kəm'plit 〕*adj.* 完全的
control[2] 〔kən'trol 〕*n.* 控制；支配　　action[1] 〔'ækʃən 〕*n.* 行動
surroundings[2] 〔sə'raʊndɪŋz 〕*n. pl.* 環境
will[1] 〔wɪl 〕*n.* 意志力；心意　　***at will*** 任意地；隨心所欲地

[2]**(B)** Experts say ***that** with practice,* all *of us* are capable of having

lucid dreams. The secret is to ask ourselves *often (even in our*

dreams!) ***if** we are awake **or if what*** we see around us might actually

be a dream.

專家說，藉由練習，我們所有的人都能做清醒夢。祕訣就是要常常（即使是在夢中！）問自己，我們是否清醒，或是否我們所看到的周圍事物，可能其實是個夢。

* expert[2] 〔'εkspɝt 〕*n.* 專家　　practice[1] 〔'præktɪs 〕*n.* 練習
be capable of + *V-ing* 能夠…　　***have a dream*** 做夢

secret² ('sikrɪt) *n.* 祕訣　　awake³ (ə'wek) *adj.* 清醒的

actually³ ('æktʃʊəlɪ) *adv.* 事實上

³**(E)** There is no doubt *that the world of dreams is a boundless*

*universe **where** we have no limitations.* ***If** we pay attention to them,*

dreams can teach us much *about ourselves **and*** they can provide us

*with very useful insight **or** creative inspiration.*

　　無疑地,夢的世界是個無窮盡的宇宙,我們在那裡可以不受限制。如果我們注意夢,它們能教導我們許多關於自己的事,而且也能提供我們非常有用的洞察力,或很有創意的靈感。

* doubt² (daʊt) *n.* 懷疑　　***there is no doubt that*** 無疑地

boundless⁵ ('baʊndlɪs) *adj.* 無限的;無窮的

universe³ ('junə,vɝs) *n.* 宇宙

limitation⁴ (,lɪmə'teʃən) *n.* 限制　　***pay attention to*** 注意

provide² (prə'vaɪd) *v.* 提供　　useful¹ ('jusfəl) *adj.* 有用的

insight⁶ ('ɪn,saɪt) *n.* 洞察力;深入的見解

creative³ (krɪ'etɪv) *adj.* 有創造力的

inspiration⁴ (,ɪnspə'reʃən) *n.* 靈感;激勵

***Since** the average person spends over 20 years of his **or** her life asleep,*

it seems like a waste *not to spend this time enjoying dreams **and***

*exploring the incredible worlds to **which** they allow us to travel.*

因為一般人一生當中，會有二十年以上的時間在睡覺，所以如果不把這段時間用來享受做夢，並探索夢境能讓我們遊覽的不可思議的世界，似乎是種浪費。

> * average[3] ﹝'ævərɪdʒ﹞ adj. 一般的　　the average person 一般人
> asleep[2] ﹝ə'slip﹞ adj. 睡著的　　waste[1] ﹝west﹞ n. 浪費
> explore[4] ﹝ɪk'splor﹞ v. 在…探險；探討
> incredible ﹝ɪn'krɛdəbl﹞ adj. 令人難以置信的
> allow[1] ﹝ə'laʊ﹞ v. 讓；允許

[4](A) Do you remember many *of your dreams*?　Most people wake up *and immediately* start thinking of *what* they have to do that day. This *often* prevents us from remembering any dreams *at all*.

　　你記得許多你做過的夢嗎？大部分的人醒來後，會立刻開始想到他們那天必須做的事。這常會使我們完全無法記住任何的夢。

> * *wake up* 醒來
> immediately[3] ﹝ɪ'midɪɪtlɪ﹞ adv. 立刻；馬上
> *think of* 想到　　*prevent sb. from V-ing* 使某人無法…
> *at all* 全然

[5](D) *Instead*, remaining lying *in bed with your eyes closed for a few minutes after you start to wake up.*　Focus your thoughts *on what* you were just dreaming *and* you'll be surprised *how much* you can remember with a little practice.

相反地,在你開始醒來之後,要閉上眼睛幾分鐘,一直躺在床上。將你的思緒專注於你剛剛夢到的,只要稍加練習,你就會對於自己能記得多少,感到驚訝。

* instead[3] ﹝ ɪn'stɛd ﹞ *adv.* 取而代之;相反地;不…而~
  remain[3] ﹝ rɪ'men ﹞ *v.* 依然;繼續
  lie[1] ﹝ laɪ ﹞ *v.* 躺【lie-lay-lain-lying】
  focus[2] ﹝ 'fokəs ﹞ *v.* 使專注 < *on* >
  thought[1] ﹝ θɔt ﹞ *n.* 思想;想法
  surprised[1] ﹝ sə'praɪst ﹞ *adj.* 驚訝的

If you are already good at remembering your dreams, try challenging yourself to remember them *in even more detail*. What sounds, smells, tastes *and* feelings did you experience?

如果你已經很擅長記住你的夢,那就挑戰自己,看能不能更詳細地記住這些夢。你體驗了什麼聲音、氣味、味道,和感覺?

* *be good at* 精通;擅長　　challenge[3] ﹝ 'tʃælɪndʒ ﹞ *v.* 挑戰
  detail[3] ﹝ 'ditel ﹞ *n.* 細節　　*in detail* 詳細地
  smell[1] ﹝ smɛl ﹞ *n.* 氣味　　taste[1] ﹝ test ﹞ *n.* 味道
  experience[2] ﹝ ɪk'spɪrɪəns ﹞ *v.* 經歷;體驗

TEST 31

說明： 第 1 至 5 題，每題一個空格。請依文意在文章後所提供的 (A) 到
(F) 選項中分別選出最適當者。

On the northern frontier of ancient China, there lived
a man who was particularly skilled in raising horses.
People called him Sai Ong—literally "Old Frontiersman."
One day, one of his horses got loose and ran off into the
Hu territory beyond the Great Wall. The Hu tribes were
hostile toward the Chinese, so ____1____. Horses were very
valuable to the people living at the frontier, so people
visited Sai Ong to express their sympathies, but ____2____.
He simply asked, "Who says this cannot be some sort of
blessing?"

Months later, the horse returned to the stable with a
companion—a fine horse of the Hu breed. And ____3____.
Everyone came by to marvel at the new horse and to
congratulate him, but again his elderly father showed no
great emotion but said, "Who says this cannot be some
sort of misfortune?"

Sai Ong's son enjoyed riding and took the new horse
out for a ride. An accident occurred, causing him to fall

badly and break a leg. Again ___4___. Again they heard the grandfather say, "Who says this cannot be some sort of blessing?"

One year later, the Hu people assembled and crossed the border into China. All the strong and healthy young men were summoned into the army to take up arms in defense. But Sai Ong's son did not go into battle due to his broken leg. Because of this, he was spared that terrible fate. Thus, ___5___. They change from one to the other endlessly.

(A) it was as if Sai Ong's wealth suddenly doubled

(B) everyone assumed the horse was as good as lost

(C) blessings may turn out to be misfortunes, and misfortunes blessings

(D) Sai Ong's elderly father surprised them by remaining calm and unaffected

(E) sympathetic people came to console the family

(F) the horse chose to take a different path

TEST 31 詳解

On the northern frontier of ancient China, there lived a man *who was particularly skilled in raising horses*. People called him Sai Ong—*literally "Old Frontiersman."*

在中國古代的北方邊境，住著一個特別擅長養馬的男子。人們叫他塞翁──字面意思是「邊境的老先生」。

* northern[2] 〔ˋnɔrðən〕 *adj.* 北方的　　frontier[5] 〔frʌnˋtɪr〕 *n.* 邊境
  ancient[2] 〔ˋenʃənt〕 *adj.* 古代的
  particularly[2] 〔pəˋtɪkjələlɪ〕 *adv.* 特別地
  skilled[2] 〔skɪld〕 *adj.* 熟練的；精於…的
  raise[2] 〔rez〕 *v.* 飼養　　literally[2] 〔ˋlɪtərəlɪ〕 *adv.* 照字面意義地

One day, one *of his horses* got loose *and* ran *off into the Hu territory beyond the Great Wall*. The Hu tribes were hostile *toward the Chinese*, so [1](B) everyone assumed *the horse was as good as lost*.

有一天，他有一匹馬掙脫，逃跑到長城外的胡人境內。胡人部落對中國人是有敵意的，所以每個人都認為那匹馬就像是遺失了一樣。

* loose[2] 〔lus〕 *adj.* 釋放的；自由的；鬆開的　　*get loose* 掙脫
  run off 逃跑　　Hu 〔hu〕 *n.* 胡人　　territory[6] 〔ˋtɛrəˌtorɪ〕 *n.* 領土
  beyond[2] 〔bɪˋjand〕 *prep.* 在…之外　　*the Great Wall* 萬里長城
  tribe[2] 〔traɪb〕 *n.* 部落　　hostile[2] 〔ˋhɑstḷ, ˋhɑstɪl〕 *adj.* 有敵意的
  toward[2] 〔tord〕 *prep.* 對於　　assume[6] 〔əˋsjum〕 *v.* 假定；推測
  as good as 和…一樣；事實上等於　　lost[2] 〔lɔst〕 *adj.* 遺失的

Horses were *very* valuable *to the people living at the frontier,* **so**

people visited Sai Ong *to express their sympathies,* **but** [2](**D**) Sai Ong's

elderly father surprised them *by remaining calm* **and** *unaffected.* He

simply asked, "Who says *this cannot be some sort of blessing?*"

馬對住在邊境的人而言,是非常珍貴的,所以大家都去拜訪塞翁,表示
同情,但令他們驚訝的是,塞翁年老的父親一直保持冷靜,而且不受影
響。他只是問說:「誰說這不會是某種幸福?」

* valuable[2] (ˈvæljəbḷ) *adj.* 珍貴的　　express[2] (ɪkˈsprɛs) *v.* 表達
  sympathy[4] (ˈsɪmpəθɪ) *n.* 同情　　elderly[3] (ˈɛldɚlɪ) *adj.* 年長的
  remain[3] (rɪˈmen) *v.* 保持　　calm[2] (kɑm) *adj.* 冷靜的
  unaffected[3] (ˌʌnəˈfɛktɪd) *adj.* 不受影響的
  simply[2] (ˈsɪmplɪ) *adv.* 僅僅　　some[1] (sʌm) *adj.* 某一
  sort[2] (sɔrt) *n.* 種類　　blessing[4] (ˈblɛsɪŋ) *n.* 恩賜;幸福

Months later, the horse returned *to the stable with a companion—*

a fine horse of the Hu breed. **And** [3](**A**) it was **as if** *Sai Ong's wealth*

suddenly doubled.

　　幾個月之後,那匹馬回到馬廄,還帶了一個同伴——一匹胡人飼養
的很好的馬。而這就好像塞翁的財富突然變成了兩倍。

* later[1] (ˈletɚ) *adv.* …之後　　stable[3] (ˈstebḷ) *n.* 馬廄　*adj.* 穩定的
  companion[4] (kəmˈpænjən) *n.* 同伴　　breed[4] (brid) *n.* 品種
  as if 就好像　　wealth[3] (wɛlθ) *n.* 財富
  suddenly[2] (ˈsʌdṇlɪ) *adv.* 突然地　　double[2] (ˈdʌbḷ) *v.* 變成兩倍

Everyone came by *to marvel at the new horse **and** to congratulate*

him, ***but*** *again* his elderly father showed no great emotion ***but*** said,

"Who says *this cannot be some sort of misfortune*?"

每個人都來拜訪,對那匹新的馬感到驚訝,並且祝賀他,不過他那年老
的父親又沒有顯現出太大的情緒,而是說:「誰說這不會是某種不幸?」

* ***come by*** 順道拜訪　　marvel[5] ('marvl) v. 驚訝 < *at* >
  congratulate[4] (kən'grætʃu,let) v. 祝賀　　show[1] (ʃo) v. 顯示
  emotion[2] (ɪ'moʃən) n. 情緒　　***not** A **but** B* 不是 A,而是 B
  misfortune[4] (mɪs'fɔrtʃən) n. 不幸

Sai Ong's son enjoyed riding ***and*** took the new horse *out for a*

ride. An accident occurred, *causing him to fall badly **and** break a leg*.

Again [4](E) sympathetic people came to console the family. *Again*

they heard the grandfather say, "Who says *this cannot be some sort*

of blessing?"

塞翁的兒子很喜歡騎馬,所以就帶那匹新的馬出去騎。發生了一場
意外,使他重重地摔落,並折斷了腿。很有同情心的人們又去安慰這一
家人。他們又聽到那位祖父說:「誰說這不可能是某種幸福?」

* ride[1] (raɪd) v. n. 騎馬　　accident[3] ('æksədənt) n. 意外
  occur[2] (ə'kɝ) v. 發生　　cause[1] (kɔz) v. 導致;造成;使
  badly[3] ('bædlɪ) adv. 嚴重地;厲害地　　break[1] (brek) v. 折斷
  sympathetic[4] (,sɪmpə'θɛtɪk) adj. 同情的
  console[5] (kən'sol) v. 安慰　　grandfather[1] ('grænd,faðɚ) n. 祖父

One year later, the Hu people assembled **and** crossed the border

into China. All the strong **and** healthy young men were summoned

into the army to take up arms in defense. **But** Sai Ong's son did not

go into battle *due to his broken leg.* *Because of this*, he was spared

that terrible fate.

一年後，胡人集結起來，越過邊界，進入中國。所有健壯的年輕男子，都被召集進入軍隊，拿起武器來防衛。但是塞翁的兒子因為腿斷了，所以並未投入戰鬥。因為如此，他才能免除那可怕的命運。

* assemble〔ə'sɛmbḷ〕v. 集合　　cross²〔krɔs〕v. 越過
border³〔'bɔrdɚ〕n. 邊界　　healthy²〔'hɛlθɪ〕adj. 健康的
summon⁵〔'sʌmən〕v. 召喚；召集　　army¹〔'ɑrmɪ〕n. 軍隊
take up 拿起　　arms⁴〔ɑrmz〕n. pl. 武器
defense⁴〔dɪ'fɛns〕n. 防禦；防衛　　battle²〔'bætḷ〕n. 戰役
go into battle 投入戰鬥　　**due to** 由於
broken¹〔'brokən〕adj. 折斷的　　**because of** 因為
spare⁴〔spɛr〕v. 使免除　　fate³〔fet〕n. 命運

Thus, [5](C) blessings may turn out to be misfortunes, **and** misfortunes

blessings. They change *from one to the other endlessly.*

因此，幸福可能最後變成不幸，而不幸最後可能會變成幸福。它們會不斷地從這個變成另一個。

* thus¹〔ðʌs〕adv. 因此　　**turn out to be** 結果是
misfortune⁴〔mɪs'fɔrtʃən〕n. 不幸
the other （兩者的）另一個　　endlessly¹〔'ɛndlɪslɪ〕adv. 不斷地

TEST 32

說明：第 1 至 5 題，每題一個空格。請依文意在文章後所提供的 (A) 到
(F) 選項中分別選出最適當者。

Few men have ruined the lives of so many others as Joseph
Stalin. He probably killed more people, sent more people to
prison, and forced more people into hard labor than anyone
before or since. ___1___

But Stalin also transformed a poor, agricultural nation into
an industrial and technological superpower. Under Stalin, the
USSR defeated Hitler's mighty German army, developed nuclear
weapons and ran a space program to rival that of the United States.

It is not surprising that many Russians still have mixed
feelings about Stalin. ___2___ However, Stalin also sacrificed
the personal freedom of nearly everyone and created a backward
police state.

When he died on March 5, 1953, at the age of 74, millions
breathed a sigh of relief. His successor, Nikita Khrushchev,
immediately began a process of de-Stalinization to normalize the
country. Stalin's death remains a mystery. Officially, he died of
a stroke, but many believe he was poisoned by members of his
inner circle. ___3___ At the time of his death, it seemed clear
that Stalin wanted to lead the USSR into another war—a World
War III to export socialism to all of Europe. This was the dream
of his predecessor and leader of the Russian Revolution, Vladimir
Lenin, but Stalin had originally argued against such goals.

Lenin said the socialist revolution begun in 1917 could not succeed without several countries working together. ___4___ He launched the first "Five-Year Plan" and began to collectivize farming. He also created a cult of personality around both himself and Lenin. Stalin became the focus of massive adoration and even worship.

In his old age, Stalin had grown increasingly paranoid. Though millions still saw him as a godlike hero, his inner circle knew he was a weak man inside. Perhaps the greatest danger sign was his growing hatred of Jews.

___5___ This would have provoked war with the West, and while the USSR had nuclear weapons, its economy and military were still weak. If Stalin's death was in fact a natural one, it is likely that an unnatural one was already being planned.

(A) Under his highly organized bureaucracy, Russia achieved her greatest glory and made the whole world recognize her power.

(B) Under Stalin, they suffered great hardship both economically and personally.

(C) But Stalin, in 1928, decided to face reality and focus on self-sufficiency.

(D) Thus, he is widely considered the most terrible dictator of all time, even surpassing Adolph Hitler in his brutality.

(E) Such an assassination is not hard to imagine.

(F) Many believe he was about to follow in Hitler's footsteps and order their slaughter.

TEST 32 詳解

Few men have ruined the lives *of so many others* ***as Joseph Stalin.***

He *probably* killed more people, sent more people *to prison*, ***and***

forced more people *into hard labor* ***than*** anyone before ***or*** since.

　　很少人會像史達林一樣，毀滅這麼多人的生命。他所殺的、關進監獄的、強迫做苦工的人，可能比在他之前或之後的任何一個人，都還要多。

* ruin[4]〔'ruɪn〕v. 毀滅；毀掉
  Joseph Stalin〔'dʒɔsəf 'stɑlɪn〕n. 史達林【1879-1953，蘇聯的獨裁者】
  send[1]〔sɛnd〕v. 送　　prison[2]〔'prɪzn̩〕n. 監獄
  force[1]〔fors〕v. 強迫　　***force sb. into*** sth. 強迫某人從事某事
  hard[1]〔hɑrd〕adj. 辛苦的　　labor[4]〔'lebɚ〕n. 勞動
  hard labor 苦役；苦工　　since[1]〔sɪns〕adv. 從那時以後

[1](**D**) *Thus*, he is *widely* considered the *most* terrible dictator *of all time, even surpassing Adolph Hitler in his brutality.*

因此，大家普遍認為，他是有史以來最可怕的獨裁者，殘忍的程度甚至超越希特勒。

* thus[1]〔ðʌs〕adv. 因此　　widely[1]〔'waɪdlɪ〕adv. 廣泛地；普遍地
  consider[2]〔kən'sɪdɚ〕v. 認為　　***be considered (to be)*** 被認為是
  terrible[2]〔'tɛrəbl̩〕adj. 可怕的　　dictator[6]〔'dɪktetɚ〕n. 獨裁者

of all time 有史以來　　surpass[6] 〔 sə'pæs 〕 *v.* 超越

Adolph Hitler 〔'ædɑlf 'hɪtlə 〕 *n.* 希特勒

brutality[4] 〔 bru'tælətɪ 〕 *n.* 殘忍

But Stalin *also* transformed a poor, agricultural nation *into an*

industrial **and** *technological superpower*. *Under Stalin*, the USSR

defeated Hitler's mighty German army, developed nuclear weapons

and ran a space program *to rival that of the United States.*

　　但是史達林也將一個貧窮的農業國家，轉變成一個工業與科技的超級強國。在史達林的統治之下，蘇聯打敗了希特勒強有力的德國軍隊，研發核子武器，並進行一項太空計畫，要和美國競爭。

* transform[4] 〔 træns'fɔrm 〕 *v.* 使轉變

agricultural[5] 〔ˌægrɪ'kʌltʃərəl 〕 *adj.* 農業的

industrial[3] 〔 ɪn'dʌstrɪəl 〕 *adj.* 工業的

technological[4] 〔ˌtɛknə'lɑdʒɪkl̩ 〕 *adj.* 科技的

superpower 〔ˌsupə'pauə 〕 *n.* 超級強國

the USSR 蘇聯 (= *the Union of Soviet Socialists Republics*)

defeat[4] 〔 dɪ'fit 〕 *v.* 打敗　　mighty[3] 〔'maɪtɪ 〕 *adj.* 強有力的

army[1] 〔'ɑrmɪ 〕 *n.* 軍隊　　develop[2] 〔 dɪ'vɛləp 〕 *v.* 發展；研發

nuclear[4] 〔'njuklɪə 〕 *adj.* 核子的

weapon[2] 〔'wɛpən 〕 *n.* 武器

run[1] 〔 rʌn 〕 *v.* 經營；管理；進行　　space[1] 〔 spes 〕 *n.* 太空

program[3] 〔'progræm 〕 *n.* 計畫　　rival[5] 〔'raɪvl̩ 〕 *v.* 與…競爭

在 that of the United States 中，that 是指 the space program。

It is not surprising *that many Russians still have mixed feelings about Stalin.* ²(A) *Under his highly organized bureaucracy,* Russia achieved her greatest glory *and* made the whole world recognize her power. *However,* Stalin *also* sacrificed the personal freedom *of nearly everyone and* created a backward police state.

　　許多俄國人仍然對於史達林有矛盾的感情，並不令人驚訝。在他那非常有組織的官僚政治之下，俄國獲得最大的榮耀，並且讓全世界認同她的力量。然而，史達林也幾乎犧牲了每個人的個人自由，並創造了一個落後的極權國家。

* surprising¹〔sə'praɪzɪŋ〕*adj.* 令人驚訝的
  Russian〔'rʌʃən〕*n.* 俄國人　*adj.* 俄國的
  mixed²〔mɪkst〕*adj.* 混合的
  have mixed feelings 懷著錯綜複雜的感情；懷著相矛盾的感情
  highly⁴〔'haɪlɪ〕*adv.* 非常
  organized²〔'ɔrgə,naɪzd〕*adj.* 有組織的
  bureaucracy⁶〔bju'rɑkrəsɪ〕*n.* 官僚政治；官僚作風
  achieve²〔ə'tʃiv〕*v.* 達成；獲得
  glory²〔'glorɪ〕*n.* 光榮；榮耀
  在 Russia achieved *her* greatest glory... recognize *her* power 中，
  　　因為「國家」被視為陰性，所以代名詞用 she，所有格用 her。【詳見「文法寶典」p.92】
  recognize³〔'rɛkəg,naɪz〕*v.* 承認　　power¹〔'pauɚ〕*n.* 力量
  sacrifice⁴〔'sækrə,faɪs〕*v.* 犧牲　　personal²〔'pɝsn̩l〕*adj.* 個人的
  freedom²〔'fridəm〕*n.* 自由　　nearly²〔'nɪrlɪ〕*adv.* 將近；幾乎
  create²〔krɪ'et〕*v.* 創造　　backward²〔'bækwɚd〕*adj.* 落後的

police[1] 〔 pə'lis 〕 *adj.* 警方的　　state[1] 〔 stet 〕 *n.* 國家
police state 警察國家；極權國家

When *he died on March 5, 1953, at the age of 74,* millions breathed

a sigh *of relief.* His successor, *Nikita Khrushchev, immediately* began

a process *of de-Stalinization to normalize the country.*

當他 74 歲，於 1953 年 3 月 5 日死亡時，數百萬人都鬆了一口氣。
他的繼任者赫魯雪夫，立刻開始了去史達林化的過程，要使國家正常
化。

* million[2] 〔 'mɪljən 〕 *n.* 百萬　　breathe[3] 〔 brið 〕 *v.* 呼吸；呼出
sigh[3] 〔 saɪ 〕 *n.* 嘆氣；嘆息　　relief[4] 〔 rɪ'lif 〕 *n.* 放心；鬆了一口氣
breathe a sigh of relief 鬆了一口氣
successor[6] 〔 sək'sɛsɚ 〕 *n.* 繼任者
Nikita Khrushchev 〔 njɪ'kjitʌ 'kruʃtʃɔf 〕 *n.* 赫魯雪夫【1894-1971，
　蘇聯總書記】　　immediately[3] 〔 ɪ'midɪɪtlɪ 〕 *adv.* 立刻
process[3] 〔 'prasɛs 〕 *n.* 過程
de-Stalinization 〔 dɪ,stalɪnɪ'zeʃən 〕 *n.* 非史達林化
normalize[3] 〔 'nɔrml̩,aɪz 〕 *v.* 使正常化

Stalin's death remains a mystery. *Officially*, he died of a stroke,

but many believe *he was poisoned by members of his inner circle.*

[3]**(E)** Such an assassination is not hard *to imagine.*

史達林的死仍然是個謎。按照官方說法，他死於中風，但很多人相信，
他是被他的親信毒死的。這樣的暗殺並不難想像。

* remain³〔rɪˋmen〕v. 仍然是　　mystery³〔ˋmɪstrɪ〕n. 謎；奧祕
officially²〔əˋfɪʃəlɪ〕adv. 官方地；正式地
die of 死於（疾病）　　stroke⁴〔strok〕n. 中風
poison²〔ˋpɔɪzn̩〕v. 下毒　　member²〔ˋmɛmbɚ〕n. 成員
inner³〔ˋɪnɚ〕adj. 內部的
circle²〔ˋsɝkl̩〕n. 圓圈；集團；同夥；（交友的）範圍
inner circle（接近權力中心的）親信；內圈人物
assassination⁶〔ə͵sæsn̩ˋeʃən〕n. 暗殺
hard¹〔hard〕adj. 困難的　　imagine²〔ɪˋmædʒɪn〕v. 想像

At the time of his death, it seemed clear ***that*** *Stalin wanted to lead the*

USSR into another war—a World War III to export socialism to all of

Europe. This was the dream *of his predecessor* ***and*** *leader of the*

Russian Revolution, Vladimir Lenin, ***but*** Stalin had *originally* argued

against such goals.

在史達林死的時候，他很顯然想要帶領蘇聯，參與另一場戰爭——第三次世界大戰，將社會主義出口到全歐洲。這是他的前輩，俄國革命的領導者列寧的夢想，但史達林最初是反駁這樣的目標。

* lead¹ˑ⁴〔lid〕v. 帶領　　***World War III*** 第三次世界大戰
export³〔ɪksˋport〕v. 出口
socialism⁶〔ˋsoʃəl͵ɪzəm〕n. 社會主義
Europe〔ˋjurəp〕n. 歐洲
predecessor⁶〔ˋprɛdɪ͵sɛsɚ〕n. 前輩
leader¹〔ˋlidɚ〕n. 領導者　　revolution⁴〔͵rɛvəˋluʃən〕n. 革命

Vladimir Lenin〔'vlædɪmɪr 'lɛnɪn〕*n.* 列寧【1870-1924，蘇俄共產黨領袖】　originally[3]〔ə'rɪdʒənḷɪ〕*adv.* 最初；原本
argue[2]〔'ɑrgju〕*v.* 爭論；主張　***argue against*** 反駁
goal[2]〔gol〕*n.* 目標

Lenin said *the socialist revolution begun in 1917 could not succeed without several countries working together.* [4]**(C)** ***But*** Stalin, *in 1928,* decided to face reality ***and*** focus on self-sufficiency. He launched the first "Five-Year Plan" ***and*** began to collectivize farming.

　　列寧說，開始於 1917 年的社會主義革命，沒有幾個國家一起合作，是無法成功的。但是，史達林在 1928 年決定要面對現實，並且專注於自給自足。他推出了第一個「五年計畫」，並開始農業集體化政策。

* socialist[6]〔'soʃəlɪst〕*adj.* 社會主義的　***work together*** 合作
face[1]〔fes〕*v.* 面對　　reality[2]〔rɪ'ælətɪ〕*n.* 現實；事實
focus[2]〔'fokəs〕*v.* 對準焦點；集中　*n.* 焦點；中心
focus on 專注於
self-sufficiency〔'sɛlfsə'fɪʃənsɪ〕*n.* 自給自足
launch[4]〔lɔntʃ〕*v.* 發起　　collectivize[6]〔kə'lɛktɪ,vaɪz〕*v.* 集體化
farming[1]〔'fɑrmɪŋ〕*n.* 農業

He *also* created a cult *of personality around both himself **and** Lenin.*

Stalin became the focus *of massive adoration **and** even worship.*

他也創造他自己與列寧的個人崇拜。史達林成為大規模景仰，甚至是崇拜的中心。

* create[2] (krɪˋet) v. 創造　　cult (kʌlt) n. 狂熱崇拜
  personality[3] (͵pɝsn̩ˋælətɪ) n. 名人
  around[1] (əˋraʊnd) prep. 以⋯爲中心
  massive[5] (ˋmæsɪv) adj. 大規模的
  adoration[5] (͵ædəˋreʃən) n. 崇拜；景仰；敬慕；鍾愛
  worship[5] (ˋwɝʃɪp) n. 崇拜

In his old age, Stalin had grown *increasingly* paranoid. ***Though***
millions still saw him as a godlike hero, his inner circle knew *he*
was a weak man inside. *Perhaps* the greatest danger sign was his
growing hatred *of Jews*.

　　在老年時，史達林已經變得越來越偏執。雖然數百萬人仍然視他爲
像神一般的英雄，但他的親信都知道，他的內心是個脆弱的人。也許最
大的危險信號，就是他日益憎恨猶太人。

* ***old age*** 老年　　grow[1] (gro) v. 變得
  increasingly[2] (ɪnˋkrisɪŋlɪ) adv. 越來越
  paranoid (ˋpærə͵nɔɪd) adj. 偏執性的；過分猜疑的
  see A as B 認爲 A 是 B
  godlike (ˋgɑd͵laɪk) adj. 如神的；神聖的
  hero[2] (ˋhɪro) n. 英雄　　weak[1] (wik) adj. 虛弱的；軟弱的
  inside[1] (ˋɪnˋsaɪd) adv. 在心中　　sign[2] (saɪn) n. 徵兆；跡象
  growing[1] (ˋgroɪŋ) adj. 增大的；增強的
  hatred[4] (ˋhetrɪd) n. 憎恨；討厭
  Jew[1] (dʒu) n. 猶太人

[5](F) Many believe *he was about to follow in Hitler's footsteps*
***and** order their slaughter.* This would have provoked war *with the*
West, ***and while** the USSR had nuclear weapons*, its economy ***and***
military were *still* weak.

　　許多人相信，他即將要跟隨希特勒的腳步，下令屠殺猶太人。這會
引發和西方國家的戰爭，而且雖然蘇聯有核子武器，但它的經濟和軍事
力量仍然很弱。

> * *be about to V*. 即將…　　 follow[1] (ˈfalo) v. 跟隨
> footstep (ˈfʊtˌstɛp) n. 腳步
> *follow in* one's *footsteps* 跟著某人走；步某人的後塵；效法某人
> order[1] (ˈɔrdɚ) v. 下令　　 slaughter[5] (ˈslɔtɚ) n. 屠殺
> provoke[6] (prəˈvok) v. 激起；引起　　 *the West* 西方國家
> while[1] (hwaɪl) conj. 雖然　　 economy[4] (ɪˈkɑnəmɪ) n. 經濟
> military[2] (ˈmɪləˌtɛrɪ) n. 軍隊；軍方

If Stalin's death was in fact a natural one, it is likely ***that** an*
unnatural one was already being planned.

如果史達林事實上是自然死亡，那就很可能，一場非自然的死亡已經在
計畫中。

> * *in fact* 事實上　　 natural[2] (ˈnætʃərəl) adj. 自然的
> likely[1] (ˈlaɪklɪ) adj. 可能的
> unnatural[1] (ʌnˈnætʃərəl) adj. 非自然的
> plan[1] (plæn) v. 計畫；規劃

TEST 33

說明：第 1 至 5 題，每題一個空格。請依文意在文章後所提供的 (A) 到 (F) 選項中分別選出最適當者。

Le Corbusier was a master in architecture. He was a Swiss-French architect, designer, painter, urban planner, writer, and one of the pioneers of so-called modern architecture. __1__

As an early pioneer of Modern Architecture, Le Corbusier strove to conceive a new style of architecture that would best suit the 21st century. He later proposed the Five Points Towards a New Architecture. __2__ These were Le Corbusier's ideals for a new architectural aesthetic, and Villa Savoye, constructed between 1928 and 1931, embodied the Five Points. The bulk of Villa Savoye was lifted off the ground. Le Corbusier utilized pilotis, reinforced concrete stilts, instead of supporting walls, to bear the load of the structure. __3__ Without the concern for supporting walls, the non-supporting walls could be designed as the architect wished and the floor space was free to be configured into rooms. On the second floor, there were long strips of horizontal windows, which allowed unobstructed views of the large surrounding garden. ___4___ Villa Savoye represented the basis of modern architecture. It was very influential in the 1930s, and imitations of it can be found around the world. ___5___

(A) The five points include a different design in supports and roof gardens, the free design of the ground plan, the free design of façades, and the horizontal window.

(B) By incorporating new materials, he created a logical modern space to live in.

(C) His career spanned five decades, and included buildings constructed throughout Europe, India, and America.

(D) Le Corbusier also designed a roof garden to compensate for he green area consumed by the building.

(E) These pilotis allowed him to clarify his next two points: a free façade and an open floor space.

(F) It also manifested the dominant status of Le Corbusier in the architecture.

TEST 33 詳解

Le Corbusier was a master *in architecture.* He was a Swiss-French architect, designer, painter, urban planner, writer, ***and*** one *of the pioneers of so-called modern architecture.* [1](C) His career spanned five decades, ***and*** included buildings *constructed throughout Europe, India,* ***and*** *America.*

　　勒‧科布西耶是建築學的大師。他是出生於瑞士的法國建築師、設計師、畫家、都市規劃師、作家,也是所謂現代建築學的先驅之一。他的事業橫跨 50 年,包括遍及歐洲、印度和美洲的建築物。

　　* master[1] ('mæstɚ) *n.* 大師
　　architecture[5] ('ɑrkə,tɛktʃɚ) *n.* 建築;建築學
　　Swiss (swɪs) *adj.* 瑞士的
　　architect[5] ('ɑrkə,tɛkt) *n.* 建築師
　　designer[3] (dɪ'zaɪnɚ) *n.* 設計師
　　painter[2] ('pentɚ) *n.* 畫家
　　urban[4] ('ɝbən) *adj.* 都市的　　planner[1] ('plænɚ) *n.* 規劃者
　　pioneer[4] (,paɪə'nɪr) *adj.* 先驅者　　*so-called* *adj.* 所謂的
　　career[4] (kə'rɪr) *n.* 職業;事業;生涯
　　span[6] (spæn) *v.* 跨越;長達
　　decade[3] ('dɛked) *n.* 十年
　　construct[4] (kən'strʌkt) *v.* 建造
　　throughout[2] (θru'aʊt) *prep.* 遍及

As an early pioneer of Modern Architecture, Le Corbusier strove

to conceive a new style *of architecture **that** would best suit the 21st*

century.

　　勒‧科布西耶是現代建築學早期的先驅，他努力構想出一種最適合
21世紀的建築新風格。

* strive[4] 〔 straɪv 〕 v. 努力 < *to* >
conceive[5] 〔 kənˈsiv 〕 v. 構想出
suit[2] 〔 sut 〕 v. 適合

con　+ ceive
　|　　　|
with + *take*

He *later* proposed the Five Points Towards a New Architecture.

[2]**(A)** The five points include a different design *in supports **and** roof*

gardens, the free design of the ground plan, the free design of façades,

***and** the horizontal window.*

他後來提出「新建築五點」。這五點包括支柱和屋頂花園不同的設計、
地面方案的自由設計、建築物正面的自由設計，以及橫向水平的窗戶。

* later[1] 〔ˈletɚ〕 adv. 稍後；後來　　　propose[2] 〔 prəˈpoz 〕 v. 提議
include[2] 〔 ɪnˈklud 〕 v. 包含　　design[2] 〔 dɪˈzaɪn 〕 v., n. 設計
support[2] 〔 səˈport 〕 n. 支柱；地基　　roof[1] 〔 ruf 〕 n. 屋頂
ground[1] 〔 graʊnd 〕 n. 地面
façade 〔 fəˈsad 〕 n. (建築物的) 正面
horizontal[5] 〔ˌharəˈzantḷ〕 adj. 水平的

These were Le Corbusier's ideals *for a new architectural aesthetic,*

and Villa Savoye, *constructed between 1928 and 1931*, embodied

the Five Points.　The bulk *of Villa Savoye* was lifted *off the ground.*
這些是勒・科布西耶對於新建築美學的理想，而興建於 1928 到 1931 年
的薩伏伊別墅則具體表現了這五點。薩伏伊別墅的地面大部分都挑高。

* ideal³〔aɪ'diəl〕*n.* 理想
aesthetic〔ɛs'θɛtɪk〕*adj.* 美學的　　*n.* 美學
villa⁶〔'vɪlə〕*n.* 別墅
embody〔ɪm'bɑdɪ〕*v.* 具體化
bulk⁵〔bʌlk〕*n.* 大部分
lift¹〔lɪft〕*v.* 抬起；提高

Le Corbusier utilized *pilotis, reinforced concrete stilts, instead of*

supporting walls, to bear the load of the structure. ³(E) These pilotis

allowed him *to clarify his next two points*: *a free façade and an*

open floor space. Without the concern for supporting walls, the

non-supporting walls could be designed *as the architect wished and*

the floor space was free *to be configured into rooms.*

勒‧科布西耶沒有用承重牆，而是利用底層架空柱，也就是強化的混凝土支撐柱，來承擔整棟建築物的重量。底層架空柱使他能夠說明他的下兩個重點：自由的建築物正面和開放的地面空間。不必擔心承重牆的問題，非承重牆就可以依照建築師想要的去設計，地面空間也可以自由地設置成房間。

* utilize[6] 〔'jutḷ,aɪz〕v. 利用
piloti 〔pɪ'lɑtɪ〕n. 底層架空柱
reinforce[6] 〔,riɪn'fɔrs〕v. 加強
concrete[4] 〔'kɑnkrit〕adj., n. 混凝土（的）
stilt 〔stɪlt〕n. 支撐柱   ***instead of* 而非**
bear[2,1] 〔bɛr〕v. 支撐；承擔
load[3] 〔lod〕n. 負擔；重擔
structure[3] 〔'strʌktʃɚ〕n. 結構；建築物
allow[1] 〔ə'laʊ〕v. 允許；使能夠   clarify[4] 〔'klæsə,faɪ〕v. 說明
floor[1] 〔flor〕n. 地板；地面   space[1] 〔spes〕n. 空間
concern[3] 〔kən'sɝn〕n. 擔憂   configure 〔kən'fɪgɚ〕v. 配置

> utilize *v.* 利用
> = use
> = employ
> = make use of

On the second floor, there were long strips *of horizontal windows*,

which allowed unobstructed views of the large surrounding garden.

[4](D) Le Corbusier *also* designed a roof garden *to compensate for the green area consumed by the building.*

二樓有長排橫向水平的窗戶，能看到周圍大片的花園，視野毫無阻礙。勒‧科布西耶還設計了一個屋頂花園，以彌補因建築物而被消耗掉的綠色空間。

* strip³ ﹝strɪp﹞ *n.* 長條

unobstructed ﹝ˌʌnəbˈstrʌktɪd﹞ *adj.* 沒有障礙的

【obstruct ﹝əbˈstrʌkt﹞ *v.* 阻礙；阻擋】

surrounding³ ﹝səˈraʊndɪŋ﹞ *adj.* 周圍的

compensate⁶ ﹝ˈkɑmpənˌset﹞ *v.* 補償；彌補 < *for* >

consume⁴ ﹝kənˈsjum﹞ *v.* 消耗

Villa Savoye represented the basis *of modern architecture.* It was

very influential *in the 1930s,* **and** imitations *of it* can be found

around the world. ⁵**(F)** It *also* manifested the dominant status *of*

Le Corbusier in the architecture.

薩伏伊別墅表現出現代建築的基礎。它在 1930 年代影響力非常大，全世界都可以找到模仿它的建築。它也顯示出勒・科布西耶在建築學上崇高的地位。

* represent³ ﹝ˌrɛprɪˈzɛnt﹞ *v.* 表現　　basis² ﹝ˈbesɪs﹞ *n.* 基礎

influential⁴ ﹝ˌɪnfluˈɛnʃəl﹞ *adj.* 有影響力的

imitation⁴ ﹝ˌɪməˈteʃən﹞ *n.* 模仿（物）

manifest⁵ ﹝ˈmænəˌfɛst﹞ *v.* 顯示

dominant⁴ ﹝ˈdɑmənənt﹞ *adj.* 佔優勢的；崇高的

status⁴ ﹝ˈstetəs﹞ *n.* 地位

TEST 34

說明： 第 1 至 5 題，每題一個空格。請依文意在文章後所提供的 (A) 到 (F) 選項中分別選出最適當者。

Having a headache is nothing unusual to modern people. When we have a headache, we may associate it with too much stress or too little sleep or a hangover, etc. Headaches seem to be a part of life and thus we may just take painkillers to ease the pain, to make it disappear. __1__ In some cases, we have continual headaches because we suffer from a brain tumor or certain deadly diseases, whereas in other cases, we get headaches merely because we're exposing our heads daily to cell phone radiation. __2__ Nevertheless, if we look more closely, we'll find that a lot of studies have come to the conclusion that there is certain correlation between cell phone radiation and a number of symptoms and diseases. __3__ The helmet recorded brain activity when put on a person's head. The cell phone signals were turned on for the same period of time that a person is normally on his cell phone. The brain waves were measured while the cell phone was on and while it was off. __4__ The results showed that the cortical area of the left side of the brain, which is responsible for language and for movement, was indeed more active when the phones were on. ___5___

Some other independent scientific studies also indicate that the radiation from hand-held mobile phones does pose serious health risks and can increase the incidence of brain tumors. With all the evidence, perhaps we should have the courage to act on what we have found out for our own good.

(A) The participants were unaware of when the cell phone signals were turned on or off.

(B) Years ago, a study was conducted with participants wearing a specially-designed helmet with a cell phone near the left ear.

(C) Cell phones work by relaying low levels of radio waves from their antennas to a nearby base tower.

(D) Yet sometimes headaches continue to be chronic, and no matter what we do and no matter how we change our lifestyle, they just don't go away.

(E) What's more, the increased activity in the brain continued for up to one hour after the cell phone was turned off.

(F) So far, no one has told us that cell phone radiation is proven to be dangerous.

TEST 34 詳解

Having a headache is nothing *unusual to modern people.* ***When***
we have a headache, we may associate it *with too much stress **or** too*
*little sleep **or** a hangover, etc.*

頭痛對現代人來說沒什麼不尋常。當我們頭痛時，我們可能會聯想
到壓力太大、睡太少，或宿醉等等

* headache〔'hɛdͺek〕*n.* 頭痛
　unusual[2]〔ʌn'juʒʊəl〕*adj.* 不尋常的
　associate[4]〔ə'soʃͺet〕*v.* 聯想 < *with* >
　stress[2]〔strɛs〕*n.* 壓力　　hangover〔'hæŋͺovɚ〕*n.* 宿醉

Headaches seem to be a part *of life **and** thus* we may *just* take
painkillers *to ease the pain, to make it disappear.* [1]**(D)** ***Yet** sometimes*
headaches continue to be chronic, ***and no matter what** we do **and no***
***matter how** we change our lifestyle,* they *just* don't go *away.*

頭痛似乎是生活中的一部份，因此我們也許只會吃個止痛藥，減輕疼痛
讓它消失。然而，有時頭痛持續成爲長期的問題，無論我們做什麼，無
論我們如何改變生活方式，它們就是不會消失。

* painkiller〔'penͺkɪlɚ〕*n.* 止痛藥【pain[2]〔pen〕*n.* 疼痛；痛苦】
　ease[1]〔iz〕*v.* 減輕　　disappear[2]〔ͺdɪsə'pɪr〕*v.* 消失

chronic⁶〔'krɑnɪk〕*adj.* 長期的；慢性的
no matter what 無論什麼　　***no matter how*** 無論如何
lifestyle〔'laɪf,staɪl〕*n.* 生活方式【style³〔staɪl〕*n.* 風格；方式】
go away 離開；消失

In some cases, we have continual headaches ***because*** *we suffer from*

*a brain tumor **or** certain deadly diseases*, ***whereas*** *in other cases*, we

get headaches *merely **because** we're exposing our heads daily to cell*

phone radiation. ²(F) *So far*, no one has told us ***that*** *cell phone*

radiation is proven to be dangerous.

在有些情形中，我們會有持續的頭痛，是因為腦部有腫瘤，或是罹患某
些致命的疾病，然而在有些情況中，我們會頭痛，只是因為我們的頭部
每天都暴露在手機的輻射中。到目前為止，沒有人告訴我們，手機的輻
射被證明是危險的。

＊case¹〔kes〕*n.* 情形；例子
continual⁴〔kən'tɪnjʊəl〕*adj.* 持續的
suffer from 受～之苦；罹患　　brain²〔bren〕*n.* 腦部
tumor⁶〔'tjumɚ〕*n.* 腫瘤　　certain¹〔'sɝtn̩〕*adj.* 某些
deadly⁶〔'dɛdlɪ〕*adj.* 致命的　　whereas⁵〔hwɛr'æz〕*n.* 然而
merely⁴〔'mɪrlɪ〕*adv.* 僅僅
expose⁴〔ɪk'spoz〕*v.* 使接觸；暴露
daily²〔'delɪ〕*adv.* 每天　　***cell phone*** 手機
radiation⁶〔,redɪ'eʃən〕*n.* 輻射　　***so far*** 到目前為止
prove¹〔pruv〕*v.* 證明

*Nevertheless, **if** we look more closely*, we'll find ***that*** *a lot of studies have come to the conclusion* | ***that*** *there is certain correlation between cell phone radiation **and** a number of symptoms **and** diseases.*

然而，如果我們仔細看看，我們會發現很多研究得到結論，認為手機幅射以及一些症狀和疾病之間，有某些相互關係。

* neveltheless[4] 〔ˌnɛvəðəˈlɛs〕 *adv.* 然而

closely[1] 〔ˈkloslɪ〕 *adv.* 接近地；仔細地

conclusion[3] 〔kənˈkluʒən〕 *n.* 結論

come to a conclusion 得到結論

correlation 〔ˌkɔrəˈleʃən〕 *n.* 相互

關係【relation[2] 〔rɪˈleʃən〕 *n.* 關係】

a number of 一些　　symptom[6] 〔ˈsɪmptəm〕 *n.* 症狀

cor	+	re	+	lat	+ ion
together	+	back	+	bring	+ *n.*

[3]**(B)** *Years ago*, a study was conducted | *with participants wearing a specially-designed helmet with a cell phone near the left ear.* The helmet recorded brain activity ***when*** *put on a person's head.* The cell phone signals were turned on *for the same period of time **that** a person is normally on his cell phone.*

幾年前進行過一項研究，參加者戴著一個特殊設計的頭盔，手機靠近左
耳。這個頭盔戴在頭上時，會記錄這個人的腦部活動。手機信號在這個
人平常使用手機的同時，也被打開。

> * conduct[5] 〔kən'dʌkt〕v. 進行
> participant[5] 〔par'tɪsəpənt〕n. 參與者
> design[2] 〔dɪ'zaɪn〕v. 設計　　***specially-designed*** 特殊設計的
> helmet[3] 〔'hɛlmɪt〕n. 頭盔　　record[2] 〔rɪ'kɔrd〕v. 記錄
> activity[3] 〔æk'tɪvətɪ〕n. 活動　　signal[3] 〔'sɪgnḷ〕n. 信號
> ***turn on*** 打開　　period[2] 〔'pɪrɪəd〕n. 期間
> normally[3] 〔'nɔrmḷɪ〕adv. 正常地；通常

The brain waves were measured ***while*** the cell phone was on ***and***
while it was off. [4]**(A) The participants were unaware of *when the***
cell phone signals were turned on or off.
當手機打開和關掉的時候，腦波都被測量。參加者並不知道手機信號何
時被打開或關掉。

> * wave[2] 〔wev〕n. 波；波浪　　measure[2,4] 〔'mɛʒɚ〕v. 測量
> unaware 〔ˌʌnə'wɛr〕adj. 不知道的【aware[3] 〔ə'wɛr〕adj. 知道的】
> ***turn off*** 關掉

The results showed ***that*** the cortical area of the left side of the brain,
which is responsible for language ***and*** for movement, was ***indeed***
more active ***when*** the phones were on. [5]**(E) *What's more*, the**

increased activity *in the brain* continued *for up to one hour **after the***

cell phone was turned off.

結果顯示，負責語言和動作的左腦皮質層，在手機打開時，的確比較活躍。此外，大腦增加的活動在手機被關掉後，還持續長達一小時。

* result² 〔 rɪˈzʌlt 〕 *n.* 結果　　cortical 〔ˈkɔrtɪk!〕 *adj.* 大腦皮質的
  be responsible for 負責　　movement¹ 〔ˈmuvmənt〕 *n.* 動作
  indeed³ 〔 ɪnˈdid 〕 *adv.* 的確　　active² 〔ˈæktɪv〕 *adj.* 活躍的
  what's more 此外 (= *besides²*)　　***up to*** 高達；長達

Some other independent scientific studies *also* indicate ***that*** the

radiation from hand-held mobile phones does pose serious health risks

and *can increase the incidence of brain tumors. With all the evidence,*

perhaps we should have the courage *to act on **what** we have found out*

for our own good.

　　還有一些其他獨立的科學研究也顯示，手持行動電話的輻射的確會造成嚴重的健康風險，可能增加腦瘤的發生率。有了所有這些證據，也許為了我們自己好，我們應該要有勇氣按照我們所發現的來採取行動。

* independent² 〔ˌɪndɪˈpɛndənt〕 *adj.* 獨立的
  indicate² 〔ˈɪndəˌket〕 *v.* 指出　　***hand-held*** 手持的
  mobile³ 〔ˈmob!〕 *adj.* 行動的；機動的　　***mobile phone*** 行動電話
  pose² 〔 poz 〕 *v.* 造成　　serious² 〔ˈsɪrɪəs〕 *adj.* 嚴重的
  risk³ 〔 rɪsk 〕 *n.* 風險　　incidence 〔ˈɪnsədəns〕 *n.* 發生率
  evidence⁴ 〔ˈɛvədəns〕 *n.* 證據　　courage² 〔ˈkɝɪdʒ〕 *n.* 勇氣
  act on 按照…行動　　***for** one's **own good*** 為了某人好

TEST 35

說明： 第 1 至 5 題，每題一個空格。請依文意在文章後所提供的 (A) 到 (F) 選項中分別選出最適當者。

Tomatoes are a good source of antioxidants and beta-carotene. But if you eat a tomato without adding a little fat, say a drizzle of olive oil, your body is unlikely to absorb all these nutrients. __1__ They recruited graduate students to eat bowls of green salads with tomatoes and various types of salad dressings, from fat-free to regular Italian. Researchers put IV lines into the participants' veins and drew blood samples before and after they'd eaten the salads in order to get precise measurements of the absorption of nutrients. __2__ But when researchers analyzed their blood samples, it was found that people who had eaten fat-free or low-fat dressings didn't absorb the beneficial carotenoids from the salad. __3__

How food is prepared is also important. Many people believe that a tomato is a tomato, no matter how it is eaten. __4__ It suggests that some cooking methods may be better than others and won't deteriorate the nourishment contained in raw vegetables. Researchers at the University of Murcia in Spain cooked 20 different kinds of vegetables in six different ways. __5__ They found that microwaving helped maintain the antioxidants, whereas boiling and pressure cooking led to the greatest losses. So, if you are going to eat tomatoes, it may help to cook them gently.

(A) Scientists at Iowa State University figured this out a while ago.

(B) Then they analyzed how well the foods retained antioxidants.

(C) Only when they had eaten the oil-based dressing did they get the nutrients.

(D) However, a recent study of nutrition research goes against the grain of trendy food ideas.

(E) The salads might have all tasted the same to the participants.

(F) The project will offer these groups the information they need to better understand the benefits.

TEST 35 詳解

Tomatoes are a good source *of antioxidants **and** beta-carotene.*

***But if** you eat a tomato without adding a little fat, say a drizzle of*

olive oil, your body is unlikely to absorb all these nutrients.

[1](A) Scientists *at Iowa State University* figured this out *a while ago.*

　　蕃茄是很好的抗氧化劑和 β 胡蘿蔔素的來源。但如果你吃蕃茄沒有加一點油脂,例如一點點橄欖油,你的身體不可能吸收所有這些養分。這是愛荷華州立大學的科學家在一陣子之前所了解到的。

* source[2] 〔sors〕 *n.* 來源
  antioxidant 〔͵æntɪˈɑksədənt〕 *n.* 抗氧化劑【oxidant *n.* 氧化劑】
  beta 〔ˈbetə〕 *n.* 希臘字母的第二個字母 β
  carotene 〔ˈkærə͵tin〕 *n.* 胡蘿蔔素　　add[1] 〔æd〕 *v.* 添加
  fat[1] 〔fæt〕 *n.* 脂肪;油脂　　say[1] 〔se〕 *v.* 例如【常用於插入】
  drizzle[6] 〔ˈdrɪzḷ〕 *n.* 毛毛雨　　***a drizzle of*** 一點點
  olive[5] 〔ˈɑlɪv〕 *n.* 橄欖　　unlikely[1] 〔ʌnˈlaɪklɪ〕 *adj.* 不可能的
  be unlikely to V 不可能　　absorb[4] 〔əbˈsɔrb〕 *v.* 吸收
  nutrient[6] 〔ˈnjutrɪənt〕 *n.* 養分　　***figure out*** 了解
  while[1] 〔hwaɪl〕 *n.* 一會兒;一陣子

They recruited graduate students to eat bowls of green salads *with*

*tomatoes **and** various types of salad dressings, from fat-free to regular*

Italian.

他們招募了研究生來吃蔬菜沙拉，裡面加蕃茄並搭配各種沙拉醬汁，從零脂肪的到一般的義式醬汁都有。

> * recruit[6] (rɪ'krut) v. 招募　　graduate[3] ('grædʒuɪt) adj. 研究所的
> bowl[1] (bol) n. 碗　　salad[2] ('sæləd) n. 沙拉
> **green salad** 蔬菜沙拉　　various[3] ('vɛrɪəs) adj. 各種的
> type[2] (taɪp) n. 類型　　dressing[5] ('drɛsɪŋ) n. 調味醬
> **fat-free** adj. 無油脂的；零脂肪的
> regular[2] ('rɛgjələ) adj. 普通的；一般的

Researchers put IV lines *into the participants' veins **and** drew blood samples **before and after** they'd eaten the salads in order to get precise measurements of the absorption of nutrients.* [2](E) The salads might have all tasted the same *to the participants.*

研究人員在參加者的靜脈中，插入靜脈注射導管，在他們吃沙拉之前和之後都抽取血液樣本，以得到養分吸收的精確測量值。這些沙拉可能對參加者而言吃起來味道都一樣。

> * **IV** adj. 靜脈內的；靜脈注射的 (= *intravenous* (ˌɪntrə'vinəs))
> participant[5] (pə'tɪsəpənt) n. 參加者
> vein[5] (ven) n. 靜脈　　draw[1] (drɔ) v. 抽取
> blood[1] (blʌd) n. 血液　　sample[2] ('sæmpḷ) n. 樣本
> precise[4] (prɪ'saɪs) adj. 精確的
> measurement[2] ('mɛʒəmənt) n. 測量；測量值
> absorption[4] (əb'sɔrpʃən) n. 吸收
> taste[1] (test) v. 吃起來

But when researchers analyzed their blood samples, it was found *that*

people who had eaten fat-free or low-fat dressings didn't absorb the

beneficial carotenoids *from the salad*. [3](C) *Only when they had eaten*

the oil-based dressing did they get the nutrients.

但是當研究人員分析他們的血液樣本時，發現吃了零脂肪或低脂沙拉醬的人，都沒有從沙拉中吸收到有益的類胡蘿蔔素。只有當他們吃了以油脂爲基底的醬汁才得到養分。

* analyze[4]〔'ænlˌaɪz〕*v.* 分析　　beneficial[5]〔ˌbɛnə'fɪʃəl〕*adj.* 有益的
  carotenoid〔kə'ratnˌɔɪd〕*n.* 類胡蘿蔔素
  based〔best〕*adj.* 以～爲基礎的；以～爲基底的
  【base[1] *n.* 基地；基礎；根據】

How food is prepared is *also* important.　Many people believe

that a tomato is a tomato, no matter how it is eaten. [4](D) *However,*

a recent study *of nutrition research* goes against the grain *of trendy*

food ideas.　It suggests *that some cooking methods may be better*

than others and won't deteriorate the nourishment contained in raw

vegetables.

　　食物如何準備也很重要。許多人相信蕃茄無論怎麼吃，就是蕃茄。然而，最近一項有關營養的研究，則違反了流行的基本食物概念。這個研究表示，有些烹調方法可能比其他的好，不會讓生的蔬菜裡含有的營養成分變糟。

* recent[2] (ˈrisn̩t) *adj.* 最近的　　nutrition[2] (njuˈtrɪʃən) *n.* 營養

against[2] (əˈgɛnst) *prep.* 違反　　grain[3] (gren) *n.* 紋理；基本特質

trendy (ˈtrɛndɪ) *adj.* 流行的【trend[3] (trɛnd) *n.* 趨勢】

suggest[3] (sə(g)ˈdʒɛst) *v.* 建議；暗示；表示

method[2] (ˈmɛθəd) *n.* 方法　　deteriorate[6] (dɪˈtɪrɪəˌret) *v.* 惡化

nourishment[6] (ˈnɝɪʃmənt) *n.* 營養品；食物

contain[2] (kənˈten) *v.* 包含　　raw[3] (rɔ) *adj.* 生的

Researchers *at the University of Murcia in Spain* cooked 20 different

kinds *of vegetables in six different ways.* [5](**B**) *Then* they analyzed

***how** well the foods retained antioxidants.*

西班牙莫夕亞大學的研究人員，以六種不同的方法來烹煮 20 種不同種
類的蔬菜。然後，他們分析各種食物抗氧化劑被保留下來的情況。

　　* retain[4] (rɪˈten) *v.* 保留

They found ***that** microwaving helped maintain the antioxidants,*

***whereas** boiling **and** pressure cooking led to the greatest losses. So,*

***if** you are going to eat tomatoes,* it may help to cook them *gently.*

他們發現，以微波烹調有助於維持住抗氧化劑，而用水煮和高壓烹煮則
導致最大的流失。所以，如果你要吃蕃茄，清柔地烹煮【即指不要太熱、
不要高壓】可能比較有好處。

　　* microwave[3] (ˈmaɪkrəˌwev) *n.* 微波（爐）　*v.* 用微波烹調

maintain[2] (menˈten) *v.* 維持　　whereas[5] (hwɛrˈæz) *conj.* 然而

boil[2] (bɔɪl) *v.* 沸騰；用水煮　　pressure[3] (ˈprɛʃə) *n.* 壓力

loss[2] (lɔs) *n.* 損失；喪失　　gently[2] (ˈdʒɛntlɪ) *adv.* 輕柔地

TEST 36

說明： 第 1 至 5 題，每題一個空格。請依文意在文章後所提供的 (A) 到
(F) 選項中分別選出最適當者。

Situated in the corner of the North American
continent, Alaska is the largest state of the United States.
Originally discovered and owned by Russia, this vast land
was initially a place for fur trading and whaling. Then, as
fur became difficult to acquire, few Russians were willing
to inhabit Alaska because of the harsh cold.   1
Because of these reasons, in 1867, Russia gave up the
right of possession of Alaska to the United Stated for
$7.2 million, less than two cents an acre. Alaska became
a colonial possession of the United States and was called
"Seward's Folly" because it was U.S. Secretary of State
William Seward that arranged the purchase.   2   At
that time, there weren't many settlers, and only some
salmon canneries were set up there. Alaska remained
a wilderness without any infrastructure.

It was widely believed that Alaska had nothing to
offer until the discovery of gold in the 1890s changed

its fate. Hundreds of thousands of miners, prospectors and settlers rushed there. ___3___ With the growing population in Alaska and the increasing conflict over the unclear border with Canada, its inhabitants urged an official declaration of the possession as a U.S. territory. In 1903, an international commission set the present boundary, and in 1912, the Alaskan Territory was established, with Juneau as the capital. ___4___

The need for road construction coincidentally met the demand for jobs during the Great Depression. The government sent people to construct roads there through a program called The New Deal. This program made a great contribution to the development of Alaska. Nevertheless, the government still felt the need to take further measures to protect the land. ___5___ Finally, in 1959, Alaska obtained its statehood, and became the 49th state of the U.S. Further infrastructure was built and more settlers moved in, which brought about the discovery of oil in Prudhoe Bay. Americans were thrilled. Looking at this precious land with rich oil and other natural resources, who would think that the purchase was a mistake?

(A) Because of this, the government built the Alaska Highway, which connects Alaska with Canada and the United States.

(B) Most people in the U.S. ridiculed this arrangement and few could see the benefits of this remote and white land far away from their country.

(C) Most of them gathered in the towns of Juneau, Nome and Fairbanks, for these towns were the first ones where abundant gold was found.

(D) Protests against the ignorance of the land border were constantly held, so the government had to send troops to clamp down on the riots.

(E) Soon, towns of miners of gold, coal and copper prospered, which made road construction necessary.

(F) On top of that, the land was separated from mainland Russia by the Bering Sea, which made it hard for the Russian government to govern it.

TEST 36 詳解

Situated in the corner of the North American continent, Alaska

is the largest state *of the United States*. *Originally discovered and*

owned by Russia, this vast land was *initially* a place *for fur trading*

and whaling.

　　阿拉斯加州位於北美大陸的一個角落,是美國最大的州。最初由俄羅斯發現並擁有,這片廣闊的土地,剛開始是一個毛皮交易和捕鯨的地方。

* ***be situated in*** 位於　　corner[2] (ˈkɔrnɚ) *n.* 角落
continent[3] (ˈkɑntənənt) *n.* 洲;大陸
Alaska (əˈlæskə) *n.* (美國) 阿拉斯加州
originally[3] (əˈrɪdʒənḷɪ) *adv.* 最初;原本
discover[1] (dɪˈskʌvɚ) *v.* 發現　　own[1] (on) *v.* 擁有
Russia (ˈrʌʃə) *n.* 俄羅斯　　vast[4] (væst) *adj.* 巨大的
initially[2] (ɪˈnɪʃəlɪ) *adv.* 最初地　　fur[2] (fɝ) *n.* 毛皮
trading[2] (ˈtredɪŋ) *n.* 貿易;交易
whaling (ˈhwelɪŋ) *n.* 捕鯨 (業)【whale[2] (hwel) *n.* 鯨】

Then, *as fur became difficult to acquire*, few Russians were willing

to inhabit Alaska *because of the harsh cold*.

　　然後,隨著毛皮變得難以獲得,因為嚴寒,很少有俄羅斯人願意居住在阿拉斯加。

* acquire[4] 〔əˋkwaɪr〕 *v.* 獲得；學會

Russian 〔ˋrʌʃən〕 *n.* 俄國人　　willing[2] 〔ˋwɪlɪŋ〕 *adj.* 願意的

inhabit[6] 〔ɪnˋhæbɪt〕 *v.* 居住於　　harsh[4] 〔hɑrʃ〕 *adj.* 嚴厲的

harsh cold 嚴寒（= *severe cold* = *bitter cold*）

[1](F) *On top of that*, the land was separated *from mainland Russia by the Bering Sea,* **which** *made it hard for the Russian government to govern it.*

除此之外，這片土地隔著白令海與俄羅斯大陸分開，這使得俄羅斯政府難以管理。

* ***on top of that*** 除此之外；另外

separate[2] 〔ˋsɛpə‚ret〕 *v.* 使分開

mainland[5] 〔ˋmen‚lænd〕 *n.* 大陸

Bering Sea 〔‚bɛrɪŋ ˋsi〕 *n.* 白令海

government[2] 〔ˋgʌvənmənt〕 *n.* 政府

govern[2] 〔ˋgʌvən〕 *v.* 統治；管理

Because of these reasons, in 1867, Russia gave up the right *of possession of Alaska to the United States for $7.2 million, less than two cents an acre.*

因為這些理由，俄羅斯在 1867 年把阿拉斯加的擁有權，以一英畝不到兩美分，720 萬美元的價格讓給了美國。

* ***give up*** *A* ***to*** *B* 把 A 讓渡給 B　　right[1] 〔raɪt〕 *n.* 權利

possession[4] 〔 pə'zɛʃən 〕 *n.* 擁有;所有物
cent[1] 〔 sɛnt 〕 *n.* 一分錢　　acre[4] 〔'ekə 〕 *n.* 英畝

Alaska became a colonial possession *of the United States **and*** was called "Seward's Folly" ***because*** it was U.S. Secretary of State *William Seward **that*** arranged the purchase.

阿拉斯加成為美國的殖民地,且被稱為「西沃德的愚蠢」,因為就是美國國務卿威廉・西沃德安排了這項買賣。

* colonial[4] 〔 kə'lonɪəl 〕 *adj.* 殖民(地)的
  folly 〔'falɪ 〕 *n.* 愚行;荒唐的事
  Secretary of State 國務卿　　arrange[2] 〔 ə'rendʒ 〕 *v.* 安排
  purchase[5] 〔'pɜtʃəs 〕 *n.* 購買;買賣 (= *buy*)

[2]**(B)** Most people *in the U.S.* ridiculed this arrangement ***and*** few could see the benefits *of this remote **and** white land far away from their country.*

大多數的美國人都嘲笑這種安排,很少人能看到遠離美國本土的這片偏遠白色土地的好處。

* ridicule[6] 〔'rɪdɪˌkjul 〕 *v.* 嘲笑
  arrangement[2] 〔 ə'rendʒmənt 〕 *n.* 安排
  benefit[3] 〔'bɛnəfɪt 〕 *n.* 利益;好處
  remote[3] 〔 rɪ'mot 〕 *adj.* 遙遠的;偏僻的
  far away 遠離;(離…)很遠

At that time, there weren't many settlers, ***and only*** some salmon

canneries were set up *there*.　Alaska remained a wilderness *without*

any infrastructure.

在當時，那裡並沒有很多移民，只有一些鮭魚罐頭工廠設立在那裡。阿
拉斯加仍然是沒有任何基礎設施的荒野。

＊settler[4]〔'sɛtlɚ〕*n.* 殖民者；移民　　salmon[5]〔'sæmən〕*n.* 鮭魚
cannery〔'kænərɪ〕*n.* 罐頭工廠【can[1] *n.* 罐頭　*v.* 裝罐】
set up 建立；創立　　remain[3]〔rɪ'men〕*v.* 仍然是
wilderness[5]〔'wɪldɚnɪs〕*n.* 荒野
infrastructure〔'ɪnfrə,strʌktʃɚ〕*n.* 基礎建設

It was *widely* believed ***that*** *Alaska had nothing to offer* ***until*** *the*

discovery of gold in the 1890s changed its fate.　Hundreds of

thousands of miners, prospectors ***and*** settlers rushed *there.*

　　人們普遍認為阿拉斯加是沒有東西可提供的地方，直到 1890 年代
黃金的發現後才改變了它的命運。數十萬的礦工、探礦者以及移民湧至
那裡。

＊widely[1]〔'waɪdlɪ〕*adv.* 廣泛地；普遍地
offer[2]〔'ɔfɚ〕*v. n.* 提供　　discovery[3]〔dɪ'skʌvərɪ〕*n.* 發現
fate[3]〔fet〕*n.* 命運　　***hundreds of thousands of*** 數十萬
miner[3]〔'maɪnɚ〕*n.* 礦工
prospector[5]〔'prɑspɛktɚ〕*n.* （礦山等的）探勘者；採礦者
rush[2]〔rʌʃ〕*v.* 衝進；湧至

³(C) Most *of them* gathered *in the towns of Juneau, Nome and Fairbanks*, *for* these towns were the first ones *where abundant gold was found*.

他們大部分聚集在朱諾、諾姆以及費爾班克斯等城鎮，因為這些城鎮是最早發現豐富的黃金的地方。

* gather² 〔ˋgæðɚ〕 v. 聚集
Juneau 〔ˋdʒuno〕 n. 朱諾【美國阿拉斯加州的首府】
Nome 〔nom〕 n. 諾姆【美國阿拉斯加州人口普查區】
Fairbanks 〔ˋfɛr͵bæŋks〕 n. 費爾班克斯【美國阿拉斯加州中央東部的城市，是該州第二大城市、阿拉斯加內陸地區最大的城市】
abundant⁵ 〔əˋbʌndənt〕 adj. 豐富的；充足的

With the growing population in Alaska and the increasing conflict over the unclear border with Canada, its inhabitants urged an official declaration *of the possession as a U.S. territory.*

隨著阿拉斯加人口不斷增加，以及與加拿大邊界不明的衝突越來越多，阿拉斯加的居民敦促屬地正式聲明為美國領土。

* population² 〔͵pɑpjəˋleʃən〕 n. 人口　　conflict² 〔ˋkɑnflɪkt〕 n. 衝突
border³ 〔ˋbordɚ〕 n. 邊境　　Canada 〔ˋkænədə〕 n. 加拿大
inhabitant⁶ 〔ɪnˋhæbətənt〕 n. 居民　　urge⁴ 〔ɝdʒ〕 v. 催促；呼籲
official² 〔əˋfɪʃəl〕 adj. 正式的；官方的
declaration⁵ 〔͵dɛkləˋreʃən〕 n. 宣言；公布
territory³ 〔ˋtɛrə͵torɪ〕 n. 領土

In 1903, an international commission set the present boundary, ***and***

in 1912, the Alaskan Territory was established, *with Juneau as the*

capital. [4](E) *Soon*, towns *of miners of gold, coal **and** copper*

prospered, ***which made road construction necessary.***

1903 年，一個國際委員會設定了現在的邊界，然後在 1912 年，阿拉斯加領土建立，朱諾爲首都。不久，黃金、煤炭、銅礦的礦工城鎮繁榮了起來，使得道路建設成爲必要。

* international[2] ﹝͵ɪntɚˋnæʃənḷ﹞ *adj.* 國際的
  commission[5] ﹝kəˋmɪʃən﹞ *n.* 委員會
  set[1] ﹝sɛt﹞ *v.* 設定；制定　　present[2] ﹝ˋprɛzṇt﹞ *adj.* 現在的
  boundary[5] ﹝ˋbaʊndərɪ﹞ *n.* 邊界　　establish[4] ﹝əˋstæblɪʃ﹞ *v.* 建立
  capital[3] ﹝ˋkæpətḷ﹞ *n.* 首都；首府
  coal[2] ﹝kol﹞ *n.* 煤　　copper[4] ﹝ˋkɑpɚ﹞ *n.* 銅
  prosper[4] ﹝ˋprɑspɚ﹞ *v.* 繁榮；興盛
  construction[4] ﹝kənˋstrʌkʃən﹞ *n.* 建設
  necessary[2] ﹝ˋnɛsə͵sɛrɪ﹞ *adj.* 必要的

The need *for road construction coincidentally* met the demand

for jobs during the Great Depression. The government sent people

to construct roads there through a program called The New Deal.

This program made a great contribution *to the development of Alaska.*

　　道路建設的需要，碰巧滿足了經濟大蕭條時期的就業需求。政府透過一項名爲「新政」的計劃，派人到阿拉斯加修建道路。這項計劃對阿拉斯加的發展有很大的貢獻。

* coincidentally〔ko͵ɪnsə'dɛntḷɪ〕*adv.* 碰巧地；巧合地
  demand[4]〔dɪ'mænd〕*n.* 要求
  meet demands for⋯ 滿足⋯的需求
  depression[4]〔dɪ'prɛʃən〕*n.* 沮喪；不景氣
  the Great Depression 經濟大蕭條【1920 年 10 月股市大崩盤後，
  　　發生在美國及其他資本主義國家的經濟危機，持續至 1930 年代】
  construct[4]〔kən'strʌkt〕*v.* 建造
  program[3]〔'progræm〕*n.* 計劃　　deal[1]〔dil〕*n.* 交易；政策
  contribution[4]〔͵kɑntrə'bjuʃən〕*n.* 貢獻
  development[2]〔dɪ'vɛləpmənt〕*n.* 發展

Nevertheless, the government *still* felt the need *to take further measures to protect the land.* [5](A) *Because of this*, the government built the Alaska Highway, ***which*** connects Alaska with Canada ***and the United States.***

　　不過，政府仍然覺得有必要採取進一步措施，來保護這片土地。因此，政府修築了阿拉斯加公路，來連接阿拉斯加與加拿大和美國。

* nevertheless[4]〔͵nɛvəðə'lɛs〕*adv.* 然而；仍然
  further[2]〔'fɝðə〕*adj.* 更進一步的
  measure[4]〔'mɛʒə〕*n.* 措施　　protect[2]〔prə'tɛkt〕*v.* 保護
  highway[2]〔'haɪ͵we〕*n.* 公路　　connect[3]〔kə'nɛkt〕*v.* 連接

Finally, *in 1959*, Alaska obtained its statehood, ***and*** became the 49th

state *of the U.S.* Further infrastructure was built ***and*** more settlers

moved in, ***which*** *brought about the discovery of oil in Prudhoe Bay.*

Americans were thrilled.

最後，阿拉斯加州於 1959 年取得州的地位，成爲美國的第 49 個州。更
進一步的基礎設施被建立、更多的移民移入，這導致了在普拉德霍灣發
現石油。美國人非常興奮。

* obtain[4] 〔əb'ten〕*v.* 獲得
    statehood〔'stet,hυd〕*n.* 州的狀態；州的地位
    move in 移入   ***bring about*** 導致；造成
    bay[3]〔be〕*n.* 海灣
    Prudhoe Bay〔'prʌdho 'be〕*n.* 普拉德霍灣
    thrilled[5]〔θrɪld〕*adj.* 興奮的

*Looking at this precious land with rich oil **and** other natural resources,*

who would think ***that*** *the purchase was a mistake?*

看著這片有豐富石油和其他自然資源的珍貴土地，誰還會認爲這項買賣
是一個錯誤呢？

* precious[3]〔'prɛʃəs〕*adj.* 珍貴的
    natural[2]〔'nætʃərəl〕*adj.* 天然的
    resource[3]〔rɪ'sors〕*n.* 資源
    natural resources 天然資源

7000字篇章結構詳解

The Most Used 7000 Words in Reading
Comprehension: Complete the Passages

定價：250元

主　　編 / 劉　毅

發　行　所 / 學習出版有限公司　　　☎ (02) 2704-5525

郵撥帳號 / 05127272 學習出版社帳戶

登　記　證 / 局版台業 2179 號

印　刷　所 / 裕強彩色印刷有限公司

台北門市 / 台北市許昌街 10 號 2 F　　☎ (02) 2331-4060

台灣總經銷 / 紅螞蟻圖書有限公司　　☎ (02) 2795-3656

本公司網址 / www.learnbook.com.tw

電子郵件 / learnbook@learnbook.com.tw

2018 年 5 月 1 日初版

4713269382904

版權所有，本書內容未經書面同意，不得以任何
形式複製。

高三同學要如何準備「升大學考試」

考前該如何準備「學測」呢？「劉毅英文」的同學很簡單，只要熟讀每次的模考試題就行了。每一份試題都在7000字範圍內，就不必再背7000字了，從後面往前複習，越後面越重要，一定要把最後10份試題唸得滾瓜爛熟。根據以往的經驗，詞彙題絕對不會超出7000字範圍。每年題型變化不大，只要針對下面幾個大題準備即可。

準備「詞彙題」最佳資料：

背了再背，背到滾瓜爛熟，讓背單字變成樂趣。

考前不斷地做模擬試題就對了！

你做的題目愈多，分數就愈高。不要忘記，每次參加模考前，都要背單字、背自己所喜歡的作文。考壞不難過，勇往直前，必可得高分！

練習「模擬試題」，可參考「學習出版公司」最新出版的「7000字學測試題詳解」。我們試題的特色是：
①以「高中常用7000字」為範圍。②經過外籍專家多次校對，不會學錯。③每份試題都有詳細解答，對錯答案均有明確交待。

「克漏字」如何答題

　　第二大題綜合測驗（即「克漏字」），不是考句意，就是考簡單的文法。當四個選項都不相同時，就是考句意，就沒有文法的問題；當四個選項單字相同、字群排列不同時，就是考文法，此時就要注意到文法的分析，大多是考連接詞、分詞構句、時態等。「克漏字」是考生最弱的一環，你難，別人也難，只要考前利用這種答題技巧，勤加練習，就容易勝過別人。

準備「綜合測驗」（克漏字）可參考「學習出版公司」最新出版的「7000字克漏字詳解」。

本書特色：

1. 取材自大規模考試，英雄所見略同。
2. 不超出7000字範圍，不會做白工。
3. 每個句子都有文法分析。一目了然。
4. 對錯答案都有明確交待，列出生字，不用查字典。
5. 經過「劉毅英文」同學實際考過，效果極佳。

「文意選填」答題技巧

　　在做「文意選填」的時候，一定要冷靜。你要記住，一個空格一個答案，如果你不知道該選哪個才好，不妨先把詞性正確的選項挑出來，如介詞後面一定是名詞，選項裡面只有兩個名詞，再用刪去法，把不可能的選項刪掉。也要特別注意時間的掌控，已經用過的選項就劃掉，以免重複考慮，浪費時間。

準備「文意選填」，可參考「學習出版公司」最新出版的「7000字文意選填詳解」。

特色與「7000字克漏字詳解」相同，不超出7000字的範圍，有詳細解答。

「閱讀測驗」的答題祕訣

① 尋找關鍵字——整篇文章中，最重要就是第一句和最後一句，第一句稱為主題句，最後一句稱為結尾句。每段的第一句和最後一句，第二重要，是該段落的主題句和結尾句。從「主題句」和「結尾句」中，找出相同的關鍵字，就是文章的重點。因為美國人從小被訓練，寫作文要注重主題句，他們給學生一個題目後，要求主題句和結尾句都必須有關鍵字。

② 先看題目、劃線、找出答案、標題號——考試的時候，先把閱讀測驗題目瀏覽一遍，在文章中掃瞄和題幹中相同的關鍵字，把和題目相關的句子，用線畫起來，便可一目了然。通常一句話只會考一題，你畫了線以後，再標上題號，接下來，你找其他題目的答案，就會更快了。

③ 碰到難的單字不要害怕，往往在文章的其他地方，會出現同義字，因為寫文章的人不喜歡重覆，所以才會有難的單字。

④ 如果閱測內容已經知道，像時事等，你就可以直接做答了。

準備「閱讀測驗」，可參考「學習出版公司」最新出版的「7000字閱讀測驗詳解」，本書不超出7000字範圍，每個句子都有文法分析，對錯答案都有明確交待，單字註明級數，不需要再查字典。

「中翻英」如何準備

可參考劉毅老師的「英文翻譯句型講座實況DVD」，以及「文法句型180」和「翻譯句型800」。考前不停地練習中翻英，翻完之後，要給外籍老師改。翻譯題做得越多，越熟練。

「英文作文」怎樣寫才能得高分？

① 字體要寫整齊，最好是印刷體，工工整整，不要塗改。

② 文章不可離題，尤其是每段的第一句和最後一句，最好要有題目所說的關鍵字。

③ 不要全部用簡單句，句子最好要有各種變化，單句、複句、合句、形容詞片語、分詞構句等，混合使用。

④ 不要忘記多使用轉承語，像 *at present*（現在），*generally speaking*（一般說來），*in other words*（換句話說），*in particular*（特別地），*all in all*（總而言之）等。

⑤ 拿到考題，最好先寫作文，很多同學考試時，作文來不及寫，吃虧很大。但是，如果看到作文題目不會寫，就先寫測驗題，這個時候，可將題目中作文可使用的單字、成語圈起來，寫作文時就有東西寫了。但千萬記住，絕對不可以抄考卷中的句子，一旦被發現，就會以零分計算。

⑥ 試卷有規定標題，就要寫標題。記住，每段一開始，要內縮5或7個字母。

⑦ 可多引用諺語或名言，並注意標點符號的使用。文章中有各種標點符號，會使文章變得更美。

⑧ 整體的美觀也很重要，段落的最後一行字數不能太少，也不能太多。段落的字數要平均分配，不能第一段只有一、兩句，第二段一大堆。第一段可以比第二段少一點。

準備「英文作文」，可參考「學習出版公司」出版的：